A Harlot's Progress

DAVID DABYDEEN

Jonathan Cape
LONDON

Published by Jonathan Cape 1999

2 4 6 8 10 9 7 5 3 1

Copyright © David Dabydeen 1999

David Dabydeen has asserted his right under the Copyright, Designs
and Patents Act 1988 to be identified as the author of this work

First published in Great Britain in 1999 by
Jonathan Cape
Random House, 20 Vauxhall Bridge Road,
London SW1V 2SA

Random House Australia (Pty) Limited
20 Alfred Street, Milsons Point, Sydney,
New South Wales 2061, Australia

Random House New Zealand Limited
18 Poland Road, Glenfield,
Auckland 10, New Zealand

Random House South Africa (Pty) Limited
Endulini, 5A Jubilee Road, Parktown 2193, South Africa

Random House UK Limited Reg. No. 954009

A CIP catalogue record for this book
is available from the British Library

ISBN 0-224-05972-6

Papers used by Random House UK Limited are natural,
recyclable products made from wood grown in sustainable forests.
The manufacturing processes conform to the environmental
regulations of the country of origin.

Printed and bound in Great Britain by
Creative Print and Design (Wales), Ebbw Vale

A Harlot's Progress

David Dabydeen was born in Guyana. He read English at Cambridge and presently teaches at the University of Warwick. He has published three books of poems and four novels, which have won many awards, including the Commonwealth Poetry Prize.

To Tim Cribb, Fredrick Nicholas Dabydeen,
and in memory of Sandra Latiff (d. 1997)

Prologue

22nd April 17—. Mr Pringle sits at the table in Mungo's garret, a table which Mungo uses as a desk, a place to eat and a place to lay out his Bible. He shuffles his blank papers into a neat pile. He jabs the nib of his pen into the inkwell and stirs nervously, awaiting word. This is the third visit, but at least he has made a start, if only to record the date of the meeting.

Mungo is huddled in his bed, covered over in a new blanket, a present from the Abolition Committee, which has been keeping him in food and clothing for months. He appears to be ungrateful. He will not return their benevolence with the gift of confession.

'Something must be said,' Mr Pringle urges, 'there must be a story.' He withdraws his pen from the inkwell and looks at Mungo with a dog's imploring eyes.

Mungo, master of the situation, squints at Mr Pringle, as if barely making out the shape of the younger man. He makes a heroic effort to lean his head in Mr Pringle's direction, groaning in the act.

'A beginning, Mungo,' Mr Pringle beseeches him, but Mungo is overcome with deafness. Mr Pringle moves his chair closer to the bed, so that Mungo can read his lips. 'A beg-inn-ing,' he says, and Mungo nods weakly. Mr Pringle moves the chair back to the table, takes up his pen and waits. He doodles over the date, drawing a series of ears, some drooping and mutilated, others like the heads of daffodils he had seen at the wayside on his journey to the garret; daffodils bright against the blackened frost of the city, defiant in their proclamation of survival into newness, a new season, a new beginning.

True, a man, even a nigger, has got to be respectful to other people's charity, though he would prefer to hoard the past and squirrel on it through miserable seasons. In a winter of England each time a man opens his mouth there is a plume of frost, which he can suck back into himself and be satisfied. The cold has flesh to it, I was never one to complain how I miss the tropic heat of Africa. And it is age, and service, that bend my back over the years, not like the whites who curl against the blasting ice to keep warm and remain in that posture even when sun come, as if crippled and fixed by memory. Memory don't bother me, that's why I don't tell Mr Pringle anything. I can change memory, like I can change my posture, fling the blanket away, spring out of bed, dance a step or two of a cotillion, and babble into his blank pages the most lively of syllables. But a man has got to be grateful and feed Mr Pringle's curiosity in return for all the pity he lavish on me, the shilling here, the new breeches there.

Mr Pringle asks questions, writes down and annotates Mungo's responses which are brief to the point of uncouthness. *Mungo says that he cannot recall the name of his village but 'it sound like Barambongdodo.' 'It be somewhere in Africa.' Question: tell me something about the landscape of your birth? Answer: a hot place. The only feature of the country imprinted in his mind is its heat. To variations of my question, designed to provoke his memory, he merely repeats, 'Hot-hot place.' Apparently no birds, no wild animals, no trees existed; which is impossible to believe. He is, I opine, in the initial stages of dementia, brought on by the tribulations of a Negro's life as much as by his advanced years. After a length of grim silence, lying in his bed like a picture of rigor mortis, he suddenly bolts upright and whispers to me, 'Hot-hot place. Fire! Fire! The katran bush burn down. White. The world turn white-white, smoke, thick like Manu beard.' Then he drops back into his bed, stares at the ceiling and falls asleep with his eyes open.*

Mr Pringle, realizing that Mungo is a ruined archive, resolves to colour and people a landscape out of his own imagination, thereby endowing Mungo with the gift of mind and eloquence. For the book Mr Pringle intends to write will be Mungo's portrait in the first person narrative. A book purporting to be a record of the Negro's own words (understandably corrected in terms of grammar, the erasure of indelicate or infelicitous expressions, and so forth) would bring great dividends for the Committee for the Abolition of Slavery. As its young Secretary, Mr Pringle would of course be universally applauded for his dedication and achievement in recording the Progress of the oldest African inhabitant of London: Mungo, brought to England by Captain Thomas Thistlewood and sold into the service of Lord Montague, then passed on to the notorious Jewish trickster Mr Gideon, and his mistress, Mary ('Moll') Hackabout; reputed to have resided in Charing Cross for two decades or more. Mungo has not been seen for many years, being attic-bound through severe arthritis (or melancholy?), but before he was a celebrity of slum and mansion alike, his presence greeted with equal excitement in seedy bagnio or baroque gallery. Beggars and nobility were his equal friends, and they flocked to him as he made his entrance to whore-house or High Church. This much Mr Pringle imagines, for his only source of information is Hogarth's portrait of Mungo as a boy-slave to the harlot Moll Hackabout. Some thirty years have elapsed since Hogarth's celebrated print, and Mungo has disappeared from memory. Only by the most dedicated effort of the Abolition Committee, in compiling a census of London's blacks, has Mungo been unveiled. Mr Pringle's resolve is to make him visible again, like a comet summoned into view by God's design; and though too advanced in age for the enjoyment of it, the book would endow Mungo with the fame, if not fortune, he once possessed.

Who are your mother and father? Where and what is the country called Africa you come from? When and how did you arrive in London? The who, the when, the what, the how, the why of this and that: Mr Pringle hungers for understanding as to the link between barracoon and brothel, rank nigger and perfumed pet. He seems to believe that one moment I was a dusty black child playing in a sand-dune, crinkle-mouthed from the sun, then many rivers later I found myself in an English boudoir, a feathered turban on my head, my skin polished as bright as my teeth, and I am rollicking and sipping at Moll's lush bosom. I forgive Mr Pringle his error because he is a man of true civility and wig. Still, I delay answering, I mumble and pause, and I pray that he will put my tardiness down to deafness, or to the natural docility of the African who cannot come to the point howsoever instructed by the whip or by the clergy. Only when I reach for his shilling did my resolve weaken, and I let go my classical breeding when I say to him, 'Sir, I am unworthy of your subscription,' and I catch myself and right away I start humming a street ballad and working some froth to the side of my mouth and spluttering and behaving stupid. He is utterly consternated at my words. He cannot believe me capable of speech as polished as my teeth once were. No, nigger does munch and crunch the English, nigger does jape and jackass with the language, for he is of low brow and ape resemblances.

No, I am not uncouth, I can write the story myself, for I have imbibed many of your mannerisms of language, and the King James Bible is at hand to furnish me with such expressions as could set your soul aglow with compassion for the plight of the Negro. Bah! I could sting you for a bounty of reparations, but keep your money and let me talk like dis and dat, let me say I come from the tribe of Bongo-Bongo; that I am germane and first-cousin to jungle beasts like anthropophagi, hermaphrodites, salipenters and all the other creatures dreamt of by your writers or discovered by your travellers. But such revelations will not do for Mr Pringle. He wants a sober testimony that will appeal to the Christian charity of an enlightened citizenry who will, on perusing my tale of undeserved woe, campaign in the Houses of Parliament for my emancipation and that of millions of my brethren. Pish! Where the bee sucks there suck I. Let me talk like dis and dat till the day come that I die, soon.

Mr Pringle begins to write Mungo's murmurings into an epic, the frame of which he has already constructed in his mind. All it awaits are the droolings of a decrepit nigger. He has invested in an expensive leather-bound notebook in which to record Mungo's story. It creates an image of dignity and professionalism which his previous loose-leafs of paper lacked. Although Mungo has uttered only cryptically so far and threatens to expire in body and speech at any moment, Mr Pringle does not regret his investment. He is, at heart, a Christian, and believes in the inexhaustible generosity of the Almighty Divine, that He will deliver up Mungo's true character and adventures, howsoever in the telling blemished by frailty of mind and heathen grammar. Mr Pringle, as the humble instrument of the Divine, will purge the story of its imperfections, to reveal Mungo in his unfallen state. He will wash the Aethiop white, scrubbing off the colours of sin and greed that stained Mungo's skin as a result of slavery.

He orders his notebook with a series of chapter headings:

1 Africa.
2 Voyage to the Americas in Slave Ship.
3 Plantation Labour.
4 Voyage to England with Captain Thistlewood.
5 Service in the Household of Lord Montague.
6 Purchase of Mungo by Mr Gideon, a Jew.
7 Debauched by Service to Moll Hackabout, a Common Prostitute.
8 Descent into the Mire of Poverty and Disease.
9 Redemption of Mungo by the Committee for the Abolition of Slavery.

He crosses them out and begins again.

1 The Beloved Homeland of My Birth: Africa.
2 Paradise Lost: The Terrors of my Expulsion to the
  Americas in the Bowels of a Slaveship.
3 The Pitiless Sun: My Plantation Travails.
4 etc., etc.

Yes, I tempt him, with meanness, for weeks have passed
since our first meeting and still I have not started off Mr
Pringle. And so his hand is poised over the inkwell whilst
the other is deep in his trouser pocket, fingering the coins,
calculating whether to part with any or to keep me
deprived. *Radix malorum est cupiditas*, as the Ancients put it.
He can see that I am hungry, for my mouth is dry, and
three bright sores have appeared on my lips, foretelling
malnutrition. But Mr Pringle is so eager for a snippet of my
memoirs that he would rather see me starve than surrender
his myrrh to me. Perhaps I should not make such a trial of
his Christian soul and convert him to the ways of slavery. I
watch his fingers bunch into a secret fist, as if he would cuff
me for my rebelliousness. He struggles to hide his anger,
plunging his hand more deeply into his trouser pocket. The
pen is in the other as if waiting to sign a warrant for my
arrest, or my sale.

He clears his throat but swallows, successfully resisting
the impulse to kindliness. He withdraws his coinless hand
from his pocket and places it palm down on the table in a
show of meanness. He shakes the ink from his pen and rests
it on the blank paper. His face twitches like an excited
poodle twitching its tail, working up sufficient rage for an

intimidatory growl. 'A beginning,' he says at last, his voice breaking over me with such unexpected passion that I yield to him immediately.

Part I

Put this down in your book Mr Pringle, properize it in your best English:

Pa is far. He is never here. He is never. He is tilling field or fighting war. One time he come home. I bury in my mother, sleeping, so he part me from her and put me away, by the door. I could cry but I am glad he is here, at last. He spread a warm cloth over me and because it is dark he run his fingers along my face, tracing me in his mind. He will recognize me forever by tracing me so, howsoever dark things be.

One time, a man come to our hut. It must be my father, for he part me from my mother and place me far from her. I am sleeping. I don't cry because I want him to be my father. He spread a warm cloth over me and feel my face. I don't trace him back because I want him to think I sleep, but in secret I sniff his hand. It is, I remember now, a melon smell, clean and young and without sin, so I lay still and let him go to my mother.

My mother bathe me, feed me, place me at the doorway of the hut to blot the morning light. My father is gone so she don't want to see herself, how lonely she is. I guard her from the sun of her eyes.

What she looks like is vague. So many years gone by, I mix her face up with Moll and all the rest. Is she as haggard as I recall or do I think of a white woman? My mother's eyes are big with grief. One morning in particular her face runs and runs, and although she say nothing I know somehow that my father will not come back. He has become spirit, and will live invisibly in the katran bush where no one is permitted to walk.

The katran bush is at the edge of our village. Don't walk there, my mother tell me. Why? Don't walk there, she say again, this time her voice stern. She screw up her face to look wrathful.

I don't know his name, how old he was, whose son he was, or anything else. I don't recollect him and me being with other boys and girls, I don't remember any others but him and me, and then only when we are wandering in the katran bush. Afterwards we make sin there. I only know him in the katran bush and in sin, before he went away to become spirit. There must have been other children, other games, that made us live and grow and be blessed, not die. Only the game of death stay with me though.

What is the katran bush? It is the sleep in my eyes. It is the white slick on the face of Afric's land. Everywhere is black with fertile soil but the katran bush grow, a boundary between our village and another, thick with mist and white liquid which bleed from the face of rocks. Saba – for that is the name that come back to me now – and me venture there, foolishly. We left the proper spaces within the village where child-folk play, the pond where we splash, the trees where we snare kabuti with bird-lime but let them fly off afterwards for they are no good for eating, only for making melody when they are glued to the branches. You would think they would squawk and flurry and give out black odour, but kabuti facing death are still as they sing to each other and to the far sky. Plain ragged birds, poisonous to taste, but with songs that so move us that we let them go, even the most cruel child and wasteful hand.

Saba is such. He pecks at the others, he jeers, he elbows them in the chest to rob their breath or to listen to them crying. But I am not afraid of him as other children are, for I see him as a kabuti bird but full of the wrong music. He wants to speak nicely but his throat growl instead. I sense this about him. One day when he is pelting stones into the pond, I go up to him, call out his name and when he turn I slap him across the mouth. His hands, once packed with rage, fall by his sides. He is now my slave. I am like death to him. He will sing sweetly for me whenever I command, but I still will not let him go.

A sudden blow can make you into a slave forever. If you creep up to someone, as I do to Saba, and with a quick blow knock all the stuff from his head, words and all, then you make a fresh space where only you can dwell. 'Come here' and 'go yonder' and 'do this', you can say, and he will obey, for he is now you and not himself nor no one else.

Everything in his head gone, and blood run down his face. But heed, to make a slave you have to move quick and lash in one clean stroke, or else he will stay stale, his old self stubborn, and one day will rebel and curse you.

Saba pick fruit for me when I so direct him. He collect firewood for my mother when I should be so doing. Sometimes I make him do nothing useful all day but dig a hole in the ground. Then fill up the hole, I say, and make another. When I am satisfied I send him away to his own home. One day I am bored with him. He has weeded our garden, he has destroyed ants' nests, he has hollowed me a flute, he has shaped me a stone with sharp edges, best to skip across the pond from one bank to the other as a knife opens the belly of a fish with two–three nips. But now I have no more task for him. Come to the katran bush with me, I say in a sudden urge, and when he look at me like a beggar look at his sores, I know that I have at last overcome him totally, and will have no pity on him.

The broad path through our village paved with caree shells dwindles to a dust trail. Saba is before me but as a goat foreruns its keeper to a place of slaughter. He pauses slyly to look around for another route but there is none. He makes to turn back and bolt past me but I block him, I drive him to the katran bush. In a last panic he will try to rebel and charge at me, but words come to my mind from somewhere strange that *I will brook no disobedience*, I am come armed with knives of stone.

Now I remember when my father died, but not how. It was

beautiful. All the women went to the chatree hut in the middle of our village and danced all night. There men usually stayed, smoking, wrapping wounds, picking chigoes from their feet, feeding the fire, arguing, sometimes fighting over the last mouthful of changa-wine left in the pan. But tonight only women, naked, painting each other's breasts and bellies with the resemblances of animals, and howling in mirth, and drinking as greedily as men would, and banging their fists upon the earth, and only I am permitted to be among them, all the men and child-folk banished to their huts. My mother too. She is in our garden, watching over my father who is wrapped in breta-bark which yields a soft powdery incense. Her eyes witness him, as candles rage against the gloom and stillness of an English chapel.

In this whirl and canvas of dye I move. A jungle of breasts is offered me, for tonight, only tonight, my father dead, all the women are my wives, by antique custom. I can choose to hunt the young gazelle or the red-lipped snake. The women stamp their feet around me, and drink and drink. They shudder and fall to the ground, pretending to be slain beasts. They offer me a knife to skin them, to rip from their bellies my patrimony, which are pictures of my father's lust, the young gazelle, the red-lipped snake.

Now I remember, and have new words to remember, how beautiful it was, the chorus and the exhibition of shameless painted women. I am brought into manhood – even as an extreme child – by the play of their nipples, and their bodies conjure forth the heat from my blood, till I grow numb, anointed in cold glues which flow from their nakedness, and breath leaves my mouth in troubling song, and I become the father whom my mother tends, her ears bent to his dead lips, listening for any trace of sound, any canticle of the love which once hardened within her, scraping and paining like a sackful of ebo-flints, forming the child which gave birth to me.

Now I remember, but then, in an uncreated time, when there were no words, only a small boy there was, driving a bully to his death.

The dust trail dwindles to a single thread of path broad enough only for two feet. The katran bush leaks a white mucus which sucks us towards it. The katran bush is like a goat's heart freshly taken from its chest. It is wrapped in a white film and covered over with white fat. My mother chips away at the cobwebbed heart with a stone knife, until, the whiteness gone, it gleams in her hand.

Into a bank of mist I push Saba and he goes. When sleep leaves him and he catches sight at the other side, my father will greet his throat with a shiny tooth. Saba must go, I push him cruel hard, but he cries, he will not, and his noise is of such distress that I nearly let him free. But we are at the katran bush, my father is waiting, he will have blood, so Saba must obey.

When my mother put the tip of her knife to the cleansed heart and worked it in, there was a sudden flush of red which she let drip into the ground. Then, twisting the knife here and there she opens the flesh of the heart into the head of a flower. There are four petals – two for her, two for my dead father. She will feed them raw to his mouth and to hers, tonight, when she watches over his body wrapped in breta-bark.

Saba is entered the katran bush where my father will hack at him. I am with loud drumming heart at the edge of mist, awaiting his scream. I hear nothing, I open my eyes wide and stare in the direction of his going but see nothing. I tear the mist from my face, but sleep drapes my eyes, I call out to Saba in panic, I call and call whilst the mist leaks into my mouth like a poisonous sap.

My father is cold. I sit beside my mother and watch as she strips breta-bark and winds it around him, then covers him in breta-leaves. All day she works, intent as a spider. When she finishes garlanding him, she makes offering of meat, but he will not eat, so she takes the petals of heart to her own mouth. I sit beside her and watch her eating and weeping over him. Then the women come and take me away for the stripping and the dancing. I want to remain beside her and my father, but they remove me and she does not protest, and he lies on the ground refusing to eat. They bring me back the next morning but by that time I no longer care for him. He is gone from our yard as if someone lifted him as he was sleeping and put him at a far distance. The women place me next to my mother who is resting in the hut. They make me lie naked beside her, they will not cover me over with a warm cloth. And she does not protest.

Saba comes to my call, just at the moment I go to collapse. The sight of him jolts me back to myself. I am glad to see him, and that he is whole, nothing eaten from him, no wound, no torn chest. I am sorry that my father is remaining dead, but still glad for Saba, that he is not flowered into sacrifice. When we get back to our village I will let him free and end my game with him. But for now he jabbers, his face wild with grief. He will not tell me what he has looked upon. His skin is dull as if the dead had breathed ash upon him. I rip a twig off a felpan tree nearby and beat the dust from his body until he is black again. Then I notice he is holding a gourd which he has brought back from the plot of dead. He gives it to me as tribute, and when I crack it open there is food, balls of dried ocho and sarabell. Eat, I say with a new malice, eat, for then he will be my final slave, though I set him free. And I watch him eat the food of the dead and so commit his life into my service. I wait until every last piece is chewed and swallowed, then we turn away from the katran bush to home.

The women, when they put petals of flesh to my mouth, curse their fathers and their fathers' fathers with the most nasty words, telling how they entered their mothers to suck syrups which I am draining now from them, my mouth running with sinful yolk, they curse, stifling me in their nakedness, thrusting their hips at me, running their hands over me so that unknown liquids seep from me, which they behold with spite and wipe against their nakedness in a scornful act. I am a snake with its venom drawn, they laugh, a capla shorn of thorn, and they laugh again in one chorus of ridicule, that now, countless years later, I feel the power of their community still, and I know that they made me their slave, not to flesh but to their ways of suffering. I have been fated to serve Moll from such day, and yet there was courage too given to me, courage enough to slap Saba across the face, for no man, whatever his might, will be-woman me.

This I learnt from the pleasure and vile curse of women, but too from the period of my punishment when there was no speech, no food, no company, no light, and yet after the first panic, the knives of hunger and the madness of the dark, I came to a settlement with my plight so that nothing could murder me.

Swiftly it happened, in the space of a breath, though the beatings must have taken longer, except that I grew numb after the first blows so that the rest were the useless rage of our village Headman who, between words of chastisement, broke one fresh whip after another against my back, then, yanking back my head so that my forehead faced the sun, pressed a hot stone to it, branding me with a sign of my sin, for I had trespassed in the spaces of the dead, and all the while Saba was moaning in his hut, his belly churning and swelling with demons like an adulterous woman watched over and tended by no one, the doorway of the hut blocked with stone to stop even the slightest breeze from entering to form companionship, or light to fall across his face in false relief.

The Headman brands my forehead with the sign of evil, and I am put into a deep hole which my mother is made to dig, and she surrenders me to it with her own hands, lowering me into it by a cord of breta-bark, for my disobedience has brought sin upon her and the threat of destruction to our village, for our ancestors have departed in anger from the katran bush, leaving us no defence against enemies of flies, drought, malicious stars, tribes with different scars. Saba will die and remain unburied, but this will not pacify our ancestors, though he will be forever entombed in clay and stone, unable to converse with others, to smoke pipes and drink liquor with them in the chill of night, to reminisce about courtships, squabbles with wives, bountiful crops, incidence of war, nor will he spit on the ground and mould the dirt into a seed of future birth to supplement the numbers of our tribe. Saba will not seed the future, but even this total banishment from the history of our tribe is not enough to pacify our ancestors, who have migrated to another place, leaving us without memory of past and to a stillborn future.

So I am issued into a deep hole where I must stay between one phase of moon and another, the time the gods took to fashion us from pieces of sky, painting us shades of swarthiness and putting us upon a land glazed in greens and vermilions. And in a fit of afterbirth, the gods, overcome with the beauty of what they had done, dipped their hands in the glitter of stars and daubed veins of the clearest rivers and waterfalls. And they took the plainest clod and painted it in the blush of scorpion, gild of tara-crab, sable of panther, ruddle of nadar-fish, fawn of antelope, and into the mouth of each creature the gods breathed sound according to its colour, that the earth was scaled with hum and caw and guggle and flute and yawl and a million more airs that gave hurt and delight. And having formed the earth and coloured creatures upon it and placed us in lordship over all that stirred and grew sluggish and died, the gods went away to create other worlds, leaving our ancestors to guard us from forgetting the past or seeking the future blindly.

So I am lowered into a pit and dead pupil of earth where my passing will be a sacrifice to gods and ancestors, that knowledge may be restored to our tribe: the cunning to read riddles in leaf and wing that will choose how we hunt or plant; ceremonies of mask; prayers for the newly born. I am to suffer hunger till flesh loosens from its frame, till all creation is unmade in me.

But I never suffered, I have never. All died when it is me that should, but instead, them. Why? It is me who made sin, not Saba who will never hatch out of his shell of stone, and he is crying but no one can hear, nor ever will, for smoke stops all cries. I crouch at the bottom of my pit and watch it thicken like stone against the sky but the cries of my mother and our tribe will not reach the merciless ears of the gods, nor can our ancestors heed, forgetful of duty.

Light breaks and closes over me, three days, three nights now in my mother's pit, waterless, and I'm hardening to a piece of dung sucked dry by the sun, but there is no pain, no suffering, for my mind has become numb to emptiness of stomach, and my first tears have long since dried to salt which seals my eyes, making me accustomed to myself in loneliness. At first I scoured the earth for the jelly of the flesh of worms but now my mouth is as sealed as my eyes, wanting nothing. I am content with nothing. The first wailing, the first panic and stupid clawing of the sides of the pit, dreaming a ladder to climb out of my darkness to be born into my mother's gaze, is past. I am content with no one ever seeing me again, I grow almost spiteful with the thought. Spite keeps pain at bay, I will not suffer, no, instead I cackle at Saba's fate, and the useless fury of the Headman, and the dumbness of my mother's grief as she winds the cord of breta-bark around my waist as unto my father's corpse. And if the ancestors are stupid enough to desert us because of a boy's mischief, then let them go uselessly into the dark. What plague of flies, what drought, what enemies have they ever protected us from? The ancestors are weak, they are cowards, they will use a boy's misdeed as excuse to run away and leave us prey to the white hunter who comes with gun (as we have come to name this magic) and torch and chain and cup and cross.

The smell of smoke. The sky is blown with fear, the sky is a rag of birds fleeing their nests.

Properize this in your English, Mr Pringle, put in your book the noise of scream, the knives how they wade in and out of flesh like happy bathers, and smoke rising from roofs on fire like breath panting from the tongues of dogs, whitening our village that has become a katran bush. This I see when they haul me up and bend me over the lip of pit, men with different scars who have invaded our village and killed all that moves. They find me now, the last of our tribe, the last witness, for Saba moans selfishly in his cave of stone and does not see and does not hear the murder of his family, and they bend me over the lip of pit and will chop me and they pull back my head to bare my neck, and the cutlass is raised but before it can fall I look out at the ribs of our village (for only sticks that held up wattle and straw remain), the house of dancing women, the garden of my father's last night with the stars watching into his dead eyes. The cutlass glints over me and as I look out for the last time, everything I did forget or neglect to see appear in bright guise. There, in the midst of smoke, is the hand of our sorcerer throwing pebbles into a circle. His name is Manu, his back is forever bent from drawing circles in the earth, and his face is overgrown with white mane so that he resembles katran bush. He squats studying pebbles, whilst folk at a distance huddle their breath, afraid to be near in case he suddenly rears and foretells their death. Only Ellar, the lame one, husbandless, approaches, always chewing on toba-vine to keep her mouth fresh for a future lover. Ellar scans the earth over Manu's shoulder, fearless of the fall of pebbles, for no violence can be done to her that she has not already wished upon herself. And if a lover will not visit her in the dark, when her crooked limb is hidden from scorn, then let death steal her in a thousand guises. My mother sends me into Ellar's yard with a bowl of tamma-figs from our garden, for there is no man to feed her, and the hens she keeps are too nimble for her lame foot when the time for killing comes; nor will they lay eggs, out of spite, but still they eat up all her provisions. There is Tanda, nicknamed after the fruit that litter his garden for little else will grow there, no matter how he tries, no eddo or sweet-potato or pumpkin, as if his hands are blessed for one deed only. When tanda seasons and swells his land, the whole village eats, for he is free in his giving. He is a man fat with happiness, for his wife is a maker of shrimp-nets, and his children are plentiful. There is Samyat and his twin sons, their hands wet with clay, for they are the builders of

23

homes. There is Apal bearing branches, for today he is re-roofing his hut. Sanu comes, wearing a scarf of flies, for she is making mule-dung cakes for the fireside. Janga prances forth, whirling his arms as if practising pelting a stone at a treetop nest. He is a proud man, his aim is the steadiest of all hunters, and trees rain dead birds after his assaults. Baju dawdles forth with her nose upturned, sniffing the air, and her eyes closed in concentration: she can foretell thunder or good weather or a visitation by our ancestors by the slightest odour carried by the slightest breeze. Her body is always bruised from tripping over unseen things on the ground. Onya calls to her children and though they've been dead from birth, she will not give up calling. Sometimes you can hear her scolding them for hiding in the forest and not coming to her. Each evening she puts out two plates of food for them, but only the hyenas come to eat. There is Nara who usually sits all day propped against his hut smoking his pipe or sucking tamba-seeds (for he had long lost his teeth) until it is time to sleep again: he has no need to exert himself for he is aged beyond reckoning, and in his day he has killed seventy elephants, two hundred wild cats and six thousand deer. Now his mind has grown as blunt as the point of his spear. All day he smokes and sucks and falls asleep. All these, and others, emerge from the gloom of smoke to greet me with curses for bringing death to them, and they look for revenge in the light of the cutlass's blade, and they urge it to fall upon my neck, my head dropping into the pit to be buried like a seed that will bring forth only thorn and barren flower.

Part II

I

I had many beginnings, all of them marked by a long and futile wailing – not from my mouth but from my father's. I had a father, though I have utterly forgotten him. Still, my father wailed – I can now imagine the woe in his heart as he commanded me to be banished to the wilderness, there to die among widows. I cannot remember them either but they existed, for one was called Rima, and it was she who succoured me on lizards' eyes. I was, I believe, a normal malnourished child existing on an African diet of animal droppings, my hunger mollified only by the stories Rima recited to me between meals. Oh she was sparse or plentiful with stories, and even now I am haunted by the native melody of her voice, its rasp and quinsied straining. Or else imagine the cadence of a bone being sucked longingly for its ideal of flesh, then crunched in desperation, until the mouth awakens to its vacancy: Rima vacillated so, between a dreamy lyricism and a brutish grinding of teeth.

The widows – and there must have been five or thirty of them – were either incapable of child-bearing or beyond such age, and consequently destined for death. Ordinarily, a woman whose husband was killed in war or devoured by animals would be retained at first in the sanctuary of the village. The Elder's sons and his nephews would gather on her. The period of her testing lasted between the crescent and the gibbous phases of the moon. If she proved with child thereafter, her life would be saved, she would be returned to the fields for work. Otherwise she would be chased to the wilderness, her head shaved, her wrists broken, and her palms branded with the sign of evil.

Rima explained to me the anthropology of our tribal doings, or else I dreamt them out of self-loathing. She told me that all women were hysterical with anxiety the night before a battle or a hunt. They beseeched their husbands to be exceedingly careful. They rubbed a special oil into their husbands' skins, the scent of which would form shields around their bodies. They uttered prayers learned from their mothers and grandmothers. Finally they made love to their men lavishly, so that on the battlefield or the hunting ground, the men would recall the sex, and want to return alive to their wives.

'Not wives,' Rima had said. 'Slaves. The men were masters. Only the Elder and his clan allowed themselves marriage. The rest of us were slaves to the whim of any man, though we were appointed individual masters.'

Of course I discount Rima's explanation now, for she was twisted of mind, ferocious in her hatred of men. I cannot believe that we were such a pagan people, so removed from universal decency and Christian precepts that we permitted unbridled and unregulated sex. True, our subsequent fate suggests that we were the offsprings of Gomorrah, therefore erased from the earth, but *I* have survived, and *my* being can only point to God's presence amongst us. How else can *I* account for myself, a man who in two score years or more has never lifted a callous hand against a woman, much less sequestered her body? How could *I* have been severed from the immemorial practices of my forebears? By what means of

28

disobedience have *I* annihilated myself from the past? Whatever the truth, I will be faithful to Rima's account, for she loved me in spite of my sex, abided with me, nurtured me, and even when fatally wounded by gunshot, whispered to me a final blessing. Her mouth ran with blood then, and I will be as profuse in my telling of her story.

This is how Rima described the plight of our women: day and night they squatted at the entrance of their communal hut, awaiting the return of their masters. They ate nothing, they went without sleep. Then, heralded by the screaming and sudden flight of forest birds, the men appeared.

The wailing started soon afterwards as women scanned the procession frantically for their masters. For those women unfortunate enough to be widowed, weeks of plunder followed, the endurance of the glee of young men – the sons and nephews of the Elder, too young for war or stalking prey, but now in apprenticeship for such future doings. They learned the virtues of hunting in a group: the conspiracy of gestures; the awareness of each other's positionings even in darkness; the camouflaged and concentrated waiting for the perfect moment to release their pent-up strength against the prey in a hail of spears.

After the weeks of testing, some women, fearful of banishment, stuffed their wombs with breta-leaves. Their mothers had taught them that such leaves, whatever the agony, would soak up blood before any tell-tale signs could stain their thighs. Others ate mouthfuls of dirt, for poisons in the soil would pain and swell their bellies, and they could pass as child-bearing women.

Once their uselessness became evident, they were herded together and forcibly scraped with ebo-flints of a determined bluntness to make the shearing of their scalps sufficiently painful. Hot ash was rubbed into the canals opened up in their flesh, so that they took on the appearance of the most despised of birds, the jack-jack; despised because each black serration on its lush green crown marked a moment of famine in our tribe's history. The women were marked like jack-jack and sent away to starve or be devoured – in either case a propitiative sacrifice to the demons of sterility who inhabited the wilderness. But even more cruelty was to come, namely the breaking of their wrists, and the pressing of a hot stone into their palms which left the imprint of evil. It was a peculiar sign called *peia* which only sojourn in England made familiar, for my people were ignorant of mathematical formulae. The sign was a matter of superstition, originating from a distant past, when, according to Rima, strangers visited our dreams.

No one could remember them in any detail. The passage of time had rendered them into figures of mystery. The strangers were olive-complexioned, with flowing black hair. They possessed fleshy shoulders and chests, but their lower bodies were wooden barrels attached to bizarre animals and rolling magically along the ground. My ancestors were encountering the chariot for the first time. Up till then their world was circumscribed by the capacity of their feet, for we had no horses, no chariots, no wheels. What appeared to them to be dreamlike and inexplicable became knowledge to me once I encountered whitemen and their books. The incident of their visitation, once a source of terror to my tribe, became a trite historic affair to me: I knew them to be loose Alexandrians, a battalion of Greek marauders of old who had wandered off path from North Africa and somehow ended up hundreds of

30

miles away in an unfamiliar region. Muddy paths hampered their progress, they abandoned their chariots and took to roaming through swamp and jungle. In sheer desperation they slaughtered whatever and whoever lay in their path. It was the bush which altered the Greek mind, the colossal squalor of it. You who live in England in manicured gardens; you who have such melodic names for nature – rills, meadows, groves, spinneys and purling streams – cannot begin to appreciate the dreadfulness of the bush. It howls eternally, like a soul condemned to the habitation of fallen angels. It is Satan's kingdom, Hades, the Inferno, the Realms of Pluto, the Underworld. Our native word for it is *peia*, an obvious corruption of the Greek *pi*, which we also signify as π.

It was the bush – its insects, its animals, its rank vegetation, its baneful noises, its human eyes gleaming from behind dense foliage – which drove the Greeks to massacre. Legend has it that they speared, hacked, skinned, bonfired and otherwise harassed to death thousands of folk. Whole species of tribes and animals were made extinct. The Greeks became the demons of sterility. Eventually, exhausted by the gore of the doings, and giving up all hope of their returning to their countrymen, they settled down on the banks of the Cheria river. They cleared a space, built a fort, and enslaved sufficient Africans to ease their lot and tend to their sexual wants.

Their passions stilled and a comforting silence reigning for several miles around the fort, where all life had been decimated, the Greeks resumed their true character. Relieved of the burdens of toil their minds flourished once more with inherited ideas. They debated among themselves the merits of Zeno's philosophy, Xenophanes's poetry. They ground coloured stones to dust, and boiled it in animal fat to make paints. They composed a mural of their remembered home on one side of the fort, commemorating the glory of their civilization: here was the splendid Acropolis and the splendid Stadium; there was a legion returning triumphantly from the Egyptian War, bearing trophies of slaves, precious cloth, ornaments. The men were imperious in aspect, the women lissom and milky. Legend does not yield such detail, so you must excuse me if I seek to embroider my tale but fail in the process, for no English words can describe the perfection of the Greek tribe.

They painted, they philosophized. They engaged in speculations on geometry. They measured the relationship between shapes and planes. They codified these in an abstruse algebra. And all this civilization they bestowed unto their brightest slaves and mulatto offsprings. Over time a wondrous new tribe was created in the jungle clearing; a tribe of blacks of all hues who could hunt with the naked skills of their African ancestors, but whose minds were robed in the decorum of Greek learning. The novelty of their being spread like a benevolent plague throughout the region, even though over the centuries the darkness of the jungle and of the African mind proved resistant to such. The initial excitement of penetration gave way to torpor and exhaustion. The African mind stubbornly refused the ecstasy of abstraction. The new tribe, born out of the processes of extinction, became extinct in turn. Bush reclaimed its territory, overran the mural and the fort.

Legend has it differently. Legend tells of a band of marauders, cubbed of the moon, rough-faced and pallid; they descended from the sky in a multitude of chariots, purging the eyes of all who looked upon them, sterilizing the earth and all its creatures. Our tribe scurried from the dreadful white light of their presence. We sought shelter in deep caves. We daubed mud over our bodies to create a cloak of invisibility. Still the light reached us, bathing sperm and womb, so that our tribe dwindled to a few. In desperation we ventured out to shoot arrows to the moon. She must have pitied our foolish gesture, or perhaps admired our courage, for she recalled her milky offsprings as suddenly as she had discharged them. They disappeared, leaving the longest memory of our tribe.

Some germ of Greek civilization survived the suffocation of bush and blacks to flower on my forehead centuries later. I am certain that I am an imprint of a lost tribe of Greeks, for how else can I explain the sign of *Pi* inscribed on my forehead? I was born with the sign of evil on my forehead, the very sign burned into women's palms before they were sent into the wilderness. Hence my father howled when he first set eyes on me, thinking that I was a harbinger of a new darkness, a new sterility.

II

But let me cut short his grief and relate to you instead the story of Rima and her tribulations, for they are branded into my thoughts. Though I fret and seek forgetfulness she refuses to disappear. Indeed the more advanced in age I become, with all the ruination of mind that thankfully ensues, the more she bodies forth to torment me. Sometimes I am of the opinion that she is a figure that I have absorbed from books and

33

inspissated into a poisonous bead, which I swallow and regurgitate. There has been, in recent years, since the establishment of the Abolition Committee, a veritable outpouring of the most heartrending stories of African suffering, enough to furnish a library of such gloom that only a Saint or Misanthrope would seek sanctuary therein. Every day there is some new ballad being hawked in taverns, telling of some hapless Negress caged in the appetency of a West Indian planter. The print shops in Cheapside are emblazoned with images of such concupiscence, as every engraver finds topical and ready pecuniary uses for his hitherto idle burin. Rima is perhaps one of these victims, spawned out of moral indignation and profiteering; but yet she is of such vivid fabric that I think I cannot just have encountered her in a cheaply coloured picture or balladeer's scroll.

Rima was soul captured in a crooked stick, for hunger had so reduced her. She was not black, but copper-coloured, as if the sun had drained her of natural oils. When she walked her feet – a burr of thorns – tore the ground. When she spoke she made the same rasping sound. Nothing about her suggested succulence. The only thing that trickled from her was stories, and these came with such agony that it was as if she was severing an already depleted artery. In the months, or maybe days, I spent with her, I was appalled by her loss of blood, each story she told being a progress toward suicide. In Mr Pringle's society, expression is vaunted, and a book is deemed the highest achievement of man. But, for me, the book is no more than a splendidly adorned memorial and grave. To speak is to scoop out substance, to hollow out yourself, to make space within for your own burial, so I have kept in things as bulwarks against death. I have kept silence before the nib and gravedigger's spade of Mr Pringle.

Why then am I telling you of Rima? It is because she insists on bursting out of the cage of my breast. She is so insistent that sometimes I think my heart will palpitate with fatal force. I will therefore live by allowing her to leech on me. A little bleeding will becalm both of us.

To tell her story plainly – Rima was a slave in our house, with the usual domestic duties during the day, and at nights, fulfilling the usual role of giving pleasure to my father. She described my father as courteous in manner, treating her with the same respect as he showed my mother. He was tall in stature, well-proportioned, with a fine forehead signifying his powers of prophecy. In civil society he carried himself with dignity as befitted the nephew of the Elder of our village. In the jungle he was the most fleetfooted of hunters. He was intensely alert to the slightest movement of leaf or grass. He could read the signs of animal presences as expertly as he could foretell the fate of our tribe by studying the innards of a sapan.

When Rima related all this, you will understand when I confess that I scoffed at her descriptions, calling her a liar and a love-struck weakling. She turned her face away from me and wept and though a mere boy I cursed myself for my maleness, for causing her shame and grief as the men of my village had. Still, I suspect that she was bestowing adornments on my father that were undeserved, for how can you explain my own features? I am squat and smallpoxed, with bulging cheeks, an obtuse nose and a low simian forehead scarred with a Greek formula. Even as a child, when Rima ministered to me and fed me such stories of my comely father, I knew that I would evolve into a hideous shape. I arrived at this knowledge without benefit of mirror. Nor were there clear ponds into which I could peer to see reflections of my childhood. The only water in the wilderness was a stagnant trough, its surface begrimed by the bodies of insects and the droppings of animals.

No, such prophetic powers on my part were probably inherited from my father, but even that aspect of Rima's description I cannot accept, for how did he not foretell the evil of my birth? Perhaps he did, but could not contain himself out of desire for my mother. Perhaps he was so elated by her caresses that he no longer cared that he would discharge a blighted seed. Perhaps he doubted his talent for prophecy, out of lust. He refused to believe the spectre of death materializing in his mind as he made love to her. He could foretell my birth, and the doom it carried, but still he doubted. But perhaps it was a moment nobler than lust or self-distrust. It could have been that he wanted me to be born; wanted to challenge the enslavement of our women to brute traditions. He willed me to come forth, even bearing the sign of evil, for although the miracle of such birth would bring destruction to the tribe, it would also loose them into a necessary future. *I* would be the ruined archive of our tribe but also its resurrected expression, writing the discovery of the New World of Whitemen. Such an act of writing would kill me, as certainly as the first Spaniard in the Bermudas was speared on the beach by a consternated native.

III

Whatever my father's motives, addled by lust, or revolutionary in purpose, I was born to the noise of his wailing. According to Rima, my mother was not present at my birth except in a perfunctory way. She was spread wide, delivered of child, and ushered away. 'I knew your mother only as a pair of inky hands,' Rima said, explaining that my mother was a votary of some deity or the other. In the days of our dark past we worshipped ants' nests, honeycombs, the excrement of gazelles heaped up into a sacred pyramid, everything and anything that threatened, beguiled or stank. As a votary to Whatever-It-Was, my mother was veiled from head to toe and sworn to absolute silence. Cocooned in a black silence, she ruled the household by gestures which over the years became so elaborate that a new language was formed among our women. A stiffened or slack finger, like the movement of a beetle's antennae; a quivering thumb; a palm curled like a sick leaf or the hibiscus tongue at dusk – all these signals became the means of connecting with other women and with nature, a system as subtle and expressive as the communica-tion of male hunters in the savannah – 'and for our protection too' Rima added, for just as the male hunters gestured to each other of impending dangers, so the women secretly told a master's mood to a prospective victim. When he plotted to beat, the one who discovered his intention signalled to another then another, until the message spread from hut to hut, eventually reaching the unfortunate woman.

'Your mother spoke very little with her hands,' Rima said, 'whatever motion she made was succinct as befits the wife of our master. The only time she prattled was when you were in the borning.' According to Rima her hands were a tumult of emotions. She lay on the ground screaming, not in sound, but in a crazed fluttering of her fingers. All night she cried, unable to be consoled by the women who tended to her. And between spasms of pain she drifted into a storyteller's mood. She shaped an account of the origins of our tribe, so shameful an event that you will excuse me, gentle reader, if I abbreviate it and secrete its obscenity in the elegant shell of Latin; as a Lady of your society bathes her corrupt parts in rosewater, covers them over with brocaded undergarments.

My mother in her delirium told that, at the beginning, there was only nameless woman. She wandered the earth seeking a mate, but the gods had forbidden such, being jealous of the beauty of their own creation. She was destined for permanent virginal youth, so that the gods could gaze on her for all time and be delighted. But one day, the woman, bathing in a lake, was spied upon by a camboue rat. Her breasts floated on the surface of the water, ripening the eye of the rat. Whilst she luxuriated in the water, the camboue descended its tree with such stealth that even the gods were caught unaware. It slid into the lake and corpus feminae intravit. When it had finished its sport with her, camboue exeunt ex corpore feminae, climbed the tree and hid in the topmost branches. The woman was so shocked by the sudden breach of her body, the utterly unfamiliar sensation of it, that during the obscene assault she made no noise whatsoever. She hurried out of the water and tied a strip of breta-bark about her waist, clothing her nakedness as she had never done before. She felt shame for the first time, but it was quickly overcome by a desire to experience the strangeness of the water once more. So she cast aside her clothing and entered the lake. The rat watched her from its secret hiding place and knew that the gods would be distracted by her perfect naked form. In a safe moment it descended, seeking camouflage in the nest between her thighs. All day the rat stretched and swelled within her until her body erupted and bled for the first time. Afterwards she rested on the bank, appalled at the huge stain she had left in the water. Her fear gave way to unexpected glee. She lay back and laughed uncontrollably at the sky, laughed vulgarly at the virgin forest around her. She laughed with such volume that the virgin forest shook, and fruit fell prematurely to the ground, green pods burst and released their untimely seeds. It was the beginning of our time, my mother said, the birth of our torment. The nameless woman brought forth nameless pestilence. The gods, wise to her disobedience, wise to the pregnancy of her body which deformed her original perfect shape, punished her with death. Death not singly, for the gods were infuriated, not so much by her disobedience, but the glee of it. Death in countless and viciously diverse forms. Death by drowning, starvation, warfare, murder, disease, distraction, earthquake, accident, exhaustion, despair. Death especially by childbirth. For the gods, to perfect their vengeance, created man to partner her – the very man she pined for at the beginning. A man like my father, my forefathers, myself . . . It was mother, not my father, who, seeing my sex, wailed at my birth, a long and futile wailing.

IV

My mother was not descended from a bushrat's whore, in spite of Rima's assertion. Rima was crazed by the sun, and by hunger, when she told me such stories. And they were all versions of each other, involving cunning animals, willing virgins, cheated and outraged gods. Rima was crazed by frustration too.

Still, I believe her when she said that my mother babbled with her hands all night, creating a cosmology, as if my making had to be placed within some grand design. I would have expected, though, something more noble than secret couplings with a rodent, but Rima, apart from being crazed by the sun, by hunger and by carnal frustration, was plainly jealous of my mother's fertility. She described my birth as a tawdry affair achieved by a woman frantic with pain. Only a woman devoid of all sense and will would subject herself to such indignity, Rima said haughtily. Better by guile and secret potions to make your body barren, and endure the wilderness, than to satisfy a man's ambition.

And yet I surmise Rima wanted nothing else but to serve my father productively. How else can you explain, dear reader, the care with which she nurtured me? My first and only memory of Africa is of being cradled in her arms, possibly tenderly, most likely with such fierceness she appeared a beast intent on eating me. It seems that I spent all my life in that distant time and place lying in her arms, fearful of her teeth, forever listening to her melancholy tales. I recollect nothing precise but her ferocious and salivating visage, though in moments of uncertainty she resembled what I have dreamt of my mother since I first set sight on Moll: a firm-breasted woman doomed to wastage and disease. A young unblemished woman. The dream turns into a nightmare of tantalizing detail: there is a face, angular and ebony, chiselled from basalt. The eyes too, and nose, are carved in a geometry which matches with precision the proportion of the lips.

Every feature is hard-edged and rigid. The body carries itself with an appropriate sternness of movement. The limbs are planed, contained; it walks the earth with measured cunei-form gracefulness. Rima, in a moment of my mind's inventiveness, is Grecian in her poise. It is a self-possession as Grecian in its perfection as a mathematical formula. I awake to the image of a desiccated stick, a thing measureless in deformity of spirit. 'Men,' she utters, 'men have made me so in your waking mind.' And she looks upon me in her famished arms, wanting to devour me. And I look up to see Moll's ruined face, like an alabaster bust of classical times weathered by the rude handling of vandals and auctioneers.

Still, for all her cursing of men, Rima spared me. It may have been out of love for my father. I suspect her refusal to describe my mother, when I begged her for a semblance of her face, was the result of jealousy. She promised to draw my mother's visage in the earth. She took up a twig and squatted on the ground, and whilst I stood peering over her shoulders she began to delineate the features of my mother. But the dust would not settle, a sudden gust abducted my mother and Rima tired of the effort. The wind dispersed the dust blindingly into my eyes and when I cried Rima could not comfort me. I refused to be consoled, for Rima was not my mother, and had no right to soothe me. 'In any case she was always cloaked,' Rima said out of sheer malice, contriving the story of my mother's invisibility.

And yet her descriptions of my father were never hesitant or contradictory, which is why I suspect she loved him. His appearance was congruent with travellers' tales in books such as Adamson's *Voyage to Africa* which I later perused in England; he was your normal naked savage – swift of foot, steady in his spearing, and in sexual attributes serene. She took delight in describing the giftedness of his hands, his ability to plant, even in the most stubborn soil, and yet conjure forth orchards. In drought or flood everything he seeded bloomed. Our tribe was resentfully rooted. Before, we migrated from one auspicious spot to another, but some unknown cause of calamity made us settle. We retained our skills at hunting, but only my father knew how best to choose the right soil and furrow it with exactitude of depth; what grains to bury, and in what season of the moon. So Rima claimed, without explaining the origin of his talent. None among our tribe could – they speculated that it was because his wife worshipped a deity so covetous of her complete devotion that he was compensated with another form of fertility. And how abundantly he produced, and in what details Rima described the succulence of a pomegranate seed, or a squashed berry, its gum and sap and mucilage. Hunger textured her mouth. She spoke eloquently of fruit moonwashed and lactescent; fruit sluttish with colour; fruit staunch in flesh; fruit brazen on the tongue. And it was in such a cornucopia of recollection she would bare her teeth. It was my birth, she snarled, which shrunk her body. For when they cut my cord, the past was utterly extinguished, the gods died, and my father's talent. The tribe died, my mother's hands were stilled, and I rolled from her inarticulate hands and fell to the earth and lay there quivering and nauseous until Rima discovered me. She looked upon the sign of swelling on my forehead, asserting itself against the skeins of afterbirth, and she wailed. It was Rima who discovered me, slimy and forlorn like a beached medusa. It was Rima, not my mother or father, who greeted me to the new world with a long and futile wailing.

V

Rima suckled on her rage, gesturing to me as if she had assumed my mother's habit. I read in the accusation of her hands a tale of unfulfilled and forbidden love. 'It was your father who cheated the gods and spawned you,' she said, charging him with stealing under my mother's veil and raiding her virginity like a common bushrat ransacking a nest of eggs. The gods thereafter punished the tribe by presenting it with a cursed child – a male child bearing on its forehead *peia*, the sign of evil reserved only for women. The world would be thrown into confusion, men and women no longer obedient to roles appointed by nature and tradition. Men would lose the discipline of hunting and eventually in breeding their wives. They would chew toba-seeds to get drunk, then paint their faces like whores and indulge in debauchery. The women were forsaken, but the lack of control by men would create new freedoms for them. They too would discover the thrill of each other's bodies. Out of all these perversions new diseases would arise to cripple the tribe's ability to procreate. 'Our barrenness is your father's fault,' Rima asserted, gesturing to the colony of women who shared the wilderness with us. 'If only he had raided me instead of your mother!'

When her rage waned, Rima presented a completely contrary view of my origin. In this version, my father loved her uncommonly as his secondary wife. She was no mere concubine, subject to arbitrary blows from man and wife alike. He never let his companions take her in celebration of a successful hunt. He never let her out to other men in exchange for this or that trinket with which to please his wife.

43

He never tethered her to a post like an animal needing to be tamed by constant beatings and rewards of food. No, he made love to her tenderly, and then only when she acquiesced.

When Rima miscarried, he was dumb with grief, knowing that she would be removed from his reach forever. At first he refused to divulge her failure, instructing her to feign illness and retreat into their hut, away from the gaze of the envious. Only his wife – my mother – was allowed to tend to her, on the pretext that it was an unknown illness that could endanger other women. He planted the fields in a new frenzy. The earth could not bear enough for her, although he dug and seeded it obsessively. Then one day the rains came and would not stop until his handiwork of banked soil was unravelled and washed away, leaving uprooted trees, and pods prematurely ripped.

So Rima was betrayed and sent away. She blamed it on my mother's conspiratorial hands. It was my mother who with the deftest of motion condemned her to the wilderness. My father grieved inwardly. He dared not confront traditions and court the penalty of a prolonged death. He sought a solution in the innards of various animals. He poked and prodded to the amusement and pity of folk. Once revered as our soothsayer he was now a ludicrous figure searching through slime and excrement for a salve for his heart.

'Your father took revenge on our tribe by breeding you,' Rima said fiercely, refusing to surrender to the pathos of her tale. 'He knew that you would come forth with the sign of woman's sin on your forehead. He knew the devastation that would ensue, but he still made you, so that you would go forth as a new prophecy into a new world, one which he himself could not foresee.'

All this Rima divulged to me until the slaver's gunshot blew a hole into her chest. I was lying in her lap. As if by a reflex action caused by the shock of pain, her arms lifted and pressed me against the hole in her chest. I stopped the bleeding. She leaned and whispered into my ears a final benediction and a final edict. She told me that I was special, that I was destined to survive; that I would be marooned on a faraway shore but neither self-pity nor self-loathing – the effects of intense loneliness and the loss of memory – must overcome me. And with a contrary reflexive force she flung me away from her and I travelled an endless distance across an endless sky, her blood trailing after me like a comet's tail.

VI

A noise explodes around me, Rima jerks back, shudders, then slumps forward. I roll from her lap and fall to the earth where I lay in a pool of her blood, orphaned by a whiteman's gun. Rima, who was all my mothers, died at the very moment she gendered me, and all my life in England I have sought to remake her from the glimpses I have had of women's nakedness. It was not prurience which made me peep at Moll's sleeping form, as you will come to hear, but a fitful yearning for my mother's form, one cloaked in the gloom of time past. And if my hands become stained with ink as I now compose this tale for you, it is because my mother beckons me through this cloak; her frantic silent gestures compel my pen to describe her suffering. I write for Moll, not for Mr Pringle's money. I write for Rima, who was all my mothers, who in the gentlest motion of dying or perhaps with the final crack of

45

energy of a snapped twig, surrendered me to the earth; or else I was catapulted from her lap with such force that all memory instantly emptied from me, as a stone flung against water loses weight and skips to the distant bank instead of sinking. Each word I write now is freighted, each mark of punctuation a port and anchorage, for I have skimmed along surfaces for too long and the distant bank that is my death looms. I would have reached there happily in an easeful ignorance, but Mr Pringle's probing has forced me into consciousness, as his ancestor's gun which murdered Rima forced me into birth.

And I was delivered onto a ship frantic with blood and the moaning of women. When for the first time in my life I opened my eyes, a whiskered face loomed over me. It was not Rima's, nor the imagined faces of my mother, but the distant bank of death. At that moment, being new to the world, I was ignorant of death, and I reached a freshly born hand for the bauble of its whiskers. The face moved out of my reach but when I cried out for the comfort of its touch, it leaned forward to pacify me. My fingers yanked its chin, its tendrils of red fur. It was a garden grown wild, hairs coiled and matted around its face. Later I was to wonder whether the redness of its visage was the effect of rum, and whether the vapours tangling its mouth, trapped in a brier of undergrowth, was also spiritous. But for now I savoured its breath, as utmost relief from the drought of Rima's surroundings.

And true to the prophecy of my infant mind the thing before me opened its mouth to reveal a cave resplendent with fruit. You have perused in the Old Testament a description of Solomon's vineyards, or the wondrous gardens of Babylon. Suffice it to say that there was Biblical lushness in the cave that

46

opened up for me. Its roof was a plantation of vines, nameless at first, but subsequent service in the cellars and altars of cultivated Englishmen have made them familiar: muscatel, raisin, corinth, burlet, verjuice. You will excuse me if I grow enthusiastic at the memory of this cave, for I was a mere heathen child and it was my first baptism into your religion. I met Christianity in all its luxuriance on a slaveship. For three years or thirty days, it seemed, we floated towards the distant bank of death. Beneath me, in the bowels of the ship, my fellow creatures pleaded and moaned for release, but only I was singled out for salvation. On the topmost deck of the ship I ate of the fruits of the new religion, and wished that Rima was present to feast lavishly with me, she who was devoured with a dream of my father's tillage and awoke only to the mewling of her belly. My father brought forth nothing. There were no orchards springing magically from the earth, no strange gift he possessed which transformed the dust into golden fields. I had no father, but only the vined mouth that parted to reveal a Christian bounty.

But with the satisfaction of fruit came the dreadful truth that I was dying. I can look back now and philosophize tritely that knowledge is death, that the essence of Christian thought is that unfathomable truth. In Africa there was no knowledge, therefore no death. We were progeny of rats, we lived and then we perished, that was all. We experienced only the sensations of desire and pain. Only when the Christian came were we told that there was science to our suffering: that God created us in a state of bliss but that in an instant we sinned and therefore became enslaved to death. It was a simple tale, but unfathomable because of its simplicity. If my African brethren still languish in a world of sensations in spite of your proselytizing, it is because they prefer chaos to the symmetry of Christian truth.

It was such knowledge of symmetry that came to me as I lay dying on the deck of the slaveship. I huddled in the corner like a clump of soiled and squandered rope, useless against the jaws of wind; useless against the sails bellying with pain and groaning on their cross of masts. I knew that I was born with an inheritance of sin; that man had squandered the noble gifts of reason and compassion that God had endowed him with; that lust and disobedience were the original causes of our present condition; that our fate was the jaws of hell.

Because of sin I was powerless to resist the thraldom of death. This knowledge came to me because the ship's Captain – Mr Thomas Thistlewood – singled me out for communion. I drank of the chalice of his mouth and came to an understanding of my fate. My fellow beings in the darkness of the hold and without benefit of the sacramental, cried to be relieved, enslaved as they were to a world of sensations. When the ship pitched in a sudden rough sea, the chains tightened and cracked their ankles, spines and elbow joints. Sometimes arms and legs and heads were wrenched clean off, and their torsos rolled freely about the ship. Once, after a particularly bad storm, out of curiosity I followed Captain Thistlewood, who went below to tally his losses. Apart from the stench which induced nausea and loss of concentration, it was difficult to count accurately, for there were hands sans arms wedged in the iron restraints, feet sans legs, stumps of necks. It was like a resurrection gone gruesomely wrong, for they were without benefit of the sacramental. One woman, torn from her chains, sans head and feet, rolled endlessly about, according to the rhythm of the waves battering the ship. Eventually when the ship lurched massively she was flung to the far end of the hold. She landed alongside her son and he recognized her even in her acephalous and fractured state. He yanked at his chains in a bid to embrace her. It was in such a bizarre manner that families were separated, then united, on board the slaveship. I remembered my own sudden connection and separation from Rima. This, and the hapless sight of the boy's fingers stretching towards his mother's torso, made me weep, and for days afterwards the ministrations of Captain Thistlewood could not console me.

And yet they were not fully human, for none were baptized in the body of Christ, none received the sacraments from Captain Thistlewood's, my father's, mouth. After a while I ceased feeling pity at their distress, my original mood giving way to an acceptance of the nature of things. Being heathen, it was inevitable that they would perish in irrelevant numbers. Captain Thistlewood only counted their bodies for human record, for the purpose of the insurance dividends which would be paid for loss of goods once we landed on commercial shores; or for the purpose of calculating the quantity of fresh water on board against diminishing demands. They died of cholera or heartbreak or gangrene caused by the iron manacles shearing open their flesh and flaking and rusting therein. Captain Thistlewood, to be sure, ministered to them with Christian assiduity. Every day he went below deck with salt tablets for the diarrhoeic, and bandages, and limes for the scurvied, and bread for the toothless feeble children which he chewed in his own mouth into a paste before feeding them.

He tended to them not as soulful beings but as sick animals. And when his efforts failed, and they were brought on deck to be disposed of overboard, his faced was mulched with sorrow. He was deeply affected by the loss of his creatures, and could barely bring himself to countenance the bodies warped with fever; warped canvases slipped from their frames; fevers having melted their surfaces and depths so that the deck swam in the blue oil of a ruptured liver, the vermilion of a ruptured spleen. The Captain, when he looked upon them, did not behold a scene from hell, for there were not perished souls. He saw animals innocent of crime or sin, animals discharged into his failed care and husbandry. And he was moved as fiercely as any decent man is by the sight of undeserved suffering. You, English, inhabitants of a country distinguished for its adoration of pets and charity to the lesser breed, will know the tempest of emotions that overcame my Captain. You have the nightmare of Mr Hogarth's genius, in his series of prints, *Scenes of Cruelty*, to stir you to patriotic rage. You have been so pained by their scenes of mindless destruction – the fatal beating of a horse, the tormented dog, the blinding of a dove – that you have purchased them in their thousands to adorn your mantelpiece and conscience.

Captain Thistlewood hated the business of death. He hated the classification in his ledger book of Negroes by gender and age (dead males yielding a greater sum in compensation from the insurance company than females and children). He hated the shores of commerce and its citizenry of clerks; soil-bound clerks who showed actuarial contempt for his love of his cargo, for the measureless grief he felt at the suffering of his animals.

VII

I consumed the Eucharist on board and came to the knowledge that our true slavery was temporary slavery to death, our true freedom the acquisition of a soul manacled eternally to the will of God. My Negro brethren below deck wrapped in chains and floating in their own faeces were in temporary distress. The white sailors who drank rum and went below to rape the women were in temporary insanity. They refused fresh water to the dying, deaf to the most heart-rending of supplications, or tortured them more directly by urinating saltily into their mouths – but it was a temporary cruelty of their hearts. When tempests seized the ship in a fit of palsy, the sailors vomited and soiled their breeches. They scurried here and there, jerking at ropes to adjust sails, hugging masts to steady themselves, but the sea in one long withdrawing sucking motion dislodged them instantly as rotten nails are from a rotten Cross. But all was a temporary panic and wrecking of lives. In the Christian scheme all were available to death and forgiveness and salvation.

And Captain Thistlewood, who fathered and delivered me onto a knowledge of Christ, isolated himself from the scene of distress, for he understood its temporary nature. The tempest would die down, the soul would be emancipated from slavery to its body and be rehoused in the roomy mansion and tabernacle of heaven. And yet, being human, his heart still grieved. He remained aloof in his cabin, grappling with the wheel as if challenging God for an explanation for the torture of the innocent. He could cope when his sailors maimed and molested the Negroes: he flogged them mercifully, or withdrew their wages, or read to them the epistles of St Paul urging love. However, when a tempest took Negro lives, or when his medicines failed to remedy their diseased flesh, he chafed at God.

Why then did he imperil his soul by captaincy of the vessel? I was lying at his feet like a piece of soiled and squandered rope. The skies had erupted and the ship raped of its will. Captain Thistlewood allowed me the protected shelter of his company. He fought the wheel as if willing me to stay awake, but I was a weak disciple, and the sleep of death crept onto me, and would undo me, when the Captain suddenly pressed his foot upon my groin. Then he hauled me up as the ship was hauled up to the raging sky and stripped of its sails. The shirt tore from my body, I fell from his grasp and lay naked on the floor. Instinctively I curled my body to shield myself from shame, but he stamped upon me again, and my hands withdrew automatically from my groin. I lay helpless at his feet, my testicles swollen, my penis erect in agony.

'Wipe the sleep from your eyes,' he said, loosening his necktie and tossing it at my lap, but my hands were enfeebled and the shame would not be covered by so scant a cloth. Only with the storm did the bleeding subside. Freed from the wheel, he came over to where I lay and soaked his handkerchief in his own spittle to moisten my lips. 'Forget the land, forget the land,' he said, pressing my head to his chest as if to contain some dreadful hatching.

Part III

I am at his feet, and I have no words to talk of the pain, how he press my gut, and why? There is no sense to what he does, and I know not how to ask why he beats so, why he make sweat form on his face and fall on me with the blows, and why he seem to lose his own breath as I do too when a kick and two kicks and three kicks make the air race from my mouth, and I sob and suck for the air to come back, but just as rage choke him, so pain choke me. I don't have breath and my eyes will burst from my face, then he haul back my head to face the sky so harsh that the air rush into my mouth and I live once more, like when, at the lip of the pit, the blade will fall on my neck but his voice boom out and stop the man who will chop me, and I live once more by his grace and word.

Mr Pringle's pen is poised at his notebook, and after countless years' sojourn in England I have words sufficient to tell of the ritual beatings, but I will not remember these for his seedy apprehension. He wants a story of pimps, whores and screaming nigger boys, though he will stay it in decent grammar and appropriate expressions, but I have learnt Moll's craft too well to be deceived by his purpose. Moll's hands were deft as she made knots and stays with silken cords, until her client was decorously trussed. She was as skilled with thongs as any grammarian is with language, but all was an allusion of restraint, for her client still twisted and strained rankly.

When a whiteman on the ship do bad Captain make him tie up to a mast and whip him, but it is not the same as what I get, for there is no love for the whiteman as Captain raise and fall the birch to his back, his eyes don't see the skin bulge and the blood, his hands just work at the whiteman's back as if to haul or slack a rope, to steer a sail or wipe the salt spray from his face, just one more task and act to make our way through the sea smooth. When it is done the whiteman is let loose and that is all, but Captain would take me to his room, there in the cool and dark to catch my sense and mend.

The first time, when I come to, the sting in my head and the cry still in my mouth, Captain is by the bed and he stoop and raise me and prop me up and make me drink a juice, more and more and more, till I daze and slump. Then he slide down by me, and I sleep in the feel of his breath. And in my dream a wild cry burst from my lips as my legs are spread and spread and eels are born from me like ink that drops from Mr Pringle's pen and stain a trail through his pages.

I wake, Captain is still there, and with a kind hand and a page of white bread he dab the froth from the sides of my mouth. Out of love he light a lamp and hold it to me and then to the wall of his room, so that my eyes soothe on what he hang there, the hurt dip as I dwell in a space of blue, a blue hill, blue flights of birds, and a Man who is God bent over a blue stream to wash the dirt of whores from his hands.

Captain put a cup to my mouth, tilt back my head and make me sip the blood of the blue Man. He fold my hand and teach me to pray, how His Will Be Done On Earth, that I am born of sin, that I must beg for his wrath to cleanse me. Only I can save you, he say, slap my face and draw blood, pin me to the bed and with a cry and thrust fix me to his lap where I writhe like a drawn eel. He draws sin like eels from the mud and deep of me.

Captain Thistlewood went below to inspect the sick among my brethren, and I followed him, carrying vials of medicine. I will not dwell on the sudden effluvium of air that greeted us when the hatch was lifted, for there is ample appeal to your nostrils in Abolition literature written by Englishmen truly appalled by the foulness of the African trade. Suffice to say that even the olfactory gifts of Messrs Gay and Pope, in describing London's sewers, would be paupered by the stink of nigger-sweat. They pleaded for water or a mouthful of food or for any measure to relieve them of the agony of their condition. They addressed Captain Thistlewood in the only English they knew, which were the profanities uttered nightly by the sailors. And Captain Thistlewood (who taught me language) understood them perfectly. A less experienced man, confronted with such execrations, would have abandoned my brethren, battened down the hatches and left them to their heathen state, but Captain Thistlewood (who taught me prayer) dispensed charity to them. He attended to every call, interpreting this obscenity and that as the cry of one dying of dysentery, cholera, homesickness, until I grew jealous of his attention to the toothless feeble children, feeding them bread dissolved first in his own mouth. I too cursed him with the full force of mimicry: 'Blessed are you among women and blessed is the fruit of your womb Jesus.' And suddenly, his tongue, which once had secreted these words into my ears as he mounted me, ceased ministering to the children. He pushed me to the ground in a reflex action, stamped his feet at my crotch, kicked me, and kicked me, until I fainted with the love.

When my Captain fell asleep, his rage spent, I eased myself from the weight of his body, put on my clothes, and went below to my brethren. I carried with me flasks of wine and strips of dried meat which I had taken from my Captain's store. He would not mind, since we were of one private marriage, and thus of one ownership, despite my official slavery.

In the darkness of the hold I called out Manu's name, for I would feed him first. No one answered. There was a constant low groaning which after a while sounded as normal as the groaning of the sea; their pain sounded normal, like the noise of stars, a blaze of light that after first sight, and another, and a million nights, lost its terror and became backdrop to whatever human voices broke the calm. At first there was the call of tree-frogs, twinkling and pulsating in the nights before my father died. A sound as deafening as the first light of stars, but during the ceremony for my father, we heard nothing, saw nothing. In the moment of grief, there was nothing eventful in heaven or on earth, no convulsions of light or sound, only the steady furnace of stars and the singing of tree-frogs which dimmed into such normalcy that my mother, watching over my father, heard nothing beyond the rustle of breta-leaves, saw nothing beyond the mist of her eyes. And with the dancing women I only heard in the dark the noise of my own suckling.

I called again but Manu did not answer. I called for Ellar, and Tanda and Saba and all the rest, but no voice broke the calm of Negro moaning. All were bound in one general pain, all dissolved into one mess of black suffering.

No one answered but I sensed their envy and their hatred

of me, for I had survived, and if thirst and weakness had not stopped their mouths, I could imagine the accusations hurled at me. I offered food but they scorned my charity, even in the moment of their dying. I imagined them speaking in one chorus of rejection, even as they eyed the gifts in my hands. With supreme effort and sacrifice, someone gathered the last moisture in his mouth and spat it at me. 'You have betrayed us,' one voice called, and another, 'You have become the whiteman's wife,' and another, 'You have robbed us of land.' They heaped curses on me, for Saba's sacrilege, for enslaving our tribe, for surrendering to the ways of whitemen. 'I am not the reason for your death,' I shouted in the darkness but my words merged and disappeared into their steady moaning. I left them to their ignorance and found a quiet space on the top-deck where I laid out my whole parcel of wine and meat, and I ate and drank out of spite. With each mouthful I damned them for their black and useless ways. Let them hunger and thirst, for they were surrendered to the might of the whiteman. In a moment, in the space of a gunshot, all that they owned and were ceased, all the efforts over all the ages that made them a tribe with its own scars. I bore on my forehead, in the briefest of marks, all the evidence that once we were. The Headman carved my forehead with the sign of evil: I was to be banished out of sight and memory of our tribe, but what heathen foolishness! He was dead, and all of them, our homes wasted, the fields overrun, all signs of husbandry disappeared. It is as if we had made nothing, except the mark of sin upon a boy's forehead. I drank more wine, and grew melancholy with the realization of how

59

they had burdened me to utter for them. Only my voice survived the general hum of pain.

Through the dizziness of wine, the ghost of Ellar approached, trembled into speech. 'Tell the strangers that I was fabled throughout the land for my comeliness,' Ellar said, breaking into a grin and exposing gums stained with toba-juice. She raised her skirt and winked at me. 'Look! I am shaped for dancing,' and she swayed unsteadily on her lame foot. 'Make them love me,' she laughed, throwing back her head in a gesture of frivolity, but the effort unbalanced her and she fell to the ground in an undignified sprawl. She raised her face from the dust.

'Where are your hens?' I asked, not knowing how to comfort her, and I offered her the remains of my bundle of food. 'My mother sent this for you,' I lied.

'Keep your pity, wretch,' she answered in an unexpected outburst of ingratitude, 'and as to your mother, she was as barren as a serving-boy. I am your mother, as is every other whore that walks bare-headed under the widest sky.' She caught herself, rearranged her shawl around her face in a quick nervous action. 'Tell the English I didn't long for any man, but only for what I deserved,' she said abruptly, and then fell silent as if parading in her mind all the suitors who never came her way because of her misshapen form.

Other villagers spun into view. They joined Ellar in petitioning me to remember them in the best light. They thrust their face at me and slobbered their demands, the most nauseous being Kaka, the village beggar. He, the lowliest of our tribe, one whose entrances were heralded by a buzz of flies, now commanded me to represent him as the body of wisdom. He was a small man with an overlarge

60

head all the more prominent by its baldness and stunted ears. His face was the face of an idiot: ageless, changeable, deformed in a striking, almost beautiful, way. When he was happy he could barely speak, gurgling like a child, and his shiny face took on the appearance of extreme innocence. When he was angered he snarled and butted like a deceived harlot, his skin coarsened with his voice and people ran from his path as from a foul spirit. Now, his begging gourd tied around his neck like a badge of shame, the cloth around his loins frayed, his head swollen to an even bigger size because of malnutrition, his body bruised with pebble marks (I too used to chase him from my mother's yard when he came seeking food, by pelting him with stones), he still insisted on being pictured otherwise. 'What can a madman like you know?' the villagers taunted him, and with utmost assurance he replied, 'I know a field plentiful with worms.' He addressed me with concern in his voice. 'Come, I'll take you there to feast,' he offered.

'I have enough to eat,' I replied, pointing to my harvest from Captain Thistlewood's store. He looked uncomprehendingly at the whiteman's food. There was a little froth at the side of his mouth, betraying hunger. I reached to wipe it, but the villagers beat away my hand. One took up the stick to shoo him away, and voices arose to mock him.

'I know Saba,' he shouted above the din, and there was a sudden prolonged hush, broken only by the intermittent sobbing of a woman, whom I recognized as Saba's mother. 'Ask them what they have done to Saba,' Kaka commanded, turning to face them with such fierceness that they forgot his condition of beggary. 'Let them be judged by the light of stars,' he said, gesturing to the night-sky with unexpected eloquence, 'and when they are pronounced guilty let me be their executioner!'

'What have they done to Saba?' I asked, my voice weighed with stones of guilt. I raised a flask of wine to my mouth, wanting to obliterate them from my mind, when Manu suddenly emerged from their midst, took the flask away gently and rested it on the ground.

'Stay awake. Stay awake. Remember the land,' he whispered. He combed his beard with his fingers, soothing its unruliness, all the while speaking calmly to me. 'Look at the whitemen, look at what they do,' he said, pointing to two sailors bailing out water or reefing in sails. 'Day and night they work the sea but they catch nothing but wind, they make nothing but speed.'

'What else should they do? I asked, perplexed.

'Our hands tilled and wove and built,' he said, gently evading my question, 'but the whiteman is busy only with death. We are his only harvest.' And he turned away from me to face our villagers with defiant eyes. 'Look again at Kaka, look,' he urged, but when I did, Kaka's sores still gleamed. He was the same, accompanied by the same flies. His head was as comically big. He was the same stinking nigger as when I pelted him with stones. Nor did Ellar's limbs straighten, howsoever I willed them to elegance. 'Remember us as we are, not as the whiteman will make you,' he told me.

'You are beggars and fools,' I cried out in defence, for he spoke to me knowingly, as if, even in the darkness of solitude of Captain Thistlewood's quarters, he had witnessed my Conversion. The gaze of the villagers filled me with shame. I reached for the flask of wine again, but Manu stopped my hand.

'We *are* beggars and fools,' he said in the calmest of voices, easing the sting of anger from me.

'Then it is not I who have killed you?' I asked, wanting to be forgiven.

'No, it is not you. How can a boy be responsible for such death?' He smiled at me lovingly.

'Where is my mother? Where is my mother?' I demanded with sudden courage, seeking from him confirmation of her raped body. (She was lying at the lip of the pit. Her clothes were taken from her body. They hauled me up to look upon her. Her head was broken, but she was not yet dead, for her feet shuddered, until Captain Thistlewood delivered her. He put his gun into her mouth. Everybody laughed and howled but the explosion shut them up, and there was my mother's blood and bone everywhere on their skin, so that they had to scrub themselves with dust to make themselves white again.)

'Your mother died at your birth,' he said, and as if to placate me, added, 'as women often do.'

I reeled at his revelation of my past, but recovered to doubt him, to curse him for his stupid testimony. 'You lie. All your prophecies have been lies. You ate all our food and took gifts but none of your pebbles warned us of the coming of Captain Thistlewood.'

'Yes, I failed you and all of us,' he confessed, readily, but still stroking his beard wisely. 'I was useless. Perhaps the whiteman could not be foretold.'

'You *were* useless,' I told him.

'Perhaps the whiteman could not be foretold,' he

63

repeated. 'He is neither storm nor drought. He is not the will of sky nor earth. An iron needle guides him across water. He points an iron stick at us from afar and kills. He is not naked flesh, and could not be foretold for my power is only to warn of our enemies who are yet our brethren and our likeness.'

I made to scoff at Manu's belief in Captain Thistlewood's unearthly power, I who knew his slobbering, the way he cried in surrender over me, and grew limp, and rolled away to the edge of the bed like a drained bottle, but before I could, Manu read my thoughts.

'You have tamed him in truth, you have made him your slave.' He looked at me with abiding pity in his eyes. 'You have become a woman's ache and guile.'

'You made us so,' I answered, accepting my status, becoming my mother, and women, surviving by trickery and self-abasement.

'Save yourself. We are dead already, but you must remain.' His voice grew urgent as when, pebbles strewn at his feet, he suddenly discovered a solution to whatever had been troubling our sleep. Once he was the most famous interpreter of signs in our land. Different tribes – even our enemies – came to the village to consult him. Now he was a mere figure in my dream, begging to be heeded.

'You must remain,' he repeated, 'but enslaved as you are, Captain Thistlewood will try to kill you.'

'He has saved me and has baptized me,' I said fearlessly, 'and when he beats me, it is that I too must know the suffering of the Cross.'

'He will not kill you with blows but with new words,'

64

Manu warned. 'He will plant in your mind pictures of his land, and root up ours.'

'But the pictures he shows me are beautiful, and I desire to see England. And what was our land but widows scavenging in the wilderness?'

'There were no such women, only in your imagining. Our tribe was content, each with each. There were ceremonies of love by which we lived, each with each and in communion with the gods of earth and sky.'

'Then why was it so easy to destroy us?' I interrupted, disregarding his sentimentality.

'Do you not remember your father?' he asked, evading my question a second time. 'Do you not remember how, for sixteen years, he cared for you, all the time mourning for your mother? After she died in bearing you, he did not take another wife, out of respect for her. He would disappear for many days and nights, hunting alone, for he was searching the forest for your mother. And he would return bruised and cut and empty-handed. There was no trophy of deer or pig. He could no longer kill, taking pity on each creature, the rare and sacred life in each of them.'

'I remember nothing but a man who came to me drunk, with a pocketful of sour fruit. I was always hungry, no one fed me.'

'We fed both of you. We tilled our own land, and his too, for it was overrun with mourning. We hunted for you, and him. We became his father, and yours. Do you not remember how we shaved your head and marked your forehead in preparation for your manhood, a duty which your father should have performed, but he was too sick with grief, so all the men gathered around you and became your father? We bathed you, like our own son, anointed you, marked your forehead. And the women came, their faces bright with paint, and they danced for you, and called the blessings of the gods upon you, and brought gifts for your future wife, bangles, perfumed cloths, mats to sleep on, gourds of sweet beverages.'

'I remember nothing but their filthy nakedness and their squealing.'

'The white Captain is a herd of wild pigs that root in our fields. He has run amok in your mind and left only dung. And all the descriptions of his own land are false, he speaks noble and beautiful words, but he has been at sea for centuries, and England has coarsened in his absence. They have laid waste to their own land, cleared their forests to make ships to carry us, gouged the earth for the ores to make our chains. When the white Captain beats you now, it is out of melancholy, for he knows he is estranged from his own herd, that his speech is antique beyond recognition. So remember us as we are, and the earth that not only suckled us but after the rains, it ran with colours, and gave astonishment and even in a season of drought, dust masked our faces in the richest dyes.'

One day with a kind hand Captain tie my limbs and stuff my mouth with cloth. He light the coal pot, put a brand in it and when it shine red he raise it to my head. I faint with the shock and when I wake I faint once more with the smell of my own burnt flesh. Captain care me for days and days, rub oil in my skin to cool it and wet me with kiss, till I grow well, and then he fetched glass for me to see how he mark my forehead, TT, and his voice is love as I gaze at the strange bites, and he tells me soon Cross will join Cross when the flesh heal and stretch, and that I am now in life, and will be in death, his own.

I remember nothing, but I pity Mr Pringle's solicitousness, and I am in need of his charity, so I must create characters, endow them with traits and peculiarities, and sow dialogue between us to make luxuriant plots of the pages of his notebook. As to Captain Thistlewood, was he a herd of wild pigs or my Christian master? I know nothing, only the regular journeys between his quarters, where I languished in a cataleptic state, to the top-deck where he stripped and beat me. There was nothing except the drugged journey from darkness below to an open sky and back again. And in all our time he never spoke, nor did I reply. But there was a painting which I awoke to every day, a blue painting, or several, before which he raised a lamp. You will know, from the accounts of seafaring life which furnish your libraries, that sea-captains are deemed the most uncouth of creatures, but he was a keeper of paintings – hardly a connoisseur, for the daubs on his wall were as nothing compared to the fine specimens of Italian art that informed my taste in Lord Montague's household. In moments of reprieve, before I was taken upstairs to be chastised, he spoke their subjects to me, his voice growing agitated and melancholy by turns. 'Here,' he said, pointing to a picture, then another, 'here is myrtle and leek and hyssop. Here is mandrake, lime and may-lilies. Take the roots of cowslips, the leaves of penny-royal, shred them small, put them into hot broth and rub upon your lids with soap and hog's suet melted together, then you will never sleep.' He thrust himself aggressively at me, his vined hair and tendrilled beard quaking like a forest suddenly disturbed by a storm. 'You cannot know whereof I speak,' he said after a while, the fierceness of his appearance waning. He lowered his head, and his hair hung tenderly over his face, like a woman's. All roughness was removed from his voice as he told me in hesitant confession of the nature of his fantasy. He twirled his forefinger in his hair in a feminine motion. 'They are mostly dead. We have killed what moved. We have even forgotten how to name them.' I looked uncomprehendingly at the pictures. 'Wolf,' he said, identifying an animal, 'the bane of our farmers, and yet if the head of a wolf be hung in a dove-house, neither cats, nor weasels, nor anything that will hurt pigeons will enter therein. And if a broth of its spittle be rubbed on the heads of boys who have eyes of different colours, it takes away the diversity.' He stared affectionately at the animal, as if he were the keeper of its ancient secrets. 'There was nothing in England that lived that had not magical properties. An adder's bite kills a man but if by charms and conjurations you draw forth its venom and if concocted with the roots of hare-bells and eaten with salt and filberts, then its malice be greatly tempered and it becomes a remedy for all wearisomeness.' He paused and looked at me weakly, gathering his thoughts, or else plucking up courage for a lover's confession. 'They deem you nigger, and will price you by your fitness to work. But I knew, as I saved you from my own countrymen, that no bride-price was sufficient to be put upon your head.'

'Why did you save me?' I asked, speaking to him for the first and only time. His weakness emboldened me, and when he did not reply, his face flush with coyness, I demanded him to tell me. 'They were about to hack off my head but you called out and commanded me to be saved. Why did you single me out, when you let all the others be massacred? Why am I special to you?' But he would not answer, and withdrew like a flower curling upon itself when touched unbearably.

In time I could name the land he held in such reverence. I came to know a heaven of falcons and kingfishers and an earth roamed by hart and noble unicorn. He taught me that the screech-owl and night-raven presaged death, but that nightingales sang of lovers' ache for secret union. He was proud of my quick learning, especially when he led me before the blue painting and made me kneel and repeat a hymn to the bounteousness of God and the mystery of his creation. And yet, even in a moment of adoration, he would suddenly turn on me and beat me cruelly. 'Forget the land, forget the land,' he urged, his voice hoarse with a pain I did not fully understand, in spite of my ready discipleship.

Still, I do not fear him, for his pain is great, more than my own, so I take his kick and blow and cease to moan and cry. I do not mind his strange ways from the time one night when he think I am in sleep, numb by wine, and he light his lamp and I peep as he goes to kneel to his blue God, and a huge sob break from his throat and his breast break in grief. He is mad in truth, mad, but I am sad for him, sad for the land he so loves but is far from, and for all the birds and beasts who are dead in the land. Set in paint, they do not stir nor crow nor sing. That is all they are, dreams of blue.

An assemblage of cheap art which moves Captain Thistle-wood to tears, and a nigger boy locked in his cabin learning England's bestiary: Mr Pringle will of course dismiss my account as subterfuge, as desire on my part to conceal the abuses that I endured. He thinks I am ashamed of public confession of the deeds wrought on my body. He wishes me to tell him that I was ripped from my mother's breast by the evil slaver Captain Thistlewood, taken to his ship and so molested that I became a willing disciple to the ways of animals. Hence my companionship in England of whores and Jews. Of course he would write of me with such compassion that my sins would be forgiven by the Abolitionists of England. All or part of Mr Pringle's conception of my Progress is, or may be, true, but I will not move you to customary guilt, gentle reader, even though you may crave that I hold up a mirror to the sins of your race. You will reward me with laurels and fat purses for flagellating you thus, especially should I, with impoverished imagination, evoke for you the horror of the slaveship's hold, the chained Negroes, their slobbering, their suffoca-tion, their sentimental condition. No, they laughed, they chattered, they gossiped, they cried, they desired, as they had always done in the villages in Africa. There were chains there too. They merely exchanged their distress for yours, when you packed them in your boat. And perhaps your distress will eventually prove to be more creative: I prophesy a time not when we will sire your kings and queens, nor lead your armies into battle, for such is fool's gold and counterfeit ambition. I prophesy a time when the love I bore Moll will be a common compact, that the ache of the nightingale's song will give way to blessed union. It is your love that I greed for, not the coinage of your guilt.

So let me not give you a portrait of Captain Thistlewood as you think he is, but as I wish him to be. Let me paint him as a man who beat me as our Saviour was beaten, so that I could come to know the weight of the Cross of my sins. And he beat me to forget the very land of his imagining, the very land he taught me to name with reverence, for it had become the distant bank of death: you had enclosed it, maimed its spirit with your commercial plough, converted it into a plantation and city and emporium. You peopled it with urchins playing in gutters, or with clerks who tallied its worth. You made merchants and factories and ships of death and slaves and whores. You dug its belly for metals. You lusted. You sinned.

So let him be with his gallery of dreams, his poorly coloured emblems of a previous England, the falcon and the unicorn.

And when in my account he spurns your rewards for a successful African venture, do not think his brain is seasick, affected by cholera or maddening thirst. It is my presence which has converted him to Christian ways. His fingers, once white with powder or stained in the oil in which he anointed his gun, now work frantically with other dyes as he remembers a previous land, and daubs the form of falcon and unicorn on his cabin wall for me to see the better world of his character. No longer does he curse as in previous voyages when his ship fastened to a chaotic wind and was dragged across the sea like a woman dragged by her hair, and the sea slammed into her with shameless fury. His sailors panicked, rushing to furl main and mizzen-topsails, struggling with whipstaff and rudder. Their lives were at peril, but also their entitlement to a portion of a cargo of blacks, so they wrestled with tarpaulin, bailed water, seared their fingers at ropes, braced masts that would crack and collapse. And all the while Captain Thistlewood screamed orders but the wind stopped his breath, forced his words back into his mouth.

No longer does he suffocate on his own words, nor does he supervise the execution of cowards – the sailors who are struck with fright, and slide below to hide among the stores, as if, when the demons of the sea come to claim their lives, they would appease them with dried fruit, rice, spices and other tributes from the earth. He used to kill such cowards by gunshot or strangulation and command that they be hung from the topmast like hare or pheasant, mocking their longing for land and reminding the rest of the seasoning of his wrath. They were *his* crew as the slaves below were collectively theirs to dispose of or to husband. Rape was allowed, not only for necessary manly recreation, nor because it calmed their craving for a shore, but because it promised to increase the stock of slaves. But it had to be a measured act, no lasting hurt done to the females, no excessive violence to exhaust them to the point of extinction. A sailor who allowed his emotions to overcome him and caused the loss of life would in turn yield his. Such carelessness was as unacceptable as the spillage of fresh water in a period of shortage. At sea, everything had to be managed with care and due control, for their lives' sake and the success of the enterprise.

No longer does he take stock of water and provisions, nor reckon in his ledger book the loss of Africans against original calculations of their yield, for I have cured him of such solicitousness. And do not ask me the how and why and wherefore of such cure, for love cannot disclose its alchemy. Bread and wine becomes the body and blood of God: you must have the same faith in my transformation of Captain Thistlewood and in my travelogue as you invest in your priests and your Gospels. And do not doubt that Captain Thistlewood even after seasons of abuse – being a veteran of a dozen slave voyages – is capable of redemption, for you have at hand, respected reader, many accounts of such conversions. Was not Revd. John Newton whose hymns honey your throat each Sunday once a slaver? And is not the regular reprinting of his *Thoughts Upon the African Trade* testimony to your charitable hearts? His descriptions of slavery are so potent that even a fiend is moved to fall upon his knees and seek mercy of God. And how many other of your clergymen found their calling from reading such treatises? No, nothing that I relate to you is beyond credibility even though I am a nigger in the telling of it, susceptible, because of what I am by nature, to hysteria, befuddlement and exaggeration.

Undoubtedly there will be among you rationalists who doubt the truth of revealed religion, and spurn the Gospels, and will not believe in miracles, therefore will not believe my tale. They will point to Mrs Tofts of Godalming, who gave birth to rabbits, to the wonderment of the learned who made pilgrimages of witness, until her trick was discovered. They will point to other false magicians of our time, like Mr Chandler who grew wings and fangs and savaged sheep in their pens at night. Not even the cannons of the Norfolk regiment, which were called into service by popular clamour and the king's consent, could shoot him from the sky whence he flew off with bloody carcasses. Of course he was revealed for what he was – a brilliant spectacle-maker bored with his work, who discovered a way of projecting an image against the night sky, therefore terrorizing his neighbours and giving himself great merriment. Or the notorious Mr Joseph Countryman, whom no prison could contain because as soon as the turnkey locked the doors and retired he changed into a flock of jackdaws and flew away. He was caught in human form days later and incarcerated in another institution, but escaped immediately: prison yards up and down the country were littered with jackdaws shot dead by wardens in an attempt to stop Mr Countryman's flights, but unsuccessfully.

Truly we live in an age of wonders, and desperate people will go to any lengths to earn a living. Paupers have learned to swallow bagfuls of nails and broken spoons in return for coppers from an astonished crowd. A whore, too old for her trade, earns her pension by flinging herself from a beam and suffocating on a rope. The crowd gasps as she swings but refuses to die. She has trained herself to induce a coma, thereby lessening her need for breath, and to awaken from it with precise timing, reaching in her bosom for a knife to cut the rope. The crowd gasps as she crashes to the ground, and they throw coins at her slumped body. Most piteous of all are the abandoned children who roam London's streets, who have learned such tricks of endurance with their orifices, for the amusement of gentlemen, that the King's censor would be shocked by an account of their performances.

Rationalists will place my testimony with such wonders,

and dismiss me as a pedlar of the bizarre. But you, my sympathetic reader, will judge whether I serve Captain Thistlewood faithfully by presenting him as a good and loving master; or whether my slavery to him is an act of self-mutilation, like the pauper's, or whore's or urchin's. Mr Pringle's version of Captain Thomas Thistlewood is untroubled. Captain Thistlewood is a demon and I his catamite. Animal favours, followed by beatings: such a simple explanation of my time aboard the ship gives a simple rhythm to Mr Pringle's lines. Worst of all he will deny that my forehead bears the sign of Greek learning and will say that Captain Thistlewood was marking his property by branding his initials into my flesh. And in one unified chorus of outrage, readers will fill the coffers of the Abolition Committee. And I, Mungo, confirmed and sanctified as a deserving buggered nigger, will get a fresh pair of breeches. But I will not so cheaply bargain away my esteem for Captain Thistlewood, for even if it is true that he stamped his foot upon my neck to stop me from wriggling so as to better brand my forehead with his initials, I felt no terror then, only gratitude for being baptized into his faith. The iron was a crucifix blinding my eyes to my own heathen past. He pressed it twice upon my forehead, the first pain so excruciating that it banished desire for Africa from my mind; the second exquisitely timed to stop my mouth from execrations, the final traces of African utter-ance.

Part IV

I

The ship plunges into the deep then rears up cruelly. The slaves awaken from the deceit of sleep, from the dreams of the relief that death alone brings. Once more irons cut into their flesh as the ship pitches, chains jangle an alarum to another day of living, another day of the comings and goings of desperate sailors. Each morning they look to Manu for guidance, but he is without magical shell and pebble and bone, he cannot foretell today whether they will be fed a richer meal than salt-fish and biscuits; whether the sailors will cheat them of their due rations by picking the meat from the broth for their own malnourished mouths; whether they will be unchained and taken upstairs for fresh air and exercise; whether the mess seeping endlessly from their backsides will be washed away and powder sprinkled on them to kill the lice; whether the dead will be removed from their midst and the boards disinfected with vinegar; whether the sailors will strap the mouths of the women and children before they enter them, so that at least the rest of the slaves can rest in peace and quiet. But Manu is hopeless. He is ashamed of his impotence. He cannot look them in the eye. He neglects to eat. He will not join in the scramble when the sailors throw their rations at them, feeding them as animals are fed. On deck their feet are whipped, forcing them to dance and to exercise, but Manu absorbs the stinging and will not move. On deck they scour the horizon for sight of their village, but Manu stares into himself without seeing anything, any sign that will prophesy a safe return.

I sit afar and watch them hop and skip as the sailors beat their legs. Captain says I do not need such exercise, he will attend to me personally in his quarters. In the meantime he gives me a chunk of cheese and tells me to go to the fo'c'sle where I can eat at my own leisure. Somehow, Kaka slips away from the crowd of dancers and comes to me. He is starving, I can tell, not so much from his bloated stomach, but from the way he gazes at the cheese in my hand. It is not that he wants a piece, for when I offer he refuses. He just wants to gaze at it and to salivate as I chew. He is too weak to move his own jaws, and in any case he has lost interest in his body. He is content to see me eat and to savour the memory of how he once would suck and savage the bones of left-overs put in his bowl, licking and re-licking his fingers afterwards. I chew slowly, to give him maximum pleasure, making loud sucking noises before I swallow. I burp for him. The vacant look on his face disappears gradually the more I eat. By the time I am finished, Kaka is transformed, his tongue straining to burst into gossip, his eyes twinkling with mischief.

II

In days before slavery, Manu's sacred task was to provide precise details of our future, to guarantee our survival, but Kaka assumed a different, impious role. He told us of the scandals of the present, relishing the confusions he sowed in our minds. As village beggar he was the humblest in our midst, with no ambition beyond the needs of his belly. He was hideous to look at, so daughters or wives were safe from threat of seduction. Nor was there any possibility that he would be permitted to enter into a household, where, left alone for a moment, he could steal a bangle or some other thing of value. He waited meekly at the gate for his alms. People therefore trusted him on special occasions with their secrets or divulged seemingly harmless information to him, in the knowledge that he would purvey them throughout the village, in the process transforming original fact into its complete opposite. Kaka could be trusted to convert truths into lies and lies into deeper lies which bore the appearance of truths. It was not a habit with him though, rather a gift used sparingly, in emergencies, when people felt an urgent need to communicate something special to each other.

And such a special occasion arose when Ellar called out unexpectedly to him. He knew from the moment she spoke his name. 'Kaka, Kaka,' Ellar called after him as he went about his begging, 'come, Kaka, come, I've got something for you.' And Kaka, bemused by Ellar's offer (not that Ellar was mean but she was half-starved herself, only the ownership of four chickens elevating her above his status as a beggar), turned around and stopped at Ellar's hut. He held out his calabash dutifully, knowing she had nothing to give but her need. She reached into her bosom and searched around. A puzzled look crossed her face. She plunged her hand deeper into her bosom, again finding nothing. 'I put it somewhere but I can't remember where,' she said.

'Try under your skirt,' Kaka offered, pandering to her madness.

She reached under the goatskin wrapped around her waist, but found nothing.

'Feel properly. And ruffle the hair. Poke your finger in deep.'

Ellar obeyed.

'Jump up and down in case it's stuck,' Kaka advised. Ellar could always be relied upon for a little entertainment. Before his progress through the village – a tedious journey receiving familiar scraps of yam or plantains – he would often stop at her door first, to lighten his mind with a little laughter. Today, however, he had awoken with a strange pang in his belly. He had hurried out of his hut, desperate to satisfy his hunger, not thinking of calling upon Ellar first.

He watched her hop feebly on her good foot, then, nothing yielding from her body, he withdrew his bowl. It was time to go. 'Don't go,' she said as he turned from her. There was an urgency in her voice, but today he didn't want to heed, driven by an overwhelming appetite for food.

'I'll come back later. I'll bring you some plantains,' he offered to pacify her.

'Don't go,' she asked of him again.

Anger welled up in him. He brushed the flies from her face and snarled, 'I can't help you, Ellar.'

'Help me,' she asked with as much dignity as she could maintain in her voice. She would not beg of him, not because it was *his* occupation to beg, but because he was a man. She would not now beg of any man, having spent all the life she remembered doing so, all the life she was desperate to forget. Kaka was moved by her dignity. As village beggar he had none, or was supposed to have none. As village beggar he was expected to sport his sores, laugh at his ugliness, display his worm-eaten gums, broadcast afflictions even if they did not exist. When he awoke with skin too flush with health, he would rub ash into his face to lessen the appearance of life, before setting off on his journey. He would graze his body against trees, or walk on sharp pebbles to bruise his feet. By the time he reached the first hut he was a picture of need. The gods had appointed him a beggar at birth, as they had done his father, and father's father. Now Ellar was asking him to disobey the gods, and he was tempted, for she revealed a dignity which was unexpected in her, being the owner of a mere four hens.

'You have to obey,' Kaka urged, walking away from her.

'Why? Why must I obey?'

'Because of the way things are,' he answered from a distance, summoning up as much cruelty as he could to give his pronouncement finality. 'You are beyond child-bearing, so you must be sent away. Animals must have you.'

Animals must have me? Why? Nasty man! All of you. All. Ellar looked maliciously at her hens, and suddenly decided upon revenge. *Wait and see! All of you will rue this day.* 'Come, children, come,' she called to her hens, scattering corn before them. She snatched at one of them. It squawked and defecated. She wrung its neck, then took a stone and pounded it. Blood spurted everywhere. She dipped a finger in the blood and marked the earth, making the sign of evil. She took up a stick and drew in the earth all the houses of the village. Then she marked each with blood. *Now we'll all go to the wilderness. Man and woman and child, barren or not.*

Kaka was troubled. He wished Ellar had not disclosed to him her condition and burdened him with the responsibility of broadcasting it differently to the village. She had told him things before, things which she wanted told to people in the form of lies. When food was short for instance and she was too ashamed to seek help, it was Kaka who would go to Tanda's yard on her behalf. 'Ellar give me this for you,' he told Tanda, handing over an ordinary coba-stone. 'She say that if you plant it, your trees will flourish with plenty fruit as her own. There are so many gedips and fraps on her trees that they fall to the ground and rot, she wished she had a herd of swine to eat them up.' Tanda looked at the coba-stone, seeing in it the hunger hardening Ellar's body.

'Tell her thanks, and that I will bury it specially,' he said, throwing the stone away. Kaka followed its flight with mournful eyes, uncertain as to whether Tanda would hand over any food, for it was a season of drought and even Tanda had barely enough for his family. 'Last month I borrowed three eggs from her because my own fowls were sick,' Tanda lied, 'but now that her trees are blooming and her hens multiplying, she will not need me to repay her.'

'No, she has more than enough for now, she wants nothing,' Kaka reassured him. 'In fact she has got news that things are bad with you, that's why she sent you a coba-stone to help you out.'

'Still, I have my pride. A man has got to keep his pride, don't you think so Kaka?'

'I am a beggar, I have nothing, but I still have my pride,' Kaka agreed. 'You are right. You should repay her. It wouldn't look good to owe such a trifle to a woman.'

'Give her these,' Tanda said, handing over a parcel of stunted figs, 'tell her when the rain falls the fruit will be more full. They are so ill-looking that she will probably feed them to the fowls.'

'At least you've repaid her,' Kaka told him, his own mouth watering at the gift.

Kaka was troubled. Ellar had charged him with a secret more momentous than any information she had previously confessed to him. He wished she had not called out his name. He wished she had just packed her bundle and slipped away to the wilderness, like other women whose time had come. It was the way they followed as long as the tribe existed. Trust Ellar to refuse. She was always quarrelsome. No wonder she remained unmarried. Women more deformed than her gained husbands, it was not her body that men shunned but her disobedient tongue. Kaka was overcome by a sudden fright. What if Ellar would not go away? What if she pretended that she was still fertile, awaiting only a man to prove her worth? Such disobedience and deceit would bring great danger to all of them. He, Kaka, didn't own anything, but at least he was the village beggar. His property was the career of beggary, which no one could deny him or seize from him. His birthright was beggary, by the decision of the gods, no one could deprive him of its ownership. And he owned nothing which could be seized from him. Only if Ellar stayed, sinning against the gods, could he lose everything. The gods would revenge on the whole village, beggaring the Elder and all of them. His special status would be lost, he who never owned anything to lose. How would he go about losing? He had no experience or knowledge of losing. A feeling of panic surged through him, the same as when he once awoke from an evil dream, a dream that the gods had created havoc in the village. The Elder was deprived of all wealth, and he, the beggar, was loaded with the Elder's possessions. Bangles, sickles, bags of oat, hides, jars of liquor, a bewilderment of things. But what was he to do with them? Nor could he give them away, for he had no experience or knowledge of *giving*. It was a wonderful feeling when he awoke and realized that his torment was only a dream. Flies buzzed comfortingly around him. His sores wept happily.

Kaka worried. What was he to do with Ellar's secret? Should he go about the village and lie to everyone, so saving her from banishment? And if he didn't, how would he live with the guilt of having betrayed her to save his own tattered skin? His life, once so safe and predictable, a matter of beggary, suddenly became complicated. One moment he was resolving to protect Ellar, out of a simple human feeling; the next he was overcome with the thought of how the gods would obliterate him. Never before had he had such important choices to make. He cursed Ellar for depriving him of his peace of mind. Just because her world was about to change catastrophically didn't mean she had to disturb his. Trust her to make trouble, the broken-foot bitch!

'Man, you look foul, what's on your mind?' Tanda asked, putting in Kaka's bowl half a cardan which he had planned to feed to the goat, before the beggar turned up. If the rains didn't come soon, Tanda would lose his goat to starvation, but being irrepressibly generous he gave the piece of cardan to Kaka. Kaka looked at the goat chewing on its rope, its lips painfully dry, its side shrunk so deeply that its bones were nearly exposed. There and then he decided to save Ellar.

'It's Ellar. I worry about her.'

'Oh? Did the figs I sent not satisfy her?'

'They were so stunted she fed them to the hens as you guessed she would.'

'I'll go and fetch some fuller ones,' Tanda offered, seemingly anxious to discharge his non-existent debt to Ellar.

'It's her belly that I worry about, but not how you think,' Kaka said, stopping him from rifling through his meagre store. 'No matter how fat your figs are, they wouldn't do.'

'Oh? How is that?' Tanda asked, awaiting Kaka's explanation. Kaka shook his head, shrugged his shoulders, shifted on his feet, all in a display of indecision. He will talk and he will not talk.

'She can't bear,' he said suddenly, then bit his lips as if regretting his disclosure. He looked into his calabash bowl to avoid Tanda's stare. Tanda was at first transfixed, then slowly he looked Kaka up and down. He noticed Kaka's peeling toes, his skinny waist, his overlarge head, as if for the first time. Kaka began to shift on his feet again, this time in feigned embarrassment. He awaited Tanda's laughter, and when it came he was startled by its force. Tanda rocked with laughter so loud that it seemed to vibrate the earth beneath Kaka's feet. He clutched his bowl instinctively, to steady himself, but in doing so spilt the piece of cardan. The goat strained on its rope, snatched it up and devoured it in one go. Tanda looked at the goat, then at the disappointment in Kaka's face, and roared even louder.

'Don't tell anybody,' he begged when Tanda's laughter died.

'But Kaka, how did you get her to yield to you?'

'I am a beggar,' Kaka answered with real pride, 'I am the best beggar in the world.'

'But look at you, you are so . . .' – he paused to find a generous word, but for all the goodness of his heart he could not – 'so . . . foul, so sticky with flies.'

Kaka smiled happily at such acknowledgement of his being.

'Plus all Ellar always talked about was dreaming a man with two proper and pretty feet. And all the time she was letting *you* prime her belly!'

'But she is barren, truly, so she must be sent away,' Kaka insisted.

'You are sure?' Tanda asked.

'Don't ask me how I know. How can anybody know for sure? All I know is that I know.'

'Then you don't know. How can you talk what you don't know for sure?'

The goat, hungry again, resumed chewing its rope. 'The goat chews its rope,' Kaka said sagely. Tanda looked at the goat and nodded at Kaka's assessment of things against his will, for Kaka was not making sense. 'The land is dry. The goat chews its rope. You have nine figs left. That is all there is to know. That is all there will be. Now I must go.' He threw back his head cockily, and with unfamiliar sprightliness stepped away towards Ellar's house. It had been a successful day's begging, though it was still early morning, and his bowl was utterly empty.

III

'So, you see, I saved her,' Kaka boasts, 'and I killed the lot of you.' He looks proudly at the ghosts dancing on the deck to the rhythm of the sailors' whips. The ship dips and rears, they clutch at each other to steady themselves, observing neither sex nor rank, men hugging others' wives, children trampling upon the elderly where they fall.

I listen to him, out of pity's sake, as he rambles on about how word spread through the village that Ellar was pregnant by him. Tanda had taken Kaka's tale as sexual confession. As to Ellar's barrenness, that was only Kaka's way of intimating that a child was on the way, Tanda surmised, a child that would be born to mockery, being the fruit of a lame woman's union with a beggar. That was why Kaka wanted Ellar removed to the wilderness, so that their child could be born out of earshot of mocking laughter. Tanda was confident in his interpretation of Kaka's visit, for soon afterwards, the rains came, his trees gave out happy blossoms, the goat drank and drank. Whatever Kaka said *is* was the opposite of what *was* or what *would be*, Tanda reckoned, a little confused but all the same certain. And it was in this state of confused certainty that Tanda told the village of Ellar's pregnancy. Not knowing all the facts, his story was a halting one, to such an extent that some villagers began to suspect that the true culprit was Tanda himself.

After all, he had been giving Ellar bundles of figs even at the peak of the drought (hunger had so popped their eyes that the odd mangy fruit Tanda had given Ellar became magnified in size and quantity). Had they not seen Kaka coming and going between Tanda's house and Ellar's with sackfuls of fruit? And why else did he slaughter his goat, except for Ellar's demanding belly? At the time he said it was out of kindness for the goat, for it was starving, and he could not bear its suffering, but everybody could see that the animal was healthy and well-watered, in spite of the drought. And where did the water come from, and why was it that Tanda's trees bloomed when theirs withered? He must have discovered an underground stream, the villagers calculated, which he kept selfishly for himself, and for his lame, helpless mistress. Suddenly, Ellar's crippled condition became a measure of their own. They had been close to starvation, growing crooked and disabled as each day passed. Tanda had exploited Ellar's helplessness as he had cheated them. He took her sex in return for a drink of secret water. True, he had given them pieces of the goat-meat to relieve their hunger, but he had only done so to gain their gratitude and to put them in his debt. Suddenly Tanda, once revered for his kindness, became a common cheat in their minds. And his fabled gift of growing fruit became an ordinary deed, for he was helped by a secret underground stream denied to their own trees. And how shamelessly he blamed Ellar's pregnancy on Kaka, poor leprous Kaka!

Tanda, carrier of Kaka's tale, expected joviality from them, as he had laughed when he first heard it. They smirked instead. They refused his customary gift of fruit and went inside. They shunned his wife too, preferring to fish with torn nets than to let her mend them, as she always did freely. Tanda began to doubt whether what Kaka said *was* or *was not*. Previously, all was clear. He was the villager's provider of fruit because his trees amply repaid the love with which he tended them. What they yielded he distributed among the villagers, keeping enough, and no more, for his family. His place in their affections was as secure as his relationship with his wife and children. Now, even his wife was behaving oddly towards him. He sensed a glumness in the way she placed a plateful of food before him. It was underspiced to his taste, but he ate without complaint. She went away as quickly as she could from his presence, to attend to her nets. At nights, she was as compliant as ever, but he was clumsy and apologetic. Did she really want him for his own sake or was she being merely a dutiful wife? In his uncertainty he could not sustain his passion for her. He turned away, ashamed of his failure. He wanted her to say something – chiding or comforting, he didn't mind – but she remained silent, as if his feelings, or hers, didn't matter.

Kaka came as usual first thing in the morning to beg food for Ellar. 'She is growing more barren by the day,' he quipped, holding out his bowl, 'her belly is emptying so fast that a year's harvest can't satisfy her. We have to send her away fast before she eats out the whole village and brings disaster on our heads.'

Tanda placed a few berries in the bowl sourly. He was in a mood even unfamiliar to himself. He had a vague desire to choke Kaka by the neck. Kaka looked at the meagre gift and tried to hide his disappointment.

'Eh Tanda, I see you still have your goat,' he said, as the animal, grazing behind the hut, wandered into view. 'But they told me you slaughtered it.'

'I didn't,' Tanda replied curtly.

'But they said it was eating out the provisions you wanted to give to Ellar, so you slaughtered it,' Kaka persisted, looking accusingly at the few berries in his bowl.

'They can say what they like,' Tanda snorted, turning away from Kaka in obvious distress. He felt like grabbing Kaka's bowl, stamping upon it and chasing the beggar from his yard, but he turned away instead, his innate generosity resisting any feelings of violence.

'It's that bitch Ellar,' the villagers cursed, their pity for her swiftly transformed into hatred. 'It's she who is the cause.' News had spread of a new meanness in Tanda, how he had spat at Kaka and driven him away with a stick. 'She's turned him. Eh, but what has that hop-and-drop bitch got over him that his wife can't provide?'

'She's got a honeycomb for a cunt,' one man suggested.

'The gods took muscle from her foot and put it in her cunt, to give it more squeeze,' another said.

All manner of speculation arose on the size and form and power of Ellar's sex. She who was previously known only for her lame foot and foul mouth became a creature of uncertain potency.

Was it a hand moved by hunger that threw the stone at Tanda's head as he was bent over his seedlings, tending them with the same loyalty and kindness he showed his family and the villagers? Was it a gesture of anger, an accusation that Tanda had forsaken the villagers, providing instead for Ellar? Or was it a hand moved by jealousy that threw the stone and made Tanda pitch forward and bruise his temple against the bark of his favourite tree, a syrup-mango that never forsook him, bearing in good weather or in drought, and sometimes even out of season, as if it could not show him enough love? A hand moved by jealousy over Ellar's delicious sex, and Tanda's sole enjoyment of it? Or was it the hand of a wife anxious to protect her reputation as well as gain revenge for Tanda's infidelity? Only the goat knew. It was grazing in the bush surrounding the hut. There was a stirring, a hand scrabbling the ground. The hand found a coba-stone – the very one that Kaka had given to Tanda as Ellar's offering, which Tanda had thrown away. The hand found the stone and flung it at Tanda, then the culprit crawled away on all fours. The goat looked at the thing wading towards it like an alligator, and broke into a panicked run towards the hut. It saw Tanda crumpled against a tree and went up to him, as it always did, but this time Tanda did not stroke its skin or take hold of its horns in mock-battle or feed it special berries which he carried in his pouch. The goat stood before Tanda and called out to play, but Tanda refused as determinedly as he had refused to cut its throat, at the height of the drought, when there was barely food left for his family, never mind the animal. But he could not bring himself to do it to the goat. Each morning he gave it whatever water could be spared, and the skin or stones of fruit. He loosed it from its rope that so it could scavenge in the dust for whatever root or follicle of life it could find. Each afternoon it limped home, more hungry than at the start of day. But he could not kill it, for never in his life had he killed. They would all drag out their lives to the end; they would starve together, rather than start a massacre of their animals, which would lead to a massacre of each other. Then, at the height of the famine, the rains came, not in dribbles (like the blood running from Tanda's head) but in one mighty outpouring, as if the gods had withdrawn it to test Tanda's generosity, and now that he had proved to be the best of human beings, he would be forever blessed with excessive love from all that moved in the heavens and on earth. Hidden springs would be revealed to him. Plants would blossom at his touch. Snake and centipede would withhold their venom and hurry from his footsteps.

So, having created heaven on earth, why did the gods witness, with a goat's indifference, the human hand clutching a stone and taking aim?

IV

'I didn't kill the lot of us, only Tanda,' Kaka says suddenly, imploring me to believe him. He glances guiltily at his fellow slaves hopping and skipping to the sailors' whips. His eyes begin to mist.

'Why did you kill Tanda?' I ask to humour him, knowing him to be innocent of all crime.

'Because I thought he was seducing Ellar and taking her away from me. I believed the lies of the villagers even though I had planted them to begin with.' He looks at his empty hand as if weighing up his foolishness. 'I threw the stone, wanting to miss, or just to graze him, but I must have had more strength and straightness than I knew, because the stone killed him. All my life I was a beggar with weak eyes and crooked arms, how come all of a sudden I can kill with one simple throw?' He looks again at his empty hand, appalled at his potential. His voice drops to a terrified whisper. 'When news came that he was dead, we all gathered together, the whole village, and we overran his yard. We beat his wife and children and threw them down his well. We tore down his trees. We skinned his goat, cut it up, boiled it in the best spices from his kitchen, and we feasted. Imagine what we had become, all because of a little lie! Will the gods forgive me for bringing death to everyone? Now that we are all dead, will they still be angry?' He totters with the swaying of the ship and I get up to steady him. He falls at my feet and clutches them, begging me to forgive him. Captain Thistlewood, seeing him struggling at my feet, and thinking that he means harm to me, rushes up to protect me. He cuffs Kaka's head with such force that it cracks open, like a gourd. Two sailors come and take him away. I will never see him again. The dancing stops. The fetters are brought out, our people are padlocked and taken below deck, and I will never see them again. The last to be chained is Manu. The sailor struggles with the manacle which will not fit. All of a sudden Manu beats him off, frees himself, and rushes to the side of the ship. He climbs over the boards, and before he plunges into the sea he shouts out defiantly the name of our village (it sounded like Barambongdodo, I tell Mr Pringle, and I watch his pen struggling to spell it out on the page). A gaggle of sailors rush after Manu but he has already disappeared into the sea.

Captain Thistlewood sends me to his cabin, where I will

be safe. He fears a rebellion. Manu's freedom is bound to excite the rest of the slaves. Captain Thistlewood goes below with a dozen armed sailors, to check and re-check for himself that all the chains are secure, all the padlocks intact. He will not see me harmed. I am his only concern. He is afraid that the slaves will blame me for Kaka's death, and Manu's. He fears they will revolt, not to commandeer the ship but to kidnap me. They will secrete me in their midst, not to kill me in revenge, but to convert me back to their ways. They will not surrender me to his demands, even when he threatens their destruction. The Captain cannot bear for me to be taken from him. He'll have them all shot. But the Captain knows that his sailors will disobey him. They will not countenance the loss of their bounty by destroying the slaves. They would shoot him instead, not out of malice but for the sake of commerce. It would be an execution justifiable in any English court.

'Go to my cabin and lock yourself in,' the Captain commands as he rushes below with armed guards to make sure that the slaves are secure in their death and will not rise against him, like haunting guilt, haunting terror.

I lock myself in the cabin and await his coming, but instead a mist seeps through hidden spaces and forms the shapes of Ellar and Tanda and Kaka and Manu. Ellar's skin is flayed by a sailor's whip. She is streaked with blood like a mask of desire. She is gaudy with bruises. She wears the swelling of her lips and cheeks like haughty ornaments. 'It was I who marked you all with the sign of evil,' she announces. 'Kaka lies. How can a beggar destroy the world?' And as she twirls around to confront him, the folds of her skin loosen and lift and dazzle with the colours of her

96

suffering. Kaka gasps at the sudden revelation of Ellar's beauty, he who knew her hitherto as the plainest of women, deserving of admiration only from a base creature like himself. And as Ellar faces Kaka, she too is astonished by his image, as if the comely man she sought all her life had suddenly materialized. She lowers her eyes, overcome by shyness. Speech abandons her. Kaka's head is a palette of colours. Before, his head shone monotonously like a constant sun, tiring to look at, but Captain Thistlewood had banged his fist into it, obliterating the light. In place of an ordinary roundness, his head is indented in places, small pockets bearing unfamiliar liquids – raven-black, the pink of coral, rouge of crab-back – bubbling up through hidden spaces. Rubies of congealed blood hang from his ears. Here and there, glimpses of clean white bone exposed by the Captain's cuff subdue the viewer's eye, necessary foil to the decorative richness which threatens to overwhelm. Ellar, unable to face him, lest he is an illusion of beauty, turns to Manu for guidance. Manu opens his mouth, but he has swallowed too much sea-water to speak. In his desperation to reach the shores of Africa, he drank as much sea as he could, to shorten the distance. Instead of words, fish tumble out, gorgeous and bizarre and dreadful in shape and hue, and mingling among the catch, worms, sea-snakes, sponges and other nameless life. The new nameless and exotic world he carries in his belly spills out onto the floor, confronting them with a spectacle of their own transformation. Manu himself stares at what lies before him – as he would stare at his magical pebbles – but out of stupefaction, not wisdom. Each secretly longs for the familiarity of their ordinariness, instead of the artifice that Captain Thistlewood had made of their lives. Hence Tanda's sudden cry and agitated recognition of a particular fish. 'Look, look, a talba,' he gestures as a flat dull-looking fish, then another slithers from Manu's mouth and falls onto the floor. We all stare at the talba, a common river fish which often swelled the nets of Tanda's wife, and the realization that Manu had reached Africa makes us weep. He had swum and swum, swallowing up the distance, until he reached the mouth of the river leading to our village. Once more we turn to him for guidance, wanting news of our village. We want him to prophesy, but backwards, into the past, into a time when we were still whole, a time before Kaka's lies, or Ellar's blood-curse or my sinning with Saba, or whatever it was that caused us to be murdered by the whiteman.

Our nostalgia conjures forth other villagers from the mist, they crowd into Captain Thistlewood's cabin, swarming around Manu, looking upon him with renewed reverence for his epic effort to reach home. He who once failed to foretell our loss had found a saving trail back to our home. Jubilation breaks out in Captain Thistlewood's restricted and Christian cabin. Baju's nostrils, clogged with dirt from the assault of sailors, clears mysteriously. She raises her nose to the air and sniffs dawn mushrooms and the flowers' first opening and the breath of a newly dropped calf. The closed airs of the cabin are scented with goat droppings, or the raw earth of a freshly dug trench. She detects shrimps peeled and ready to be fried, fish hooked on twigs waiting to be smoked, dough that soon will be sugared and baked, and all the other preparations that mark the beginning of day.

And the smells and tastes of our village so revive our

senses that speech returns, not in the grunting of whiteman but in the melody of our own language.

'Bal pa sanje aru prapa sen na rahol,' Ellar says, addressing the whole group, and they all cheer with her. Her voice suddenly becomes serious as she outlines to them exactly what must be done to secure their future.

Manu, as if obliged by his profession to announce the future, disagrees partially with Ellar. 'Ji na bap apha ladu deen,' he tells them, giving credence to her advice and yet offering an alternative vision of survival. The villagers, invited to give their views, engage in agitated conversation. 'Jaray na aswan daru sen apanjat,' Kaka shouts above the din, stilling them by the force of his words. They are astonished by his wisdom and gaze upon him reverentially, for the gods have chosen to speak through the mouth of a beggarman. 'Bap ne rata shanti kyem siroje lal,' he prophesies, and they lower their heads meekly, for he speaks of worms and wounded animals and women with broken wrists. He speaks of the malnourished poor and the contempt shown to the weak. He speaks of the selfishness whereby one neighbour amasses a store of corn whilst another nibbles his fingers in desperation. 'Hare da hare da jara,' he admonishes, with the eloquence of the gods. His tattered skin has become the raiment of the gods. The light of truth radiates from him, dissolving his familiar appearance, masking the bruises and other signs of human distress. He opens his beggar's arms to embrace them, to bring them into the blue light that radiates from him. 'Reya chabrani wattie,' he says, giving of himself with the spontaneous charity of the truly poor. And we take of him with the spontaneous eagerness of the truly needy. We remake and replenish our lives in the light of his forgiveness. Manu, no longer agonized with guilt for having failed to foretell our destruction, understands that his arrogance was to blame, his certainty that the gods spoke through him and no other. Now he will proclaim his understanding of the ways of the gods, but he will also listen to the voices of others. Ellar lifts her lame foot and for the first time feels the weight of her bounty. The gods have blessed her in the making of her lameness. She will forever carry it, not as a dead and burdensome stump, but as an endowment of the gods, a mark of her special and yet ordinary condition. Onya suddenly breaks into a sob, out of an old pain for her dead children but also because she realizes that they will never be restored to her. She cries because she has now been freed to adore their memory, to attend to their graves, to plant seeds there and watch them sprout into fragile life, fragile stems, tiny leaves. Her children will never come back. They will never come back. She sits on the floor and rocks her body backwards and forwards to the rhythm of her grief. She cries and cries and will not be consoled, for now she understands the true measure of loss. We are shocked by the wild melody of her grief, and by the measureless ways of the gods. 'Om dada ke bup ji,' Kaka calls out in prayer, beseeching the gods to comfort her, and to provide some glimpse into why things must be so, but his words ring hollow and we begin to doubt his divinity. 'No cry, wipe face, every thing born new,' he stutters, in English, for his confidence has been broken by the force of Onya's suffering. Only a broken foreign language is left to us, for we are all now steeped in doubt. Tanda points to Ellar's foot, laughing at her sickness, and a chorus of English obscenities arise as we recognize each other's deformities and failings. Manu, our priest, tries to protest, but this time when he opens his mouth, only a dribble of sea-water escapes, the meagre remnant of his epic journey. Kaka, once bathed in a blue light, has become himself, speckled only by his sores. 'Merciful and beneficent are the gods,' he tells us in a better English, but in the stench of his breath, we detect the lie.

'Shut your stupidness,' Tanda tells him, raising his hand to hit Kaka. The sight of Tanda, the kindest man in our village, coming to blows with a sacred beggar (for the gods had appointed him so, and he must never be harmed) encourages violence among us. Janga gives vent to an ancient grievance by pelting a stone at Tanda's head, for he has long suspected Tanda of seducing his wife with fruit. Samyat's twin sons draw knives against each other, fighting for the privilege of inheriting Samyat's house once he is dead. Apal slaps Sanu across the face, dislodging a tooth, for the sake of it. Ellar pulls out handfuls of Manu's beard, for she has always wanted to disfigure him from the time he threw his pebbles on the ground, studied them (twirling his beard this way and that, combing his fingers through it, for an eternity it seemed, whilst she was held in suspense) and pronounced that she would be lonely all her life. And whilst such violence rages, Nara sits propped against the wall, sucking tamba-seeds and staring stupidly into space, for his mind has long since fled from him and with it the passion that moves this one to tears, that one to ambition or greed or envy. In any case he has, in his lifetime, killed such quantities of deer and wild-cats and elephants, that the spectacle of death no longer holds the least surprise. At the

height of chaos Captain Thistlewood comes in and finds me
fighting off the ghosts, begging them to leave me alone. He
flings his arms around me to still my passion. 'Scch. Scch,'
he coaxes me, 'you are safe now. I've secured them below,
no one will harm you.' And with manly strength – unlike
their wasted and spectral existence – he lifts me up
effortlessly and delivers me to his bed.

Part V

I

Mungo awakens to such darkness and blades of cold that he cries out for mercy, but the assassins will not relent. He gropes around, trying to find the measure of his habitation, but there are no walls, only a floor sprinkled with woodchips. (Later he was to know that frost had hardened the woodchips into flints, so that every movement he made over them was a passage of torture. He came to know that his confinement was a cellar, and the puddles which tripped him as he attempted to rise were of frozen urine.) When he does find the wall it is barnacled with phlegm. He surrenders all effort to move, curls his body and awaits rescue.

Many hours later there is a sudden commotion, a hatch is opened and light, soupy and weevilled, empties over him. 'Are you hungry yet, you wretch?' someone asks in Rima's voice, and without waiting for an answer, throws some bread at him and bangs the hatch shut.

Time passes, days or hours, or perhaps it is but a few moments after he had reached for the bread, dipping it in whatever moisture he could gather from the stone floor, that the hatch opens and a ladder is thrown down. A fat body descends with such care as befits a lady conscious of her dignity. Her foot feels for each rung before settling on it delicately. She has trodden that narrow ladder often enough to know that the slightest lapse of grace would cause her to tumble backwards and land in an unsightly mess in the midst of startled Negroes. (She had done so once, having taken too much liquor. As she lay on the floor struggling for breath, they emerged from the gloom of corners where they had been huddling for safety. The light poured through the hatch, illuminating her body, and the Negroes approached like Magi. She had screamed, then defecated, with such force that any intention on their part at adoration was repulsed. They withdrew to the darkness of heathen spaces.)

When she eventually reaches the ground, she turns round with the flourish of one expecting applause for her elegant performance, but there is only Mungo and his hands are frozen to the skin of his waist where he had sought to caress some warmth into his body. It is in such a posture of self-regard that she meets him, taking an instant dislike to him for not paying heed to her performance. She prises him apart with a midwife's nonchalance and prods him up the ladder, towards the opening and the light.

'Are you to eat me?' Mungo asks the fat woman as she shepherds him to a tub of hot water.

'Yes I will, you tender savage,' she replies in a playful voice, 'but first, I will scrub you, grease you, powder you and dress you. Here, in our country, we prepare our meats well. In yours, you don't even bother to season the worms.' And she shoves him into the tub and proceeds to soap him. 'Let's figure out how old you are, shall we?' she says, delving her hand under the water, seeking his crotch. Mungo is unmoved by her groping. 'Ah, you have been mastered, I can tell,' she laughs, reaching to a table nearby, and swooping a tankard of ale to her lips. 'Do you know how I can tell?' she asks, replacing the nearly empty tankard on the table with a grunt of disappointment. Mungo looks at her sympathetically. 'Boys squirm and go to escape when I hold them so, or boys leak with pleasure who are innocent. But you are Thomas Thistlewood's creature, from the mark on your forehead, so you have no feeling. He is famed throughout the profession for breaking nigger boys like you.' She weighs up his penis then lets it drop. 'Sixteen I'd say. Are you in age sixteen years?'

Mungo relaxes. Her chatter means that she is not hungry, therefore he will not be eaten. Yet, there is something about the fatness of this woman that makes him waver and doubt his safety. He could trust Captain Thistlewood but as yet he is unaccustomed to the lower breed. From her ruddy complexion, unbecoming fat and smell of swine, he can tell she is of an inferior order.

'Are you sixteen years?' she asks again, and this time he nods to placate her. 'I knew it,' she cries, 'I knew it. I have never been wrong before. You are the hundredth nigger I have prepared and I can reckon any nigger from his size.'

'Then you are a genius beyond the ability of Euclid,' Mungo offers.

'You what?' It is the fat woman's turn to be anxious.

'Euclid,' Mungo repeats, and when she looks perplexed he addresses her without condescension, indeed in the tutorial tone which is to typify his encounters with the English. 'Euclid, my forebear. He calculated, even before the birth of Jesus, that parallel lines will never meet. The godly and the savage are one, but will never meet.' And he raises her hand from the tub and places it upon his. She wants to resist, but remains obedient to his manoeuvre. In

107

bed, when Captain Thistlewood was a frenzy of manoeu-
vres, not knowing where to begin, faced with a bewilderment of pleasures, so many modes of entry, so many
possibilities of hurt, it was Mungo who became the still
point from which a perfect arc could be drawn; the still
point from which lines could radiate at perfect angles. 'Our
hands are congruent,' Mungo tells her. 'See, are we one and
yet not one?'

She looks at his black hand contrasted upon hers and
though speech abandons her she understands his meaning.

'Colour divides us though we meet, as a circle curls
within a triangle wanting to meet its three points but it
cannot, for the three points are locked by lines that will not
slacken, nor will the circle acquiesce but will round and
round in stubbornness.'

She listens to him, awed at the level of her comprehension, she, a simple unschooled washerwoman, but before
she can believe fully in herself, fright overcomes her. 'What
beast has made you?' she cries, freeing her hand and pushing
his head below the water, wanting to make him disappear.
She holds him down with such power that resistance is
useless. It is only when he grows limp from the loss of
breath that a second fright overcomes her, and she hauls
him up, shakes him about, slaps his face. She tilts his head
over the lip of the tub and seals his mouth with hers.
Memories of a previous life, as much as her drunken breath,
revive him and he calls out Captain Thistlewood's name.
'Betty, what have you done? What have you done?' she
mutters to herself, withdrawing to the table and its tankard.
She sprawls in a chair, finishes the ale and stares at her
hands. 'Dozens of savages I have washed, and oiled, and

prepared for sale, and never yet have I murdered one in my care.'

He beckons to her with the same black hand that had nearly caused his drowning.

'Get away from me you devil!' she snarls, moving the chair to a safe distance. 'I could have swung for the likes of you, not even transported to Barbados. Have you come here to kill me?'

'It was you who tried to kill me,' Mungo protests.

'A boy like you will fetch thirty pounds and a few shillings thrown in to sweeten the deal. If you had died on me I would have got a dozen lashes then swung. Even if I pleaded belly and Barbados, Magistrate Gonson would have denied me life and made an example of me.' The enormity of her action in nearly drowning him continues to distress her. 'A dozen lashes, or a hundred with the sturdiest cat, till I died, and even then they would drag me to gallows. I would end up like Mary in the College of Surgeons I would, cut open and gaped at and my liver and my heart fed to dogs.' The thought of such a surgical end, with its denial of clergy and denial of burial, makes her feel faint, and yet she continues to dwell on the tools opening her body, her intestines unspooled, scalpels and saws and hammers taking her apart.

'It was you who tried to kill me,' Mungo repeats, interrupting the curious pleasure with which she contemplates the foul spectacle of herself. She growls at him as if some bone of her own anatomy had been snatched from her.

I'll kill you yet, you sprite, don't think I mind going Mary's way.

109

Mary, I said, don't do it, Lady Montague gives us her trust, look, she hands over a bundle of the finest linen for me and you to wash and press. Mary, I said, we washerwomen must have honour, we can't go stealing her handkerchief, however the lace feels royal against your brow and makes you forget that you are of pigs-breed, so I plead with Mary. But she is a young girl and she has dreams beyond her station, but in this life a pauper is a pauper. Not any old handkerchief mind you, stained with snot or bleeding from her pox, the reckless bitch, for noble as Lady Montague is in breeding she was skunkish with the joys of adultery, Lord Montague abroad suing for peace with foreigners whilst at home she takes one such – and a Jew at that, for she's fond of that particular breed – to her bed. Mary, I warned, if Lady Montague finds out she will have no pity on you, for kindness is unknown to that unpatriotic bitch. But Mary is too far gone with dream, and must depart this life, so she steals the handkerchief, a special thing with lace fringes and silver threads which catch Mary's eye. But no, she won't listen to me, so they catch her and hang her and give over her corpse to the College of Surgeons. They cut her up, feed some of her parts to the College dogs, the rest to fish in the Thames. Poor Mary . . .

II

Such was my entry into England, a damp cellar, and a bath interrupted by the musing of a washerwoman, the water growing so cold that I shiver like the reed of her tongue modulating a low-pitched English tale of theft, adultery and betrayal of patriotism which I am forced to heed. I had thought that, in being captured by Captain Thistlewood, I had escaped the ramblings of Rima and the confusions of my past. The world of logic was promised, the logic, however cruel, of slavery. I envy Mr Pringle his quest for tidiness, but the truth is otherwise. Captain Thistlewood's resolve collapsed, and with it the triangle of commercial interests that fixed Africa to the Americas to England. And the globe too within the triangle, one so perfectly defined. All because of a weakness that inheres in love, as woodlice deform the most lofty of designs . . . Consider the fate of Captain Thistlewood. He was master of a slaveship, perhaps the most perfectly designed of sea vessels, for every inch of deck needed to be plotted to maximize the cargo. Every inch of sail needed to be measured to take advantage of the winds, given the perishable or rebellious nature of the cargo. When you ferry spices or rum or cloth across the seas, you can afford a little slackness here and there, but the Negro trade demands a precision, nay, a patriotism worthy of Newton's computations that have given England such a reputation for genius. Or consider the perfection of Mr Dryden's couplets, which give new order to the English page where before there was the rudeness of rustic or regional expressions.

It was such perfection that Captain Thistlewood betrayed because of his love for me. (Mr Pringle will call it a perversion.) Once, Captain Thistlewood was the most mature of slavers, keeping scrupulous distance between his reason and his actions. When lust took him, he went below like any common sailor and loosened his belt among the slaves, but always making certain that there was no more to his actions than a little relaxation of breath and muscle. And the slaves remained slaves, as undamaged as possible, whilst he returned to his command on deck. By these reasonable deeds he presided over several successful ventures, accumulating a fortune for himself which he properly invested in the purchase of an estate in Hampstead. His was to be an uneventful life of normal trade, and even though his actions sometimes maimed or killed a slave he made sure he put his conscience to rest by compensating the owners for the unforeseen loss.

All such equanimity was lost when he allowed himself to desire me beyond reason. He would not confess it, but when he beheld me at the lip of the pit, about to be sacrificed, something jolted him forever. He saved me, singled me out from the tribe as a special creature, and taught me Christianity. He beat me manfully but only to resist his growing love for me, his collapsing heart, which, as each day passed, weakened him to the condition of woman. I came to possess him, even as I yielded to him, and the coinage of his speech became rare, when once it dwelt only on matters of trade. He told me, in fits of distraction, of an antique world where beasts rolled in imaginary freedom, as if the age in which we actually lived was so regulated that the love he bore for a Negro youth was unlawful; the love that transformed him from master to an aspect of woman.

Mr Pringle will interpret Captain Thistlewood's deterioration as the effects of some African malady which riddled his brain; for indeed many whitemen have perished through contact with our soil and its novel diseases. And if you go to Hampstead, and come upon his estate – as Moll and I once did – you will see scenes of such desolation that you will be convinced by Mr Pringle's account. It is a veritable jungle, the gardens grown wild, the house strangled by vines. Captain Thistlewood has courted ruin, revelling in a disdain for Progress. Whilst others of his rank plant and embellish and gentrify, he presides over weeds. Whilst others stock their land with deer, he encourages mole, polecat, sow – beasts of no status or value, beasts that stink or maul or scavenge. Those who have seen him are few, for he has withdrawn from polite and vulgar society. The odd tradesman who serves him with candlewax or tobacco reports a creature overgrown with hair. His eyes are lowered as he addresses you in the modest voice of a woman. The more superstitious of his neighbours speak of him as a witch, and only his reputation as one of England's formidable sea-captains, a true patriot in the service of commerce, saves him from harm.

III

Betty – Mungo's new patron – believes he will harm her, being the devil's whelp. She is afraid of him, for as soon as her appointed tasks are done – bathing and feeding him – she locks him in the cellar. He spends endless hours in total darkness, his only companions a bowl of water and a blanket. He begins to relish his hunger and the pain of the cold, for only these sensations remind him that he exists. But those whom he has killed will not leave him alone. At the very moment he grows accustomed to his solitude they come in a throng of smells and noises. Kaka bangs his calabash to the song of flies. Onya sings a lullaby to her children. Manu's pocket rattles with pebbles. Ellar's lame foot scrapes towards him. Tanda rubs a belly swollen with fruit and belches aromatically. Clay squelches at Samyat's walk, and his sons chisel pieces of wood. Sanu rolls mule-dung between her palms, shaping them into balls of fuel. Baju sneezes and sneezes as if scenting misfortune. Apal waves a festive branch and grins. Nara blows out smoke from his pipe, imitating the sound made from his legendary spear as it whizzes towards prey. 'Where is Saba? Where is Saba?' Mungo asks, and the procession suddenly wavers, then vanishes.

'Who is it that I hear you talking to?' Betty demands, rubbing soap maliciously into his eyes. She keeps a full arm's length away from him. Mungo is unmoved by the stinging. He sits quietly in the tub, hoping that his meekness will transform her anger into pity. He is resolved not to speak, for he would only frighten her. Or at least not to speak in his previous way, when his outburst on mathe-matics startled him as much as it did her. He had no inkling of the source of his knowledge, as she had no means of comprehending it.

'You'll not be the ruin of me,' she says, placated by his silence and coming closer to bathe him properly. 'Don't think I believe in ghosts. It's only you talking to yourself in the cellar, isn't that so?' Before Mungo could nod, she presses his head forwards and pours water over him. 'Here, wash your own privates.' She throws him a rag and watches, partly fascinated, partly nervous, and he does so. 'Mary was too good for your kind,' she says, taking up a brush and scrubbing his back with such force as if intending to reveal an underlayer of white skin. Mungo still refuses to squirm, allowing his body to be the means for releasing her anger. He senses that she wants to talk, and he will listen, in case he can learn something about the strange world which has captured him; knowledge which will aid his survival. 'Mary, I say to her, as I am always saying to her, but she will never listen, Mary, save on the soap. We have sixteen nigger boys in our care each week and four cakes of soap. Just give them a quick rinse, save on the soap and use the brush to get the dirt off, I say to Mary, then we can squash all the pieces of soap left over that week into one bar, then with the other unused bar, we have two bars. The next week, if we have sixteen other boys, we can save another two bars. So at the end of the month, we can have . . . we can have . . .' She hesitates, counting the bars on her fingers. 'Anyway, if we sell what we save, each bar for a farthing, we'd make . . .' She hesitates again to do her sums.

Mungo is tempted to tell her, by instant computation, that her bounty would be eleven pennies, but his better judgement leaves her to her innumeracy. 'Are whitefolk so ignorant?' he asks himself.

'A proper sum we'd make, but no, Mary would have none of it. Do you know, the poor are the ones who never steal when they are the first who should steal? Why are we so stupid, tell me?' She looks at Mungo, expecting him to answer, but he remains silent. 'What's the matter? Thistle-wood take your tongue as well as your backside? You can talk, I promise I won't bite.' She softens the pressure of the brush to encourage him, and the sudden relief from pain makes him open his mouth involuntarily.

'Eleven pennies,' Mungo blurts out, 'and if the reconstituted cake of soap is lesser in value than a new cake, say half the price, then you'd make eight pennies and two halfpennies.'

'What? For each of us, Mary and me?' Betty asks automatically.

'No, the sum to be shared between the two of you. If equally, you'd each get four pennies and one halfpenny. If you take two-thirds of the share then you'd get seven pennies, and Mary four. If you take three-quarters, then it would be eight pennies, one farthing for you and nearly three for her.' As he proceeds on this scale of fractions, barely pausing for breath, she recovers her senses, backs off and opens her mouth in a silent and prolonged scream.

'If I were you I'd take the lot, why give any to Mary?' Mungo suggests, appealing to her greed as a means of restoring the peace.

'The lot? Take the lot? Are you sure?' she asks, catching her breath in such a quick recovery from fright. Mungo is alarmed. 'Are whitefolk so easy to please?' he asks himself.

'But what will Mary say, how can I take everything?' Betty insists, seeking an escape from the companionship with Mary which would prevent her from cheating. Her feet feel heavy, as if the guilt has drained and collected there. She hauls a chair to the tub, sits down and awaits his answer. She soaks the rag and gently dabs the marks on his back made by the bristle. Mungo brushes aside her apology by straightening and stepping out of the tub. He no longer wears the mask of a piteous black creature. He reaches for a towel and wipes himself slowly, emphasizing the area of his loins, but she will not be distracted as Captain Thistlewood used to be when, bent weeping before his blue God, he would turn, look up at Mungo and be suddenly stilled by the sight of boyish nakedness. He would lay all his grief at Mungo's innocent lap.

Betty ignores Mungo's show of generosity. Either she has a sense that as a fat and ugly thing she is disqualified from pleasure, or else she is consumed by the thought of cheating Mary. 'Don't tell Mary anything about saving soap, just do it quietly,' Mungo offers instead of his body. He ties the towel around his waist, puzzled at her behaviour in rejecting him. 'Are whitefolk so unreliable?' he asks himself. His fresh body gave hope to Captain Thistlewood, who could dream of new beginnings, and when he took the boy all thoughts of margins and returns which shaped his life disappeared. *What does it profit a man to gain the whole world but to lose his life*: the words boomed in Captain Thistlewood's mind and he snatched at Mungo desperately as at a raft. 'Save me,' he cried out hoarsely, as if Mungo must become his blue, bleeding and crucified God.

Betty seeks something other of him, the price of saved soap and how it is to be withheld from Mary's knowledge. 'I can't keep it secret from Mary, she and me bathe the boys together, we both use the soap on them,' Betty says, floundering in her attempt to figure out the method for profiteering. She is convinced by the evidence of Mungo's calculations that he can guide her to the safety of a fortune. Her weekly wage from the Negro trade is less than the value of the four cakes of soap, the six bottles of lavender oil and the store of bread, herrings and suet puddings provided for the fattening of the boys. If she could supplement her wages by half, then she would consider herself wealthy.

'Mary is dead,' Mungo says, throwing her a lifeline, 'why do you bother to worry about her share?'

'Dead? Is she dead? How do you know Mary is dead?' Betty asks, a note of panic in her voice. She grows agitated, rubbing her palms as if they itched with the promise of wealth.

'You told me so yourself. And you are here alone, I cannot see her.'

'But I hear her,' Betty whispers, stifling a desire for tears. 'Every night you and her talk, I can hear the two of you talking about me. What does she tell you about me? Does she blame me for the hanging?' She can no longer contain herself. She hides her face in her hands. She is so overcome by emotion that her nose runs. Mungo loosens the towel from his waist and offers it to her. But she resists, pushing his hand away. He insists, and after a while she lets him towel her face, as if she were the newly bathed slave.

IV

'Where is Saba? Where is Saba?' Mungo asks, and the procession suddenly wavers, then vanishes, leaving him to the damp solitude of the cellar. 'Come back to me,' he pleads, afflicted by the burden of being the remnant of his tribe. 'Ellar, come back. I promise to speak of you in excess. I will describe such pulchritude that the poets of England will cower at my eloquence.'

'You will?' a voice asks, then breaks into the kind of hissing laughter that only the toothless can produce. 'You will?' the voice asks again, this time coyly.

'I will fit you porcelain dentures, the finest Wedgwood set, for such is the company that bears His Majesty's appointment. You can speak for yourself then.' There is a long pause. He worries whether he has displeased Ellar. 'With your new teeth you can speak to the English yourself about your beauty,' he repeats, desperate to recall her.

The long pause is broken by a sucking, then a spitting noise, prelude to speech. 'Naaaw. *You* tell it for me. I'll keep quiet.'

He concedes to her shy request. 'I will tell them about canta trees bursting into pink flowers. The ground is wet with new rain, and you shelter under its pink branches. A man comes to you. He kisses your wet face. His name is Falzee.'

'No, choose another name. Falzee means a vulture's beak, have you forgotten? I wouldn't have a man pecking at me as if I were forsaken flesh. "Sarpe" is better, "the handsome". Or even "Gandu", "the plentiful".'

'Let's name him Gandu then,' Mungo agrees, glad to have attracted her attention and companionship.

'What is he doing to me?' she asks, her curiosity aroused.

'He is embracing you. He wipes the wetness from your eyes to gaze into them better. He is astonished at how soft they are, like the sound of muffled bells, all the clanging and the turmoil removed, no matter how crude hands tug at ropes.'

'What are muffled bells? Can't you talk words I know?'

'Your eyes are as deep and memorable as footprints in an empty and windless desert,' he offers in compensation.

'Naaaw,' she grumbles, then laughs at him, unable to withhold her derision.

'I was thinking of Rima,' he says darkly, by way of explanation. 'Once we went looking for food. The wilderness soon became desert which stretched for miles and miles, but we set off across it anyway for our stomachs took command of our minds. And there it was, in the middle of nowhere, where you'd think no one in their right minds would walk – a set of human footprints. We froze in surprise and expectation, as Gandu now looks into your eyes.'

'Is that all Gandu is doing, staring into my eyes searching sand? I don't want a weak man love-struck by my eyes. Make the flowers blood-red and make him fierce. Talk of sex. Make him seize me.'

'But that will hurt you and you'll bleed and sob but he'll still not stop.'

'There's more to it than you know,' she retaliates. 'Why should it only be that?'

'I only want to keep you from the hurt,' he says in self-defence.

'You only want to keep me lame and laughable,' she cries, accusing him of being like the menfolk of their tribe. 'I want to run from Gandu as he goes to kiss me, I want to run for the joy of running, not out of fright. He races after me. He catches me. I struggle, not because I am woman but to match the loss of his own breath. Then without warning I lunge at him. I wrap my arms around his neck. I buckle my legs around his waist. He is like a child's kite caught in a branch but I will not let the jealous wind free him or the tugging of a jealous hand. And there will be jealousy.'

'Will they betray you, will they banish you to a wilderness there to starve, as my mother did to Rima?' Mungo is anxious that her story should have a different ending.

'No, their jealousy will give way to new ways of being with each other, by our example. Gandu and I will usher in a new age of happiness, peace between folk, satisfying sex, sturdy children, rich harvests.' Her voice is edged with cynicism. Mungo falls silent, baffled by her meaning. The cellar suddenly feels cold again and he draws his knees to his chest and lowers his head, wanting to curl into a flower that will survive her scorn and season of despair.

'Keep your fancy teeth,' she taunts him, 'and all your fine talk of a man gazing into my eyes. Let me scrabble in the dirt for the teeth of hyenas, fix them into my gums and snarl at Gandu. I will eat his neck, his chest, his waist, all of him, the very last scrap. Each night I will eat him, over and over again.' She pauses, savouring Mungo's fright, then adds maliciously, 'Like Captain Thistlewood ate your mother.' He cries out at the mention of his mother's fate, and goes to parry Ellar from him, but she does not exist and he stumbles to the ground. She laughs at his futile effort to embody her.

'Don't you remember? You saw it all, you were chained a few yards from her. Each night the Captain came below to feed on your mother, a little at a time. Her toes. Her feet. Her ankles. Her legs. Only her torso was left, fixed to the floor by irons at her neck and hands. Then he freed her hands by eating them. When the ship tilted this way and that, she spun horizontally by her neck, making perfect circles in the shit and reek. She had shrunk so much that she had space in which to move at last, no nigger body to block her passage. Then he freed her neck too with his teeth and went away satisfied. When the ship pitched and reared, her torso rolled here and there, until it landed beside you. Can't you remember how you stretched and stretched to touch her but your hands were chained? Don't you remember the long and futile wailing that came from your mouth, stilling our pain and even the ship's shrieking?'

V

'What beast has made you!' Betty cries, freeing her hands and pushing him below the water, wanting him to disappear. His talk of lines and circles and triangles has persuaded her of his necromancy. He struggles for breath once more, as when he was on the ship, the air so thick with moaning that sucking it in was like sucking the marrow from a bone. Betty hauls him up at the last moment. 'Confess where you got all your knowledge,' she commands, 'or I'll drown you, I swear.'

'I was born with it, I inherited it from the Greeks,' he tells her. Right away she ducks his head in the water again, holding him down until he nearly drowns, then bringing him up. 'Please, please,' he begs when he surfaces, 'examine my mark and you'll see for yourself.' She scans his front, his back, his arms, his legs for the devil's signs. 'On my forehead,' he splutters, 'the sign of *pi*, look.' She looks, then gets hold of his head again.

'That's Thistlewood's mark. All it means is that you've been breached and made accustomed to men. It is his way of signalling to men with special tastes that you are a special boy. I'll ask you once more, where does your learning come from? Lie, and I'll strangle you.'

'My mother, I learned it from my mother,' he pleads, but his answer incenses her.

'Your mother was a benighted nigger, how could she know anything beyond the sight of her black dugs?' She clasps his head as if to tear it off. Her fat hand is over his face like a death mask. As he slips into unconsciousness light suddenly floods into his eyes through a hole in her palm. What he sees makes him cry out in bewilderment, yet perfect understanding, as someone, awakening from a bizarre dream, recognizes and is yet puzzled by the familiarity of his surroundings. His mother is pinned to the slaveship's boards, her body rigid as the body of a compass. Then she is freed. Sans legs, sans arms, she spins by her neck like a gentleman strolling happily to his Club twirls his pocket-watch by its chain. Freed from her neck, she lands beside him, but his hands are fastened in iron, he cannot angle them towards her. They lie together like parallel lines, like the figure 11 in a ledger book, his fixed price which cannot be changed, not by the subtlest negotiation with a Trader, nor the vulgar entreaties of a slave-mother as her child is sold away from her to another plantation. She offers a grass-bangle and an egg to the Trader, but is rejected. She rushes into her hut, brings out a wood carving of Zain, protector of travellers, presses it into his hand, but the Trader, furnished with his own compass and quadrant, flings it away into the wasteland. When it lands, it throws up a little puff of dust which quickly settles. Dust settles on the face of her god. Her god has no power before the whiteman's knowledge of science and trade. The child is to be sold for 11 guineas no less. The Trader whips her back to her hut. She ransacks it, but there is nothing left to barter with. She comes out, shows him her empty hands. 'Take,' she says, 'take them all.' She chews her wrist till rubies stream forth. He grabs at her, as at unexpected wealth, but she moves away, disappears.

Nor can he meet his mother's body. Parallel lines cannot meet, just as a seller and bidder cannot agree a price. He knows the geometry of death from the circles and the lines his mother makes in the slave-hold, the marks Captain Thistlewood makes in his ledger book. That is all he knows, but Mr Pringle will invent a Jew who wears a skull-cap over his black hair, like a moon fastened in spiteful clouds. Just before Mungo is to board the ship the Jew comes up to Captain Thistlewood and offers money for him. 'What,' he cries, 'you refuse 11 guineas? A little diarrhoeic stick of a nigger boy like him, barely worth a swig of brandy and a mouthful of tobacco, but you will not take 11 guineas?'

'Keep your bride-price, I cannot part with him,' Captain Thistlewood tells the Jew, who glares at Mungo and in his mind promises to gain revenge against the boy for his humiliation – the greatest shame suffered by a Jew being failure to seal a contract with the finality of the round stone sealing Jesu's tomb.

VI

Mungo awakens to such darkness and blades of cold that he cries out for mercy. He opens his eyes to see a round face over him, like the flattened head of a nail. 'Save me,' he begs, in his distress and confusion, thinking it to be the Man-God from Captain Thistlewood's blue painting.

'Sssch. Sssch,' a voice coaxes him, 'you are safe now,' and he recognizes it as Betty's. 'Yes, it's me,' she confirms, clasping him to her bosom and rocking him in a comforting motion. Mungo looks around, recognizes his cellar by the light let in by the open hatch. 'Don't drown me,' he sobs, 'I told you the truth.'

'Drown you? Whyever would I do such a thing to you?' she reassures him.

'I told the truth. It was my mother who taught me lines and circles and figures.'

'Yes, it was your mother,' she agrees, to pacify him, 'it was your mother, truly, God bless her soul.'

'But you doubted me. You called her a benighted and stinking nigger.'

Mungo withdraws from her in fear, but Betty draws him back to her firmly and envelopes him in her arms. 'You were dreaming, that's all. You had a nightmare.' She wipes his face with her palm. It is whole, not pierced as in his dream. She is an ordinary being. He is relieved of fear.

'Your skin is roasting with fever. Come, get up, let's go into the warmth,' she says, trying to lift him to his feet. He rises momentarily, then collapses into her arms. He is not strong enough to stand on his feet, much less climb the ladder.

'Mount my back,' she says, arranging his arms around her

neck. 'Buckle your legs around my waist.' She is too fat and his legs are too short for such an undertaking. She realizes that it is a hopeless task to move him upstairs. She spreads his blanket on the ground, lies down and pulls him to her. 'Come under my night-dress,' she says, raising it to allow him to enter. There is a rush of warmth. Gladly he rests his head on her waist, and she covers him over with her dress. He settles lovingly into her fat. He dreams that he has at last entered the tent of his mother. She is no longer lonely and unadored under her veil and cloak. She gestures to him to sleep, and, as if hypnotized by her hands, his eyes close to the cruelty that awaits him.

Mungo huddles by the freshly lit fire in Betty's parlour. She hands him a bowl of porridge and he scoops it rapidly into his mouth. 'Have some bread,' she offers, moved by his hunger, 'you act as if you've been starving forever.' He looks at her fat smiling face and suddenly likes her. She has plenty, unlike Rima. He takes the bread and stuffs it into his mouth, leaving no space in which to chew. She tuts at his greed, and then laughs at his comically puffed cheeks. 'Take some out, or you'll choke,' she says with sudden anxiety, opening his mouth and freeing it of the bread. She breaks it into smaller pieces and feeds it to him patiently. He is content. His fever has disappeared, and his fright.

'Why did you go to drown me?' he asks, emboldened by his sense of safety.

'I never. Don't go about saying such, what would people think?' she scolds him. He looks at the the far corner of the room.

'Didn't you scrape my skin off with your brush?' he asks,

looking at his body for signs of violence, but finding none.

'I swear I never. What devil has come into you? Yesterday when the Captain brought you here, I gave you a washing, and oiled you, and put clothes over you to make you decent.'

He decides he must have been dreaming after all, such is the sincerity in her voice.

'Two shillings a week I get from minding you, for one whole month, eight shillings altogether.' She points to the provisions on her shelf. 'That's all for you. Three pounds of porridge, three joints of cured ham, six bars of soap, two bottles of olive oil to rub you down and more.'

'So you can count,' he says, wondering why she had stuttered and stumbled before. His rudeness leaves her speechless. 'But you told me you couldn't,' Mungo protests, sensing her rising anger. He falls silent and lowers his eyes to show contrition.

'Anyway, it wasn't me who killed them, it was Ellar's fault,' he blurts out after a while, not knowing what else to say. It was an error on his part, for Betty grows agitated. Mungo looks at her struggling to maintain an even breathing, but choking on her emotion. He cannot understand her sudden distress.

VII

Mary, I say to her, Mary, don't tempt fate. Leave the Jew's handkerchief alone. Barbados is behind God's back, Magistrate Gonson will punish you. He'll bang down his hammer and away you go in bonds, to Bridewell jail where you'll spend months picking lice from where the turnkey has opened up your skin with blows so they can lay their eggs. And such a pretty virgin girl, the turnkey and the lice will take turns in blooding you. Mary, I plead, trying to put fright into her, they'll rid you on a transport ship, and in the two months across the seas you'll get sick, so many wifeless brutes in the hold with you, and then all the lonely crew. You'll get more sick than the sea can make you, and even when you vomit they won't give up. By the time you land your belly will be a pit, all kinds of nameless life will crawl out of it and be born. And for the rest of your days, you'll slave in a canefield to feed them, for they are your bastards. And the niggers will increase your brood. She won't listen, no, the handkerchief filled her eyes, and you should see how she traced her finger over the initials of the Jew, her mind far away from the washhouse and scrubbing board in some Jew's chamber where soap smells of perfume and she bathes her face in lavender water, and rouges her lips with carmine, and paints her face Parisian, whilst the Jew kneels before her, holding up a looking-glass. Mary, don't tempt the Lord. Remember how they killed his Son, just so the Jew will kill you. Yes, he was the murderer, for putting temptation Mary's way. It makes sense doesn't it? If he didn't seduce Lady Montague when her true Master was at sea for England's reputation, then the handkerchief would never have got into Her Ladyship's bosom. That handkerchief is like what Pontius Pilate wipe his hands on, after he betrayed our Lord. But she won't heed me warning about betrayal and killing, her mind so big with dreaming about being a Lady or Mistress to a Great Man.

And what could I do? She came to town in a York wagon, with other country girls, looking for work. She was innocent. I tried to look after her. I found her wandering the streets, hungry, and before

pimps could get hold of her I took her in. I introduced her to Lady
Montague's laundry-room. I taught her how to count the money
she got each week, and I saved it for her until it grew plentiful
enough to send home to her folk. She had no skills except if you
count opening her legs in the dark. But I got to her before nasty
men, and saved her and protected her but the Jew won in the end.
Mary, I beg, don't trust Jews, they'd come at night and try to steal
the very stone they rolled at our Lord's tomb to sell it at some other
funeral. O let the Jews do what they want with the rich, rob them
blind and wreck their lives, but not my Mary's!

VIII

Mungo suddenly understands Betty's distress. 'There was no
handkerchief, was there?'

She covers her face with her hands and refuses to answer.
Mungo looks at her calluses, from the years of scrubbing
clothes and scrubbing Negroes, and feels pity for her.
'There was no handkerchief, was there?' he repeats.

Her silence is sufficient admission of guilt.

He leans towards her and with utmost gentleness coaxes
her hands away from her face. 'Look at me,' he says. She
raises her head reluctantly, yet there is a quality in his voice
which makes her want to divulge everything to him. She
opens her mouth to speak but he interrupts her with the
only comforting words he knows. 'Scch. Scch. You are safe
now. No one will harm you.'

'No one? Will no one find out?' She places her hands in

his, comforted by the incongruity of colours. He is human, like her, but still sufficiently different. Her secret will be safe with a stranger. 'I cheated on the soap,' she blurts out. 'Captain Thistlewood found out. I blamed Mary. Magistrate Gonson made her hang.' And she explains to him the business of slavery, Captain Thistlewood coming to her three times a year with boys like himself who were to be cleaned up, polished and fattened and seasoned to the cold, before being taken to market. The boys were his entitlement, for as Captain he was granted a portion of his cargo. He brought with him sacks of wheat for their feeding – the stores allocated to sailors who had perished through sickness or execution, during the voyage. The clothing of the dead sailors had also been saved, and Betty's job was to alter these to fit the boys. The soap was what was left over from the disinfecting of the slaves, the Captain delaying the period when they were to be bathed from weekly to fortnightly, thereby gaining on their provisions. 'It's only fair. That's how I saw it,' Betty says, justifying her theft of Captain Thistlewood's goods. 'He was worse than the Jew. He'd even save their teeth.' She laughs uneasily and looks at Mungo, expecting him to be shocked at her revelation, but he is not in the least moved. His calmness makes her babble on, elaborating her tale. 'Each time he had a bag with him, full of slave teeth. A storm must have battered them out of their poor mouths. Or else he must have took pliers to them, who knows?'

Mungo remains undisturbed. She desperately wants to convince him that she is not lying. 'He would give me the bag to take to a denture-maker in Cheapside, and I got six shillings in return which was my wage. Imagine being paid in teeth!'

'In Africa, our transactions are conducted in beads and coloured glass and feathers and pieces of decorated bone, so the Captain was not abusing you,' Mungo says sagely.

'I am no savage, I am a patriot like him, pay me in proper and decent English money,' she shouts defensively, parting her hand from his. 'I should have complained, but what would that do? He'd take his business elsewhere, and I'd starve, so I traded in teeth.' She looks around her room, suddenly feeling poor and shabby. After so many years' service to the slave trade, what is she worth but a few dresses and some cheap furniture which barely raises her above the condition of a savage.

'You'll do better than me and in no time too,' she says bitterly, awaiting Mungo's response. She hates and fears the accusation implied by his silence. *What right has he, a newly come nigger, to judge me? So I stole soap and made Mary pay for it, so what? Mary was stupid from the time she was born, when she was dropped by a gin-sodden midwife. She was twenty in age but her mind didn't match her years, so when they questioned her she agreed right away she was the thief and you should see how light and gay she stepped to the gallows, as if she was on stage and the howling and hoorahing of the crowd made her happy, all the rotten fruit and rocks whistling past her ears made her happy, and she eased her neck to the halter as if she was there to be crowned, a Princess at last, all her dreams fulfilled because of me, Betty. She screwed up her eyes and leant forward, trying to spy me in the audience, but the rope suddenly tightened, she dropped, her eyes burst in their sockets.*

'It was best for her,' Betty says, addressing herself rather than Mungo. She retreats inwardly, to consider her words. 'Do you have things like money in Africa?' she suddenly asks Mungo, wanting to explain herself to him again.

'Only teeth and such,' he says.

'Well, that's why you don't appreciate what I did, getting Mary hanged and all.'

'I am strange to your country, how can I understand?' he concedes so as to encourage her to continue.

'Money rules. The king has the most, then the politicians, then the merchants, then the Church, then people like me. That's our England. Our God ordered it so, it says in the Bible. Those who preach rebellion are not patriots. They preach in open fields, and at street corners, no patriot would rent them a hall, for they claim that niggers and Englishmen are equal. Can you believe it! Give them time and they'll be arguing that men and women, noble folk and vagrants should be equal too, and they would urge people to riot and burn down all that makes this country the greatest in the world. But no Christian and true-born Englishman will heed their dangerous talk.'

Mungo listens intently, an avenue of escape suddenly open to him. He will seek out these rebels at the earliest opportunity, presenting himself as one worthy of their charity. In the meantime he will suffer Betty's ramblings, in the hope that she will divulge the meeting places of these people.

'In England, all is money,' she continues, puffed by his attentiveness, 'and if you don't deal in it then the whole world will come tumbling down, plague and starvation will overcome us. Mary was dangerous. She didn't care for money. She was no patriot. When she got her pay from Lady Montague for washing clothes or from Captain Thistlewood for service to the Negroes, she stared at the coins in her hand, not knowing what it was for. She'd give them to me and go back to her scrubbing. That's all she wanted to do, work, work, work. She was what we call an idiot. Tell me, what's the point of living if you don't have a sense of what money is?' She addresses Mungo with new confidence, as if her argument is beyond reproach.

'In Africa we live because—'

'That's Africa, not here,' she interrupts, 'here is England, and here you don't do things for free, which is how men cheated her. They took her for nothing, from the time she was old enough for it. And she didn't know how to sell it for a proper price. She let them do it to her. Twelve households she scrubbed for before she ended up working for Lady Montague, and twelve households went through her, butlers, gardeners, cooks, kitchen-hands, stewards, gentlemen guests, masters. High-life and low, in and out, backdoor and front, they came and went, busier than a Royal Banquet, and she showed nothing but the pox for her years of service. I felt sorry for her. I saved her and brought her to live with me, to protect her, and I put her to work for Captain Thistlewood, on top of her work for Lady Montague, because she loved work, she couldn't do enough of it, and all the money she made I saved for her, taking out only a tiny sum for her upkeep, and to pay for medicine for her pox.' She halts, awaiting Mungo's response to her tale of generosity. *But what is it about this nigger that makes sweat form on my forehead and my tongue loose*

*in my mouth as if I am the one to be hanged? Hundreds of them
I've prepared for market, cuddly little lambs with fleece of curls, but
I curse the lot of them because of the mess around and between their
legs which I have to scrape off with my bare hands. They should
hose them down better on board and restore them to their usual
naked state, but no, the niggers are left in their own filth which
dries out like a girdle shielding their privates from sin. The first ever
clothes niggers wear are their own shit. And why like some common
whore do I have to remove such clothes and face the threat of their
original state? But at least they were rude only in body, whereas
this new nigger wags his tongue at me, condemns me as a murderer.*

'Well, what more is there to say?' she asks, for Mungo
seems discontented with her account. He leans towards her
as if expecting a conclusion.

'So you want to know about Mary's savings, is that it?'

'Whatever you want to teach me,' Mungo replies.

'Teach you? Teach you?' she splutters, infuriated by his
serenity. 'You are nothing but Captain Thistlewood's –
Thistlewood's–' she struggles to find the right word and
suddenly it emerges from her mouth with appalling clarity
'– Jacobite.' She shrieks at the sound of the word as if it had
come from Magistrate Gonson's mouth and not hers. She
pushes him away and rushed to the safety of the door, her
hands trembling so uncontrollably that she cannot unfasten
the lock. 'Leave me alone,' she cries, sensing him looming
over her even though in truth he is huddled by the freshly
lit fire, his body so frozen that it has not yet surrendered the
calmness and serenity of a dreaming corpse.

He goes into his cellar voluntarily so as to placate her. As soon as he is below she drags the washing tub over the hatch, cursing him, savouring her victory over him. *Foul wretch! You'll never rise up to accuse me, you'll starve where you are!* She will say that his death was wilful. Slaves, she heard, shunned food, no amount of cajoling or torture could persuade them to eat. All they desired was to be thrown overboard. They cheated Captain Thistlewood of a profitable sale, leaving him as mocking compensation teeth which slackened and fell from their mouths as they starved.

No one will blame her for his death. She will show them the bags of uneaten wheat, to prove her honesty. Captain Thistlewood has placed him with her as his spy, but she will outsmart him. She is convinced that Mungo is Captain Thistlewood's agent, his purpose being to get her hanged, by reporting her as a thief. Mary's sacrifice was not enough, Captain Thistlewood wants her neck too. But why? She has served him dutifully over the years, and the loss of a few cakes of soap is hardly a drain on his wealth. Why is he bent on persecuting her?

She lights a fresh fire and goes about her daily tasks, seeking refuge in the routine of work. She sweeps and resweeps the floor. She scrubs grease from the stove. She dusts and scrapes and scours with unusual fervour. She boils some potatoes and eats them greedily, despite her lack of appetite. Afterwards she takes up needle and thread to repair the rags which are her wardrobe. A careless stitch awakens her, the needle lodging in the flesh of her thumb. It is an inconsequential hurt but given her state of mind it takes on the magnitude of a fatal wound, as if gunshot has exploded in her lap.

IX

'She bleeds,' Rima tells him, 'therefore she is doomed. Pity her.' In the sterility and hunger of the cellar, Rima returns to haunt him with remembrance of woman's plight, but Mungo dismisses her as an irrelevant myth, belonging to the past. 'It is a tale more ordinary than you know,' he replies.

'You are the cause of her suffering. You hurt women in whatever you do. Are you not a man?'

'I am a slave,' he replies, denying his sex and seeking refuge in his helplessness.

'You've made her afraid of you, are you not a man?' Rima persists. 'Hear how she cries. She is terrified that you will betray her to other men who will banish her to the wilderness.'

'It is a tale more ordinary than you know. This is England, everything makes sense. She stole and got Mary hanged. Deep down she wants to be punished and looks to me to report her to Captain Thistlewood.'

'As you did to the lot of us,' a voice exclaims. Mungo recognizes it as Ellar's. 'You betrayed us and made Thistlewood kill us even though we were innocent.'

'You even got your own mother slaughtered.'

'It's true he hates us. He killed my two children because they were girls. I blamed wild animals but it was him.'

'Leave him alone,' a new voice shouts. It is Tanda's, edged with bitterness, as if the stone that shattered his head has dislodged his natural generosity. 'Especially you,' he admonishes Ellar, 'to call you a slut is to raise a praisesong for you. Let him record it for all to know that you spread your legs, and when I refused, you spread gossip instead, how I gave you a belly. And my wife abandoned me for a beggar and they conspired to kill me.' (Kaka, hearing his name called, works up a froth in his mouth to soften the speech he is to make, or else to dissemble better, like a man sucks at a pipe to interrupt the flow of words.)

The absurdity of events which undid his life strikes him as forcefully as the stone, and he laughs involuntarily. Kaka joins in, relieved that Tanda is, after all, not taking his death to heart. 'You were always a cheerful soul,' Kaka flatters him, 'you never bore a grudge against anyone.'

'Women are for fucking,' Tanda says, and Kaka is taken aback by his bluntness. 'That was my downfall. I should have stuck it in Ellar and made her froth, then I'd have been alive today. But no, I loved my wife, and I pitied Ellar, she was starving, she'd do anything for food, and wouldn't accept that I was giving fruit to her for nothing. And none of you believed me either.'

The women shuffle guiltily. Kaka clears his throat and swallows his pride. 'I never did it with your wife,' he tells Tanda.

'More stupid you,' Tanda laughs at him.

Kaka attempts fellowship by laughing too. 'After you died they climbed on your wife, but I didn't. All I got was a piece of goat-meat.'

'More stupid you,' Tanda jeers.

'I didn't know how to do it. I was afraid she'd laugh at me. The rest of them were expert at it, and afterwards they threw her down your well.'

'Then she must have died in happiness,' Tanda says. 'You must have been eaten up by jealousy, eh, Ellar? I bet you tried to stop them, eh?'

'I tried to stop them, but your wife wouldn't let me,' Ellar retaliates, seeking to hurt him. 'She was squealing more loudly than your goat when we ripped its throat.'

Voices arise in protest, the women squabbling with Ellar, whilst Tanda continues to goad her. New obscenities break out, women denouncing men for their tyranny, Tanda mocking them for being willing victims, and Kaka denying any responsibility for the violence on account of being a mere beggar, as Mungo had invested in his slavery to avoid blame.

'Stop,' a new voice commands. It is Manu's. He pulls the head of an eel from his mouth, clearing it for speech, but the eel is endlessly coiled in his stomach. The fighting wanes, out of ancient respect for him. 'What are we doing to each other?' he cries at last. The sudden loudness of his voice stills them. 'Cursing will not revive us, we are already dead, except in him.' And he turns to Mungo, urging them to forget their individual animosities, their self-defences and self-denials. 'Except in him. He bears all our wants, all our griefs.' Manu's words are like a blinding illumination. They gaze upon Mungo adoringly. He gleams in their minds, a miraculous star that will lead them out of the obscurities of their past. Rima, seeing him naked and trembling and ravished by hunger, searches the stone floor of the cellar for living worms. Her hands discover nothing, and she is pained by her inability to provide for him. She is overcome by a sense of failure, for her duty in the wilderness was to nourish him.

Tanda delves his hand into his pocket but finds no fruit. He is overcome by remorse. He had given all his food to Ellar in exchange for disgusting sex.

Nara slides a finger along his gums, hoping to find remnants of the tamba-seeds he was always sucking, but there is nothing. He is ashamed of his former greed.

They stand before Mungo, bearing their assorted guilt. Until Ellar, true to herself, fearless, irreverent, challenges their adoration of the child.

'He is a strumpet and a thief. He walked in the katran bush and found a whiteman and led him to us to steal our lives. Afterwards he lay on his belly for the whiteman and cackled.' Her outburst, so shiningly vulgar, restores their sight. They look again at Mungo, seeing him for what he is. A wave of disgust surges through them, they remember the ship and its cruelties which at first enthralled, but lost their originality, becoming more and more ordinary as the journey continued. The glint of sailors' knives, the glint of buttons on their breeches, lost their originality.

'He is a tale more ordinary than we know,' Ellar says. And the villagers, restored to themselves, are restored to vile utterances.

'He smells like a whore's arse,' Baju announces, sniffing the air wisely, recovering her gift of prophecy. Her assessment of Mungo raises shrieks of approval among the women. They urge her on, out of self-hatred, and rebellion against their bodies. 'He smells like a seven-day menstruation,' Baju offers, wriggling her nose to arrive at a precise definition. 'Or more like . . .' and she looks to Ellar for a revelation.

Manu tries to speak, to placate the sexes, but when he opens his mouth a fat fish sits on his tongue, flapping, so that his words are a meaningless stammer.

'There was one who always sat at my feet, massaging the

hurt from my ankles, do you remember him?' a voice asks, suddenly restoring them to tenderness.

'Yes,' someone answers, 'he was more a youth than a man, you could tell, even in the darkness. By the way he just sat there, quietly, respecting my age, his mother's age. O how his touch seemed to suck up my legs and thighs, the slow massage torturing me. I could have snapped my chains with the frustration.'

'Yes, he was different, he had a name, what was it?'

'I didn't hear his name, but he was a doctor-sailor. He gave me a cordial and put a wet cloth on my forehead to cool the fever.'

'He gave me too, a strange cordial when my tongue was swelling up, which took away the pain.'

'He had a name, but I forgot it. He told it to me and when he asked me my own name I cried, for none of the other sailors were bothered, they just found my hole.'

'It's true, he never touched any of us, except to massage the hurt.'

'He was so gentle, he must have been of a different tribe from the sailors. Perhaps not even human. I never saw him for it was always so dark below deck.'

'Do you think he was a god?'

'Or a dream?'

Their voices dip, they grow wistful, remembering the stranger's kindness.

'I miss the whippings most,' Baju says boldly, returning them to obscenity. 'The sailors knew exactly where to lash you, to pucker your skin and you quiver and make sucking begging noises. Afterwards, with the exhaustion, I used to sink into such a lovely deep sleep and wake up feeling so refreshed, the air in the hold fresh, smelling of my garden, the young oranges and paw-paws, the jacaranda.'

'And their tongues!' Ellar exclaims, suddenly remembering a particular moment in the hold. 'I swear I was at a banquet. The first tongue tasted of grapefruit, a shade sharp for my taste I admit, he should have sugared it ever so slightly, but I was so happy I wasn't going to complain. The next tongue was beyond description, gingery in flavour, just the right strength, and the flesh had the texture of lightly steamed lasa-fish, you know, promising to crumble in your mouth. The third course was sheer parsemelon, I could taste the pinkness, and the seeds lodged in between my teeth. By this time I was so bloated I couldn't eat another thing but they insisted, starting to feast me all over again, with avocado and passion fruit and boiled pumpkin.'

'No wonder you died of diarrhoea,' one of the women laughs at her, jealously, for she was elderly, and on board the ship no one invited her to any festivity.

'I died of cholera,' Ellar rebukes her, anxious that Mungo should put it down correctly in his book.

'Shame I died of cholera too. I was having such fun,' Baju says, sinking into reverie.

'Dysentery killed me in the middle of a belly-laugh, his beard was tickly.'

'I was taken early,' a young voice complains, 'on the very first night on the ship. I flapped and couldn't breathe, the chains hooked me to the floor, I tried to heave out of them, and I thought this was what sex was, for it was my first time, I died thinking I was having sex, but it was only fever.'

141

The women tut, pitying her innocence, and a doleful silence descends on them.

Rima speaks their grief, addressing the men. 'They preferred slavery to what you did to them. You stubbed out their hearts.' And ignoring their mumblings, she gestures to Mungo. 'Only he can redeem you,' she says.

Manu struggles again to speak, to agree with her, but only a whimper escapes his mouth, summarizing the mood of the men.

'He will keep Betty from harm,' Rima says. 'He will not disclose her secret to men who will judge her and sentence her to slavery and the open sea. Betty loved the Jew. She was jealous of the Jew's relationship with Mary. She accused Mary of theft and had Captain Thistlewood condemn her to hanging. Or else it was the Jew who tired of Mary and discarded her and Mary thought she'd get revenge by stealing and getting herself hanged, to make him remorseful. Or else there was no Mary, except a baby which Betty bore for the Jew, and out of shame strangled it, cleansing it first in her washing-tub of sin, and baptizing it Mary, for that is the name of the mother of their Christian god. And was there or was there not a handkerchief? What do these things matter, except her tragedy?'

X

Mr Pringle's account of Betty will be an ordinary tale. She is a heartless thief, scrimping on the already meagre provisions given her for the care of hapless Negroes. She blames her friend Mary, and betrays her to Magistrate Gonson. Her deeds are characteristic of the times. Deceit and betrayal motivate people at the highest level, by their example the poor are corrupted. Jews and Jacobites and Papists and their spies are everywhere, threatening the stability of England. The ruination they cause by speculation in stock, or in creating false Bubble schemes, is a grander version of Betty's crime. The Jews by manipulating stock prices in the South Sea Scheme years ago made millions. Betty's dealings in soap gain her a few shillings. They're all thieves together, great and small, their joint actions eroding the foundation of the country. True, the Jew is worse, his money-making being part of a conspiracy with Papists and Jacobites to create chaos. He finances their plots to overthrow King and Parliament and the commercial system on which the security of the nation depends. The Jew will profit from England's demise, buying up enterprises cheaply and stripping them of their assets. The French will overtake England in business, monopolize mercantile trade, vanquish the Royal Navy and invade the country to enslave the people in Popish worship. Betty is at least a patriot of sorts and innocent of the ways her immorality contributes to national decline.

It is this concern for the moral intactness of the nation that motivates Mr Pringle's campaign for the end of slavery. Common sense tells him that mercantilism underpins the welfare of the people, giving occupation to thousands and prestige to the nation. But what is crucial to the country's economy is also morally indefensible. The enslavement of blacks, which underpins England's commerce, is sinful. And it is blindness to such sin, for the sake of profit, that makes

England vulnerable to foreign invasion. It is inevitable that the sin England commits overseas would visit it at home in the form of Jews and Papists and Jacobites. Saving me from the degradation of slavery will be to save England's Christian soul from the contamination of the foreign . . .

And I, Mungo, am to prick the nation's conscience by a testimony of suffering, which Mr Pringle will compose with as much intelligence as a Jewish conspiracy. For I am to become a crucial instrument in Mr Pringle's scheme to rescue England from its enemies. Mr Pringle will demonstrate the slavery that lies at the heart of Catholic worship – slavery to doctrine, slavery to Priests – and will contrast the freedoms fostered by Anglicanism. To do so would demand utmost care of thought and preparation of a watertight case, to convince the English merchants too of the virtues of abolition.

We are black and enslaved. We are in anguish. We have no family, no home, no money. It is such wants that Mr Pringle believes endow us with missionary power, though of heathen character. Our humility is our strength, as it was the strength of Our Lord, and Mr Pringle will unleash us in your midst, dear merchants, to worry your conscience as Our Lord worried the Temple of Jerusalem, unleashing His anger against the traders, overturning their tables. And because He wore rags gladly and declined the devil's offerings, the traders could accuse Him not of envy, nor the spirit of competition. A Negro slave is the closest England comes to having Our Lord in its midst, Mr Pringle believes. Thus I, a heathen worth eleven guineas at the outset, have become a priceless treasure. O ye Negroes who tug at your chains and curse the white hands which ordained you to slavery, think again of your condition of blessedness! What would you have been but for the whiteman's interference in your lives? Will you chafe at your Christ-like status and long for the degraded lives you led in your villages, of dust and famine and mulish labour and beastly copulation?

XI

Mungo listens to Betty with compassion. He does not condemn her. He does not betray her to the authorities. He listens with the patience of Our Lord, and being a Negro, being nothing, he becomes her conscience. She trusts him with a tale more anguished and complicated than Mr Pringle's. She blurts out a confession. It was Lady Montague's doing. A pasty malodorous bitch. But with money. Lots of it. So the Jew came. Dark, fine-boned, exotic in manner. He spoke with a musical foreign lilt. The bitch lapped him up. Betty served the refreshments. Chocolates wrapped in silver paper. Bohea tea. They giggled and flirted shamelessly, not seeing her. She came and departed from Lady Montague's boudoir unnoticed. But not when Mary came to remove the trays. Their laughter eased then. Mary was pretty. Pretty curled blonde locks. Pretty eyes. The ideal servant girl to wait upon a Master. The Jew sensed her youth. Instantly he calculated what it would take to get her. A lace handkerchief for her soft eyes. A silver box. The Jew coughed nervously. Lady Montague glared at him. She never minded Lord Montague's appetite for Mary. But the Jew was for her only. In jealousy she got rid of Mary. Betty also, to keep up appearances. Lord Montague returned from France. She told him they had stolen, so she had dismissed them both. A handkerchief and silver box were missing. Lord Montague was upset. He was used to Mary's service. There were thousands of other country girls looking for positions, Lady Montague told him. He was placated. 'And so we ended up here,' Betty says mournfully, looking around the shabby room with its shabby furniture. It is an abandoned public house, ruined by fire, only one room intact, with a cellar. Out of desperation, they had taken it, even though the rent was outrageous, for it was the height of winter. Another day trudging the streets, looking for accommodation and at nights sleeping on straw in a charity house, would have killed them. Betty cursed Mary for her decline. Once a proud servant in the Montague family, with a room of her own and inferior maids to command, she was reduced to carrying her belongings in a bundled-up bedsheet, with a young girl in tow. They journeyed through a fog of chimney smoke, seeking shelter, their faces wrapped in scarves, old cloth tied around their feet to reinforce their shoes. And she resented Mary who still gleamed with youthfulness in spite of the soot and uncleanliness through which they moved. Landlords sniffed at Betty contemptuously but as soon as they glimpsed Mary's face as she loosened her scarf to speak, they softened. There was a room, but only spacious enough for one person, they all said, inviting Mary to cross the threshold, going to assist her with her bundle, but Betty would drag her away. 'I'll give you two pounds for her,' one offered, upping the price by several shillings as Betty led Mary away.

Others offered a lowered rent, even free lodgings with food and clothing provided, but for Mary only.

'I should have sold her on the spot,' Betty says, growing bitter as she recounts in her mind the humiliation of begging passers-by for money and savouring the rotten vegetables in the soup served by the charity kitchen. 'But I took pity on her and I took in niggers to make a living.' She shudders at the extent of her fall, the humiliating ejection from the Montague household and the starvation that forced her to take up the meanest of occupations, the washing of niggers. Mungo listens compassionately. He sits before her like a sacrificial offering. If she chooses to beat him, he will submit, for it is he who embodies her fallen state. It is he who by his slavery degrades her, forcing her into the meanest of occupations. 'I should have sold her to the lowest bidder,' Betty says, wishing Mary a life of slavery to the basest of passions. With great effort she rises from her stool and walks with sluggish steps to the corner of the room. Guilt over Mary's fate has suddenly reduced her to a state of fatigue. She stoops, and lifts a loose floorboard concealing a small package wrapped in paper. She takes it up but is unable to rise to her feet. She struggles to summon her strength, but instead of rising up she slumps forward, the package falling from her hand. Mungo goes to steady her, but she shoves him away, ashamed of her condition. It is her final humiliation, letting a nigger witness her in a helpless state. She might as well have opened her bowels on a public stage, as she saw Mary do when the hangman put the noose around her neck. The crowd howled with mirth and pelted her with stones, but Betty wept at the sight of

Mary's helplessness, the spontaneous defecation, the shamefulness of it, and blood seeping from openings made by the stones. 'All her prettiness was for nothing, and her flouncing and pretending. We lived in this same hovel, but once she handled her gifts she daydreamed into a different world.' And without looking at Mungo Betty gestures to the package on the floor. Mungo picks it up and loosens the string to reveal a silver snuffbox wrapped lovingly in a lace handkerchief, the sight of which weakens him. Quickly he sits down on the floor, holding the package tightly to steady himself. He places it beside him with as much calmness as he can muster. Voices arise in his head, Saba calling as he emerges from the katran bush, his face wrapped in mist; Saba's voice tails off and a voice that Mungo recognizes as Rima's sings a lullaby as she unwraps a stillborn child of mucus and natal cord, her movements delicate as lace. She holds it up to the sky to be doused in moonlight, and when she is satisfied that it is truly dead she wraps it tenderly in breta-bark and buries it, marking her treasure with a coba-stone.

He presses his hands to his ears to stop the noises in his head, and his sudden distress arouses Betty from her fatigue. She stares at the silver box and lace handkerchief, seeing the baseness of Mary's death, the bleeding and the soiling. 'I've killed Mary and I will kill myself,' she says with sudden decisiveness. She picks herself up from the floor, takes up a broom and begins to sweep as if in preparation for her fate. She wets a cloth and wipes the shelf bearing her only ornaments, noticing with fresh pain what the years of poverty have made her accustomed to: the crack in the inside of a porcelain bowl which runs the length of the painted field like a gutter, spoiling the scene of milkmaids and shepherds. Lady Montague used to soak her teeth in it, but gave it to Betty when the colour faded and the flaw appeared. Betty had treasured it as a mark of her status in the household, for Lady Montague had presented it to no one but her. In her pride and gratitude she had overlooked the crack, seeing only the picture of her childhood. She had put it away, not wanting to handle it again, not wanting to remember. Now, as she wipes the bowl, the dirt embedded in the crack loosens, smearing the painted surface. 'I have killed them too,' she says, gazing at the soiled figures. The sadness in her voice shifts Mungo out of his self-pity. He gathers the silver box and handkerchief and takes them to her, but she spurns his gifts, turning away from him and putting the ornament back on the shelf. She picks up her broom again, raising up clouds of dust as if to cloak herself from view.

XII

Mungo watches the crazed fluttering of her hands as she works the broom and resolves that she will not suffer the fate of his mother. He will not allow her to accuse herself of sin and surrender herself to the Law which will banish her to a life of slavery in the Indies where men will slake their thirst by her as by the froth of a stagnant pool. He will withdraw to a corner of her eye and outwait her distress, and when she is becalmed he will summon her to his sight and place his hands on her head in benediction, as Captain

149

Thistlewood taught him, after the manner of his god, and send her forth to sin no more. He will free her from the Company of death, the ships that cross the seas with the flesh of the innocent. She will refuse his forgiveness, wanting to be punished for Mary's death as he wanted to be punished for the death of a tribe, but he will persist, for both their sakes. He will tell her that there has been too much death already but that they must seek redemption from guilt by learning to live again, as a slave, suddenly released from cuffs and ankle chains after months of bondage, stretches a tentative foot forward, feeling the newness of space, and gazes as if for the first time at the miracle of his native limbs. The memory of chains jangles in his mind as he walks, and he will halt, not because he thinks he will topple over but because of the awesomeness of his freedom. Like him they will have to learn to come into being again, haltingly, pausing to marvel at what surrounds them, or at what they enact. 'Consider the lilies of the field,' he will preach to her, telling her stories suckled from Captain Thistlewood, of Sparrowhawk and Owl, of Thistle and Cowslip and Pennyroyal, their ancient fame and magical properties which survive the guilt that makes men murder men, and build their shining governments of the damned. And it is then that her childhood past will become fresh in her mind again and she will speak in a strange tongue – a tongue estranged from the nigger-tub and hovel of the present – of a village in Yorkshire, a father who ploughs and harvests, a mother who weaves cloth, sisters who shape straw and clay into useful craft. She will recall – haltingly and with the astonishment of discovery – the scent of marl – honest and reassuring, telling of hard but rewarding toil with an honest earth – on her father's body; and her mother's palm like a cracked and flaking canvas – the dyes she stained cloth with drying her skin, ageing it, as the passage of centuries dignify a painting – more precious than any that adorned the walls of Lord Montague's mansion. And she will speak of hurst and weald and holt, of briar and furze and rush that survive the axe and plough; the memory of England's originality preserved in the curious ancient names for plants and vines (local names that survive the Progress of ships which transformed him into Mungo, Noah, Boy, and the like). And she will tell him, with a child's excitement, of a copse at the edge of her village, shrouded in morning mist, into which she and her sisters were sent to pick mushrooms; of the sudden hot breath of a Green Man or fugitive convict or dead hermit on her neck as she stooped to gather the mushrooms which made her scream, drop her basket and flee homewards, abandoning her sisters without the least feeling of guilt, to whatever or whoever would ravish them in the ecstasy of mist. 'It was my first memory of sin,' she will confess to him, and he will reassure her immediately that her fright was natural; she was fifteen then, no longer a child, no longer innocent of the imagination of men. But she will insist on greater guilt, confessing to him how, on a sudden whim, she had abandoned her family, packing a few belongings and slipping away to the Inn where people set off for London. 'I lied to you,' she will tell him, 'what I said of Mary was of myself. It was me who arrived in London in a wagon, packed with other Yorkshire girls. I wore a stuff frock and a white apron and a tucker over my shoulders and–' she will laugh gaily – 'a rose in my bosom to catch any stranger's fancy.' Her laughter will fade as she returns to her present shabby condition but still her words will be edged with defiance. 'It wasn't enclosure and hunger which made me go. We had what we reaped and wove, enough to keep us.'

He will not bother to enquire why she deserted her village for he knows she will stumble for an answer. Some idea entered her mind, brought into being by no particular excitement, like the quick loveless coupling of rustics which, to their amazement, gives birth to calamity. For no reason she decided to abandon them. It was neither out of malice nor ambitiousness that she wrapped a bundle of clothes, stole the necessary fare from the jar her father kept his wealth in, and set off for the wagon-inn.

XIII

He, Mungo, had made the same inexplicable decision to enter the katran bush, and just as Betty had tried to justify hers afterwards, by talk of enclosures, the tyranny of the gentry or the poverty of her family which forced her onto the degraded streets of London, so he had fabricated stories of his village; stories of bush-rat, of benighted women, or of lost Alexandrians, which he told only to himself, for fear of ridicule or incarceration in a madhouse. But for now, he is a mere youth in the care of a washerwoman, not knowing how he had arrived in London, and what would become of him. Captain Thistlewood had pressed a hot iron on his forehead, the shock of pain erasing memory of Africa which returned only in occasional glimpses and fragments of voices. As Betty discloses her true past to him, he seems to recollect something of a smaller boy, perhaps his earlier self, stumbling in the mist of the katran bush. Why he is there is impossible to tell. It may be that he is tending his father's goat which has slipped its rope and strayed into the bush. That makes sense, for why else has he wandered so far from home? He calls out – whether the name of the animal or of his mother he knows not – but there is no answer. A hand suddenly seizes his neck. There is a throng of noises. Noises of the dead. The dead swarm around him. 'Where is your village?' a voice demands (which he later recognized as Captain Thistlewood's). The mist thins to reveal colourless faces. Death has bled the colour of their skin to the colour of bone. The man shakes him again with white hands, preventing him from losing consciousness. 'Where is your village?' the voice repeats and although he cannot under-stand the language of the dead he points in the direction they seek. The man pushes him forward, commanding him to show them the way. He can easily slip away and disappear into the mist, for the dead are weighed down with strange weaponry. They trudge after him with heavy feet. He knows that they will quicken when they reach the village, killing or capturing everyone. He can easily slip away and warn the folk of their coming but he does not. He leads the dead dutifully through the mist of the katran bush towards the path leading to his village. They will quicken when they reach the village, killing or capturing everyone. The man whose voice is Captain Thistlewood's prods him on, threatening him in a language he cannot understand. Or perhaps it is a voice uttering promises, for why else does he guide them out of the mist of the katran bush? Why does he not slip away and warn folk of their coming?

Betty chides him for his self-pity, telling him that he is foolish to blame himself for leading Captain Thistlewood and his slavers to the village, for he was only a small boy; he was merely terrified by their appearance, as any small boy would be, and took them automatically to the village.

'There is too much death already,' Betty says. 'We must salvage what we can and start to live again.' And she tells him of plans to redeem them both from guilt by profiting from the past. She has resolved to sell the silver box and handkerchief, and return to Yorkshire with the money. It would be enough to buy a spinning-wheel and other tools to make cloth. She would teach him to dye. He would be safely lodged in her parents' cottage, protected from those who would want to steal and sell him. They would trade cloth in the marketplace, save their money, buy their own cottage, and even a cow or two to supplement their wages. As Betty speaks to him, outlining a new beginning, Ellar giggles in his mind.

'So you come all the way to England for this?' she taunts him. 'You mean all of us die so that you could end up sire to an English sow?'

'Halt your jealous mouth,' Kaka scolds her. 'Don't heed her, boy. Pig-meat sweet, once you scrape off the bristles, cut away the fat, and pickle it well. Trust me, I too would have sold out the tribe for a taste of English.'

'Eh? Listen to him! Which English woman, howsoever common like Betty, would give a beggar like you even a sniff, never mind a mouthful? Like your head swell with ambition as well as starvation?'

And the two of them squabble, trading insults, until Mungo shouts at them to shut up.

Betty is startled by his outburst. She is hurt by his seeming rejection of her offer to care for him, to rescue him from a future of slavery. He will not advance himself by profiting from the past, it seems, but wallow pig-like in the dirt of it. Her sense of hurt turns to anger, and then to fear. 'So you want the silver box and lace for yourself? You'll betray me to Magistrate Gonson? You'll kill me too, after all I did for you, scrubbed you and fed you and when you shivered warmed you in me?'

Her sorrow provokes a glimpse of his mother. She is standing at the doorway of their hut, staring out over the wide savannah in the direction of the katran bush. He has been missing all day. She goes out, calling for him, but a sudden storm beats her back, the rain lashing her skin with a man's anger, and the wind stopping her mouth. She retreats to her hut to wait and to call, even though the wind rages above her voice and the rain so thickens the air that she cannot see clearly. The rain mocks her by distorting her sight, making her imagine that each shape it makes in the air is the shape of her son. She grows excited and depressed in turn, thinking one moment she can discern his coming, the next riven with doubt.

And when he does arrive, bringing Captain Thistlewood and his gang, it is to condemn one who had fed him, warmed him in her body, and even as he issued forth from her, enraged, bawling, brushed his face of sorrow as tenderly as Betty now brushes the tears from her eyes.

XIV

All night the wind rages, and the rain, and Betty looks upon him and weeps, for he will wander far and never return to her. A few hours earlier she had scrubbed him for the last time, preparing him for the morning's marketplace. Now she keeps vigil by the side of his bed. He sends her away from the damp cellar but she will not go. She tries to speak to him but the noise of the storm drowns her voice. She wants to confess how, although it has been a few days at the most of being together, she has become attached to him. She has become like Captain Thistlewood, once stiff with authority, now servile before him, disorderly in her needs. But such untidiness of emotion repels him, such fickleness on their part. She wants to tell him how he has altered her life, and to suffocate him in gratitude, but just as he will resist Mr Pringle's designation of him and his brethren as Christ, so now he sends Betty away from him for the second time. He is exhausted by their need to repent, by the way they peck at themselves out of guilt and will use him to leech that guilt. He wants them to let him go, as Rima spat him away from her, or else lowered him gently from her lap to the ground and urged him to hurry away, before the gunshot stopped her life. But, like Mr Pringle, they will ensnare him in their needs. Mr Pringle will nail him down with the nib of his pen and he will struggle to wriggle free from his page, as from Captain Thistlewood's bed, and Betty's solicitations. He is exhausted. He wants to sleep. He sends Betty away again, but she denies him a third time.

All night the wind rages, and the rain, but Betty lies

under a warm blanket, happily secure in her house of stone, for it will withstand the devil's wrath, and Mary's condemnation. In dream she has returned to her Yorkshire village, where she dwells in idyll, for Mungo is beside her, warding off evil. Pagan charm or bone of saint she is unsure, but she knows that in telling her sins to him she has found rest, and in caring for him, salvation. The rain will cease, the wind decline and at morrow, she will lead him through a childhood garden, and show him vine and flower, and teach him to name the world as honeysuckle, thistle, beech, rosemary, names lyrical unlike the song of chain and whip's refrain which was his previous state. He marvels at how a people can make such sweet sounds for nature, and yet ululate in another's land, slashing with iron and blasting guns.

Betty leads him through clover and rye to a hill where he is to gauge the measure of his freedom by looking out at the vast unframed land; fields of subtly different shades, according to the crops they bear; fields flecked white with newly born lambs; and hedgerows running here and there like drips of paint. When they return home Betty bakes apples on a roaring fire, toasts meats and makes oatcakes. He feeds and grows sluggish and dozes in the glow of the fire, Betty covering him with fresh linen, but at the very moment when he drifts into forgetfulness, a sudden thunderclap rouses him from her dream. Once more the wind howls, like a tethered dog. He awakens from Betty's dream of a stone cottage set in a tableau of flowers, far from slaver and magistrate. The dog is a rack of bones for it has been left to starve. The farmer to whom it once gave such service – shepherding the new-born lambs or guarding his door of vagrants wandering the countryside – has taken it to the middle of the field and secured it to the scarecrow. Together they stop the birds from feeding, though the field is thick with corn. The farmer makes a final profit from the dog. Mad with thirst, it bites the scarecrow, bites its own paws. He awakens from Betty's dream with a dry mouth. He gathers whatever moisture he can from the floor of the cellar and wets my lips. So Saba must have searched his tomb for a scrap of nourishment and finding nothing, bitten his hands and howled to a heedless world.

XV

Betty's face is crumpled and her dress shabby as a scarecrow's. Today she is not bothered with appearances. Her grief is undisguised as she takes Mungo to Johnson's Coffee House to be sold. She walks at a furious pace, and Mungo trots behind her like a dutiful pup, slipping occasionally when his feet meet patches of frost. His progress is all the more perilous because of his oversized shoes. No one pauses to stare at them, a distracted woman and an unsteady and breathless Negro, for the streets are a bedlam of activity. The overnight storm has ripped slates and tiles from houses, and slabs of lead from church roofs. Young children, their hands wrapped in old cloth to keep them warm, are busily piling these onto carts, to repair or reinforce the hovels of the poor. They move in scum, for the gutters have overflowed onto the streets. It is early morning, and Betty, a veteran of city ways, walks with her eyes either fixed at her feet, to avoid the ordure spilt from night-carts as they bumped over dislodged coping-stones and other debris left by the storm; or else she glances upwards, anticipating windows suddenly opening and chamber-pots emptying onto their heads. People mill around her, but she steers a passage through them with the ease of an experienced street-walker.

It is Mungo's first tour of London. He is overpowered by the stench of offal and ashes littering the streets. Signboards shriek on their hinges but the people are even more distressing, wandering in all directions and bawling. 'Salt-salt-white-Wor-ster-shire salt.' 'I ha' white radish, white, and hard lettuce, white young onions.' 'Buy a mat, a mat or a hassock for your pews.' 'Buy a fine mouse-trap or a tormentor for your fleas.' 'Saloop, barley-broth, furmety, hot-pea-cods, oysters.' An apple-woman shouts pippins and hot codlings. Others tout hot spiced gingerbread, mackerel, rhubarb, water-cress, Shrewsbury cakes, oat-buns, taffety tarts, boiled tripe, pickled onions. The desperation in their voices is matched by people swarming to the baskets of food, grabbing whatever they buy and stuffing it into their mouths. Everywhere people are chewing and swallowing and belching as if recovering from a famine. Mungo is terrified by the scenes of hunger. 'Smoked, baked, bar-becued, salted, pickled, stewed Negro, freshly caught Negro, tender and mild though from the wild,' he thinks he hears someone calling out. His feet quicken to catch up with Betty.

They walk for miles through the dilapidation of poor people's quarters, spaces of low damp land intersected with ditches beside which lean sheds of wood and straw.

Children sit at doorways, sopping potatoes in bowls of fat and shoving them into their mouths. Women riddle through piles of ash collected from the hearths of the rich, seeking the cinders. The odd shop sells bread and suet-puddings and cow-heels. There is a peculiar quiet in the air, as if the day-to-day endurance of hunger and need has becalmed the poor; or else it is the calm before a riot, the poor swarming out of their hovels with patriotic torches to burn down Synagogue or Catholic Church. The scenes of desolation give way to higher ground, bearing more commodious houses, with alleyways jammed with chandlers, chimney-sweeps, knife-grinders, bellows-menders and balladeers, all offering their goods and services in compelling voices; finally, wide elegant streets lined with shops displaying the signs of draper, hatter, upholsterer, hosier, clock-maker and picture-framer, the nature of the trades a measure of the wealth of the area.

'Soon, soon we'll get there,' Betty tells Mungo in an agitated voice.

But they continue to walk all morning, going down endless lanes and crossing countless squares, as if Betty has no intention of arriving. Mungo is tired. He is no longer afraid of the people of England. He pauses to watch a man leading a bear by a rope, and followed by curious urchins. Elsewhere, a tumbler and dancing-girl set up their pitch with pipe and drum. A fop in red-heeled shoes and peruke prances by, raising his eyebrows at Mungo as if jealous of the boy's livery: Betty had dressed him as she did all her Negroes on the final day, in a sailor's jacket, its brass buttons outshining his freshly oiled face.

'Come. Come.' Betty summons him, dragging him away

from the man's attention. 'You will suffer enough of them where you're going, sure enough,' she mutters, giving the man a savage look. The man pouts, flickers his eyelids and minces away.

They arrive at Johnson's Coffee House, but Betty hesitates at the entrance and draws Mungo to her protectively, hugging him to her waist. 'Are you cold?' she asks feebly, but Mungo is distracted by the sight of a sedan chair coming towards them, borne by two men puffing so mightily that their faces are shrouded in the cold vapours of their breath. The chair is set down at the doorway to the Coffee House, the curtains part, and a gentleman – a Huguenot – steps out daintily. He is sumptuously apparelled in a black velvet coat and breeches, a silk waistcoat and shoes gleaming with silver buckles. A gold-topped stick hangs from his wrist. He looks with momentary disdain at them, noticing Betty's shabbiness and the black boy in naval uniform. Betty lowers her head reverentially as he enters the Coffee House, but as soon as he's out of sight she grimaces and spits on the ground he has trod. She turns for approval to the porters who are leaning against the handles of the sedan chair, recovering their strength. They spit on the ground in a show of solidarity.

'They stint you a ha'penny even though they weigh the heaviest,' one complains.

'It's all that English gold in their pockets which weighs them down,' his companion agrees.

'Some are so careful with their money they swallow it when they go about, to disappoint cut-purse and pick-pocket. If you slit their bellies, gold pours out.'

'There was a time we could hoot, hunt, kick and cuff

them, but not now. They buy the protection of magistrates and politicians.'

They chuckle at the memory of assaulting Huguenots, and Betty joins in. 'Shall we take you somewhere, you and your lad?' the first man offers, taken by Betty's friendliness. 'We shan't charge you nothing. Jump in, travel in style for a change.'

'Yes, jump in,' the other urges, noticing Betty's slip-shod condition, her stockings out at heels, and Mungo shin-deep in his shoes. 'We're going by Lincoln Fields if that's on your way.'

Their kindliness belies the rough faces they wear, noses crooked from years of brawling, low brutish foreheads and scars telling of foreign wars or domestic escapades.

'We can't,' Betty tells them, nodding at Mungo to inform them of her business. They look compassionately at Mungo.

'Poor lad,' one of them sighs.

'They do nothing wrong, except they're black,' the other offers.

'He'll be alright in the end, so long as a Jew don't buy him. Make sure a Christian gentleman gets him, then he'll not suffer many blows.'

'Christian or not, they're all the same,' Betty disagrees.

'Yes . . . yes . . . they're all mule-heavy. At least he'll only be carrying trays and teapots, us lot are doomed to carry plump-arsed gentlefolk.'

Mungo watches them go, wondering at the kindliness of utter strangers.

Betty leads him through the door into the Coffee House to

a scene as infernal as the slaveship's hold. An enormous stench greets him, the air black with tobacco smoke mingled with the odours of unclean spittle. The room is packed with men sucking on pipes and gobbing onto the floor. There is a pandemonium of voices: the agitation of card-players; excited babble about the prices of indigo and saltpetre; loud conversations about mortgages and tithes; the trading in wit and epigram by a table of scholars; aspiring politicians in full throat on the issues of excise and window-tax and the crisis in Calais. Betty sags, overwhelmed by the heat and the noise, but Mungo, accustomed to the callousness of men, is not in the least discomfited. When she turns and heads for the door, thirsty for clean air, he stands his ground.

'Follow me,' she urges, but he will not budge.

A man emerges from the gloom of smoke to greet them. He takes Mungo's hand and leads him to a private adjoining room. Betty has no choice but to follow them. He sits Mungo down at a table furnished with plates of boiled ham and fried sausages, richly buttered bread and a mug of coffee. 'Eat,' he tells Mungo, putting a plate before him. Mungo watches him fussing with the meat, piling it on his plate, wondering again at the kindliness of utter strangers.

The man – Captain Thistlewood's agent – watches keenly as Mungo eats the food. 'There'll be fierce bidding for him,' he tells Betty, winking cheerfully at her. 'He's the Captain's boy, broken-in and seasoned. They'll riot for such a prize.' He is to receive a percentage of the sale. He is happy. 'I've given notice of him in the newspapers, I expect at least a dozen gentlemen to turn up.' He gives Betty the newspaper to read. She scans it ignorantly. When he is gone, to make final preparation for the auction, Mungo relieves her of the newspaper and offers to read it for her. Among the advertisements for new plays, miracle cures and Mr Hogarth's latest prints, Mungo comes upon himself with a curious sense of satisfaction. He reads aloud the description, dwelling on each word to gain as full a picture as he can of his identity.

'FOR SALE, fresh from the upper coast of Dahomey, a *choice youth*, sixteen or so in age, HANDSOME in demeanour but for some slight tribal scarring on his forehead, and UNBLEMISHED in all other parts, with an eagerness to please, HAVING BEEN IN THE SERVICE OF THE REPUTABLE CAPTAIN THISTLEWOOD who has blooded him, taught him *sufficient language* and purged him of *Negro habits*. He is of excellent hygiene, carries himself with UNCOMMON DIGNITY, and will make an assured servant at table. He answers to the name of NOAH, and will be disposed of at 2 o'clock at *Johnson's Coffee House* next Friday.'

'Noah! Who gave me such a queer name?' Mungo asks, the pleasure of seeing himself in print disrupted.

'I didn't,' Betty says defensively. 'I know you as Mungo. Captain Thistlewood didn't tell me what to call you, so I baptized you myself.'

'So what was I before I came to you?'

'Don't ask me, you should know. Whatever it was you didn't seem to care. Whenever I called you Mungo you sat up.'

'But I thought "Mungo" was what whitepeople called our folk, like "Negur" and "Blackamoor" and "Boy" and other words the sailors used on us.'

'Well, can't you recall what the Captain called you? And what about your mother? Don't your lot have names where you come from? Your mother must have given you a name?'

Mungo cannot remember. He repeats aloud the word 'Noah', hoping to find some meaningful echo in it, some clue to his original state.

'It's a sweet and lovely name for a boy,' Betty reassures him, 'I'd take it if I was you. It's the only thing you'll get free from the likes of Thistlewood.'

'And where is the "upper coast of Dahomey"?' Mungo asks, equally puzzled by the description of his village.

'I can't help you there either,' Betty shrugs, but then, seeing the look of loss in the boy's eyes, decides to comfort him. 'Wait a minute . . . all Captain Thistlewood's Negroes came from the same one place. Now what was it?' She pauses, pretending to search her memory. 'A black that I was in charge of last year told me. I asked him and he said – he said – now what was it he said? It sounded something like Barambongdodo, yes, I'm sure of it.'

Mungo senses that she is lying.

'Anyway, it doesn't matter, does it? You're here and now, that's what counts.' And on impulse, she adds, 'And I care for you.' She falls silent, embarrassed by her admission. She focuses on the empty plate on the table, to avoid his gaze. 'Noah of Barambongdodo,' she says after a while, recovering her composure. 'Sounds grand doesn't it? Noah of Barambongdodo, and it says you are handsome too, and choice, and what else. In England only Great Men have titles like you. There's Lord Hood of Sherwood Forest, really famous, and people like Lord whatshisname of

Windsor Forest. Barambongdodo sounds like it has got a lot more vegetation than we have, so you're even greater than our Lords in your own forest.' She babbles on uncontrollably until Mungo stops her firmly with a distinct fiction of his past.

'There were no trees. There was only dust. And women like flints.'

It is Betty's turn to be perplexed.

'Once I saw a star explode and blanch the evening sky. And the next day the sands convulsed, the land cracked open, and Rima who had gone to search for food was sucked in, and the land covered over her and the sands were whipped up in a storm and piled over the spot where she disappeared. I dug and dug and broke my fingers trying to find her.' A vague sadness overcomes him, the only residue of a previous life. He looks at his hands, which are as unblemished as the advertisement stated, and he doubts that they ever attempted to save Rima from entombment.

'Come with me,' Betty says in partial understanding of his catastrophic past. 'Come with me,' she repeats, but he is deaf to her plea. He cocks his ear earthwards, listening out for any underground scratching that would reveal Rima's whereabouts.

'There is only you and me left and what's above the ground,' Betty tells him. 'If you stay here you'll be a dog forever, burying a bone, digging it up, burying it again. In Yorkshire we can start a new life.'

'You go,' Mungo says. 'If you steal me away they'll hang you.'

'I'll pay for you,' Betty says in desperation, pulling out the snuffbox and handkerchief from her bosom and placing

166

them on the plate like a church offering. 'This will fetch enough to buy your freedom.'

Mungo looks at them knowing that they are inadequate to redeem him.

'I'll give more,' Betty says, searching her bosom frantically but finding nothing. She stares disconsolately at her hands, bare but for the blotches made from the years of soaping slaves. Blotches the size of sovereigns.

'Will you get a commission from my sale?' Mungo asks.

'A shilling for every pound you raise.' Her voice is tinged with shame.

'Then you will gain at least three pounds,' he says, ignoring her shame. 'Take it, and with the four pounds you'll get from selling the snuffbox and handkerchief, go, find your home, find your family.'

'But what will become of you?' she asks.

'Does it rain in your village?' he asks, dismissing her question. 'Tell me what it looks like.'

'What does it matter? You'll never see it,' she says, struggling to contain her emotion.

'Tell me still,' Mungo insists, as if to force her to remember.

'There are wide fields growing turnips and barley and rape, and cherry orchards, and a thicket of beech trees, and brooks of the purest water which we divert to feed the land.' She pauses to take in the unfamiliarity of her words. But before things can make sense, the agent's footsteps are heard. Swiftly Betty snatches up the snuffbox and handkerchief and replaces them in her bosom. 'I'll send for you,' she promises, 'I'll weave and hoe and when I've saved enough I'll send for you.' She makes final preparation of him, straightening the collar of his coat, giving the buttons a quick shine with the sleeve of her dress. She goes to clean his face with her bare hands, but changes her mind, pulling out the precious handkerchief and wiping his forehead with the gentlest of touches, seeking to erase from his mind the impression of hurt that Captain Thistlewood had left there like the claw-print of an unclean animal.

XVI

I go into the smoke and disappear from her love of me. The agent takes my hand and leads me as kindly as a father might to a room smelling of lotions and freshly laundered silk, for gentlemen have gathered there to bid for me. And I will not see Betty again. I commend her to your care, gentle reader, as one of the deserving poor; one who should command your kindness, should you ever light upon her. Forgive me if I raise my voice above the noise of bidding, the unbecoming baying of the best of your people – Lords and Admirals and Connoisseurs – and address you, beseeching you to treat her with Christian charity, should you light upon her. Recognize her by *my* testimony, and not by the descriptions of thief and sinner that Mr Pringle will furnish of her. Her name is Betty. She is thirty years or so in years, the age of your crucified God. Her hands bleed with sores. She is short in stature and fat and ties her hair in a green ribbon. She wears yarn stockings and a linsey-woolsey petticoat. She has dark eyes and her face is furrowed beyond her years. She can neither write nor count, and is lacking in all cunning. Once, when I asked her why she had abandoned her village, she answered artlessly, 'May morning broke but the cuckoo would not tell my lover's name. And when I put bridecake under my pillow and fell asleep, my lover never came to me in dream.'

I pray that you will not meet her in circumstance of want but that she prospers in her cottage, making cloth, her garden plentiful, her family gathered around her to comfort her through periods of sickness and despair. But should she suffer madness, and abandon the womb of land and community, kick off her wooden pattens for dainty leather, and once more seek out the sinfulness of London streets; or should drought or landlord's guile drive her to the marketplace of its slums; then give her shelter and companionship in your hearts, as Jesus took unto Him whores and widows. Seek her out where the poor congregate in a huge morass of misery; where the men, having pawned their tools to buy gin, tumble in ditches like poisoned rats; and their wives, past scolding and past the vigour of sex which gained them a shilling for each act, sit at the doorways of their hovels, begging a piece of bread – however pasty and mixed up with chalk, alum and bone-ashes – from passers-by; and their children fresh in their filth as potatoes just turned out of the mould. Heaven tempers the wind to the shorn lamb, and you therefore must withhold your disgust at Betty's stumblings. I bid for her with Christian coinage – which is Our Lord's Sermon on love – and having purchased her I free her into your care.

Part VI

I

Lord Montague himself buy me and I praise God for the room pack with men with red faces and wild looks as if they come to eat me, a fattened calf or suckling pig. I am on a platform where all can examine what I resemble. My coat and shirt are stripped from me to show off my neck and chest and waist and arms. The agent open my mouth and run a finger along my gums to prove to them that I have all my teeth. He run his finger along Captain Thistlewood's crosses on my forehead to prove that I am tamed and trained. They shout out money and the agent write in his book 15, 20, 30, 35, 40 guineas, I can hear his heart thump and see his hand shake or in sweat struggle to grip the pen as he write down the prices, for the bidding is higher than he hope. The men grow in rage, some even stand on their chairs and wave their hands at the agent in case he miss their offer. Only Lord Montague is calm. He stay in his chair. His hand rest on the gold top of his cane. He is the best of all of them in dress. His coat is rich with gold trim and buttons. After a while he rise and walk over to the agent. The room hush as he do so. He place a bag of money on the agent's desk without a word. The agent don't even open the bag. He bang the desk with his hammer and that is the end of everything. He bang so hard that the ink pot jump off the table and pour on the floor, and his pen too. When the men go, some step in the ink and leave footprints on the floor.

They are low in breed, I think, with money but no mind, for they don't write with their hands, but with their feet.

Lord Montague lead me kindly by the hand like a father and put me in the coach to sit next to him and a picture he buy. We ride through the same dingy streets that Betty and I walk. The same pack of oyster wenches, shrimp-girls, shoeblacks and chimney-sweeps, all of them behaving mad, butting each other and bawling out prices, but I ignore them, for my sale is done already. When the coach stop here and there because of the crowds, children run up and try to shove their unwashed hands through the window, but Lord Montague done close it to keep out the smell. I hear the horseman crack his whip at them to chase them away. We ride and ride and all the time Lord Montague keep my hands in his to still me, and now and again he smile, till the filth give way to a country lane and planted fields, patches of forests, a blackbird sky. Then we turn into a broad path running uphill through acres and acres of land till at last we come to a grand yard and a grand house. A man in a red coat come out and open the coach-door. I am by now stiff with travel but Lord Montague himself help me out. Another man, in blue, come and unbuckle the horses. A man who all the time was standing at the back of the coach, also in a blue coat, take in some bags.

When we enter the house, people appear from every-where, one to take Lord Montague's stick, another his hat, another his coat, another the picture, another bags from the back-standing man, another me, and all the time the first man in red watch them coming and going with such ease. He is like a conductor at the concert house me and Moll one day will visit, except that he doesn't wave his hand about to make things work. He just watch. In quiet. Later I get to know all their names – Valet, Butler, Steward, Footman, Groom and the Women-Servants of the kitchen, the pantry, the still-room and the spinning-wheel – but for now I just gladden at the order and quiet of everything. At last I can rest, in order. And best of all, no one even look at me or say anything, for I am as unseen as Lord Montague. The rich are like spirits who you feed and worship and tend to, though you can't see them. You are afraid to look them in the eye, to touch them, to call to them. You just serve blindly. And if the rich have a friend or companion, they get the same treatment. So I get the same treatment. I am black and stumpy, my jacket is stiff with sea-salt, my face shine with cheap oil and I drag my shoes along, but I might as well be Lord Montague, who is tall and proper and marble and a man of breeding.

II

Mr Pringle presses me to tell him of Lord Montague's character, for your appreciation, valued reader, but I can say nothing for truly I knew him not. He purchased me, he took me to his mansion, keeping my company to lessen my anxiety over my future, then he summoned a servant to feed me. True to his thoughtful nature he ordered the kitchen to prepare a Negro meal, to make me feel comfortable in my new surroundings. A dish of crab-meat, pickled mangoes and West Indian potargo was placed not at the kitchen table but at the place where he supped. It was a long mahogany table with a beautifully ornate surface, and it bore on it expensive napkins and candlesticks. There was a ceiling mural of nymphs and shepherds – classical scenes which gave me greater comfort and made me feel more readily at home than the dish set before me: the spices were unfamiliar, leaving an unpleasant burning on my tongue, for I had grown accustomed to Betty's plain broth. Still I ate, out of respect for Lord Montague's consideration. He sat at the far end of the table watching me, pleased at the ease with which I seemed to accept my fate. True to his breeding, not a word passed from his lips. Everything in his household was marked by a quiet efficiency, a quiet undertaking of duties. And I was glad for such ambience, after a lifetime of screeching from Rima, sobbing from Betty, and especially the vulgar and chaotic interruptions in my inner-ear by Tanda, Kaka, Ellar and the rest, tormenting me with either descriptions of a devastated past or else with prospects of return to the innocence which was our village. In the months or years I spent in Lord Montague's household they never once appeared; as if they knew instinctively, and obeyed, the rules of England's decorum: that as lesser beings they must never trespass on noble ground, ground that was forbidden by ancient and vener-able rules of social behaviour as our katran bush was forbidden by dark superstition.

But Mr Pringle is dedicated in his endeavour, he insists that I provide a picture of Lord Montague, even though I inform him that I was largely ignorant of my patron, having been in his presence no more than half a dozen times in the months or years in his noble, silent household. Eventually my own patience wear thin under Mr Pringle's onslaught of questions, so I command him to take up pen and write down faithfully what I dictate. 'Here is the Lord Montague as I recollect him,' I say, and he draws his breath nervously like a virgin waiting to be laid bare and rested on white sheets. He takes up pen with unsteady hand, but has to blot a drop of ink that drips involuntarily from the nib before he can begin. I don't wait for him, but speed ahead, tempting him to catch up with my words, like a painted nymph sporting with her swain on Lord Montague's ceiling, running from his embrace and hiding in a thicket, so as to make his efforts worthy of her capture.

He pants across the page as I dictate. 'I knew Lord Montague by his wardrobe, for it was my duty to assist him as he dressed. He consisted of nine fashionable coats, two of which were plain, two of cut velvet, four trimmed with gold, and the last with silver lace; six frocks, three of white drab with large plate buttons, the other of blue with gold binding; one waistcoat of gold brocade, one of blue satin embroidered with silver, one of green silk trimmed with broad figured gold lace, one of black silk with fringes, one of white satin, one of black cloth and one of scarlet; eight pairs of cloth breeches, one pair of crimson, and another of black velvet; twelve pairs of white silk stockings, as many of black silk and the same number of fine cotton; three hats laced with gold *point d'Espagne*, another with silver lace scalloped, a fourth with gold binding and a fifth plain; several wigs – full-bottomed, Spenser scratch, long bob Caxon; three dozen of fine ruffled shirts and as many neckcloths; one dozen of cambric handkerchiefs and the like number of silk; a gold watch with a chased case; two diamond rings of stupendous value; two mourning swords, another with a silver handle and another of cut steel inlaid with gold; a diamond stock-buckle, and a set of stone buckles for the knees and shoes; a pair of silver-mounted pistols with rich housings; a gold-headed cane and a snuffbox of tortoise-shell mounted with silver, bearing the portrait of a lady on the lid.'

Mr Pringle gives up his struggle and rests his pen, staring at me instead in disbelief.

I interrupt my inventory, suddenly remembering my error. 'He was without the snuffbox, Betty had stolen it,' I correct myself, and instead of leaving at that, find myself speculating aloud, as a guilty man confused by being discovered volunteers additional crimes he never committed. 'Lord Montague never replaced the snuffbox, such was his love for his wife, whose portrait was set in it.' I look at Mr Pringle but he is still set in disbelief. 'He pined for the loss,' I elaborate nevertheless, 'he was a picture of ruin. He would not commission a copy, for he was a nobleman, one of true taste, not like an upstart merchant craving the status of connoisseur but out of cheapness buying counterfeits of original works.'

Mr Pringle puts his hand in his pocket, as if to hide his disappointment. I notice his hand bunch uncharitably around the coin in his pocket, the coin he has reserved for me but which he will not now surrender, for I have left him dissatisfied. He makes me feel like a strumpet whose performance is undeserving of his coin. Many a times Moll had told me of such men, to whom she yielded at Hyde Park, the men refusing to pay afterwards for the goods, like a merchant haggling over shipments of salted cod, or spices newly arrived from Jamaica, claiming that they were damp or malodorous or bored through by worms. Moll though defied them all, their cheapness, their slavery to commerce, and cursed them in the Latin I had taught her for such occasions. She wanted to spit in their faces but I had coached her in the ways of polite society. And the merchant-client was left speechless, as at the sight of a picked purse. He tottered off with breeches still ragged around his knees. 'Radix malorum est cupiditas, you piece of shit,' Moll shouted after him (my tutorship was incomplete for she died early).

III

I hear in times gone by in the Press Yard of an English jail a noble man is laid on his back on the bare ground, no litter, no straw, no clothes but a white rag to hide his privy member. They are to torture him for he will not plead guilty to wronging the King. Heavier than Captain Thistlewood's foot that day when he stamped upon my groin, the sky blown and the ship raped of its will, they place an iron weight upon the captive's chest, and another and another, till the first screaming from his full throat become a gasp then a wheeze, for he cannot breathe. The warder kneel at his side and put his ears at the man's mouth trying to catch his confession which alway come. The other jailers laugh, for the pressure put on the man's chest force down blood into his loins which swell, and his privy member rise and hoist the white rag like a flag of surrender. When the confession is writ down on paper, a priest as witness, they lift off the weights and put some brandy into his mouth to revive him. He is very faint, and almost speechless for seven days, and then he seems to recover strength for a little time, for they feed him barley bread and plain water and rumours that the King will send pardon. At the right moment, when he is sickly but still well enough to hope for the King's pardon, they take him to Tyburn and there hang him in full view of a coarse low-bred rabble – among them his own servants – who howl with laughter as the blood is forced down from his neck into his loins which stiffen once more, and as he swings and spins his member is a compass point gone wild, as when the storm did break upon our ship, Captain Thistlewood struggling to steer it, but the rudder loose and the compass gone wild, everybody will drown, then he sees me lying at his feet, and it comes to him – out of pressure to save his own life – that it is me who has done wrong, me who like a serpent at Eve's ear whispered and wheezed out a confession, telling my desire for him and my knowledge of doing it in heathen ways. And it comes to him that he will be caught doing it with me, and become the laughing stock of his fellow men, and will fall from grace with the abruptness of a hanging, and his sex will stiffen once more with shame. So he stamps upon me as upon a viper, until my sting is revealed and he can draw it from me, leaving me forever obedient to his will. He could kill me but he pardon me instead, for my mouth is stopped, I will never testify, I am forever obedient to his will.

Mr Pringle wants to hear, first about Captain Thistlewood, then about Lord Montague, and if I do not tell he will make hunger press upon my stomach not by iron weights (for England was barbarous then, without benefit of commerce) but by the lightest of coins. The cheapest coin is heavy, as if it bears memory of a barbarous past; the higher the value of England's coinage, the lighter the weight. Indeed gentlemen carry money now in the form of paper, leaving the poor to base metal. But I do not mind if I am deemed a remnant of the barbarous past, deserving only of base metal. Let Mr Pringle keep his sheaves of paper, a shilling will do me.

So what shall I give him for his shilling? If I was a fishmonger, a fillet or two, or mend his stockings like a milliner or grind his knife or make good his chair with fresh rushes, his wig with clean hair, but Mungo is old, look at me, my hands shake, I can craft nothing, and all the skill I had before was to wait upon a noble lady and dabble in a little quack medicine which was the death of Moll, as you will come to hear.

Only stories left, the breath in my mouth which I can retail for a few shillings, but Mr Pringle press me for more than I can testify of Lord Montague. But in the months and years I stay in his house, I only meet the man one–two times. He was always out of England in places with names that sound like Lizbon and Kallay and Florence, for the King send him all over the world to sign treaty or sue for peace. And that's how his house full of Jesu paintings and Greek stone and Chinee porcelain for he collect from wherever he go, so that if you walk in, whether you be Turk or Christian gentlemen you feel straight away at home. Or even a Negur like me find ease when I first go in his house, for there was a huge colouring of ships in the hallway, and I look round expecting to spy Captain

Thistlewood and to see Ellar and Manu and Tanda and Kaka rush into the room, banging calabash, slapping thighs and making merry to greet me – but nothing. Quiet – quiet. I can only hear my own breath come and go in my nose and sound like bubbles. Once the sea bore the ship and the crew rush below to unlock the slaves and save them from drowning, but the irons jammed on a few, no one could free their necks, so they just lie there trapped under water, bubbling from their mouths as if making song. Like the kabuti birds that we used to trap and glue to the branch, making such melody. I stand there in the quiet-quiet hallway of the Montague house, looking at the colouring, ships at war, cannon-shot, smoke, fire, bodies spill into the sea, dying everywhere, and I can hear my breath like the music whitepeople write down on paper. Once I open up a book on Lady Montague's piano and it full of bubbles trapped between lines, some black, some clear, and later when I come to know whitepeople ways better I learn that each bubble is a sound on its own, padlocked to its own line. And that is why I accept my slavery, for only when you are padlocked and meeting death do you sing as I do now for Mr Pringle, look how he heed my breath, straining to note everything I say, full of worry if he think he miss a remark, a crotchet or breve. He write down my bubbles on his page and make of me a memorable song, that whoever hear will weep and carry it in their heads forever and find themselves humming it when they are lonely or in broken love or bankruptcy. Outside, listen to the noises of the free: the bellows-mender, rabbit-seller, chimney-sweep, cooper and a thousand furious others crying their wares and trade, no one halting to hear in their breath the quiet-quiet music of their own dying.

Then Lord Montague is gone. He squeeze my hand as I stand before the picture, to calm me for he believe that I am in shock, for the ship-fighting and drowning men are reminding me of my time at sea, the waste of it. So he squeeze my hand and then draw me away to the table where servants bring food and when Lord Montague is content that I am sated he arise and is gone.

I stay at the table and wait but no one come. I look around the room, the rich cloths, the pictures on the wall, the ceiling edged with gold and painted with classical men and women I vaguely seem to know, and in all that time no one come. And I won't call, for the whole house is hush and I will not make a coarse noise and behave like Ellar and all of them, or the chimney-sweeps and their tribe. So I sit still and wait. The whole house is hush but for slight sounds now and then, like glass clinking, or silver, till at last the man in red appear, he look at me then turn, not a word. And I follow him from the room to another room where he scrape and bow to a Lady who look up from her needlework, see me, give me a bleak smile.

IV

She give me a fixed smile like she know me all her life as friend or kin, and she make me sit beside her on the sofa as she sew. To start with she say nothing and I come to wonder whether rich whitepeople too proper to use their tongues and have another way of talking to one another. Like my mother. I watch her hands working the needle and remember my mother and I look up to spy her face but only a smile I see like a rip across her face. Behind the rip is a secret that will never be told me but will tantalize all my life. I know that now, but how, I know not, nor really why, except that she is a woman like my mother, like Rima, and all the others, who are sent away from view by the order of men. But even though I am born in my father's sex I still want to know, so I study her Ladyface, but her smile mock me like a rip which she long ago mend with her needle to stop me now peeping. I can't seek in her eyes my mother's child, and so feel lost in spite of her smile. I crave for her to look at me so I can see how I reflect in her eyes and can then talk out my true name. But she will not throw light on who I am, her hands working the needle like a blind man's stick.

Put this in your book, Mr Pringle, that in the months or years I stay with her I never know her, for her smile was like a rip in my own eyes. I can only tell my mother's veil and I can only tell the Lady's outwardness. She had on blue clothes, ruffled like waves of the sea, little nips here and there like the beaks of fish, Captain Thistlewood's care of all living creatures making him empty us overboard as meal. I can tally too the nature of her body. Imagine skin of bleached sugar, bales of cotton her breasts, veins of gold running along her arms, her lap a mine of inexhaustible ores, and yet all the cargoes of Empire but a trifle compared to the effort that went into her creation, the centuries and centuries of constant progress, the harbouring of the seed to ensure purity of race and lineage, the gradual accumulation of riches and reputation, like a stately ship starts from rude forest, a mansion from rude stone. Her mothers were ovoviviparous, securing their inheritance from the foul and the foreign by Law and Religion and Language and Title, and Moat and Castle Wall and the King's Militia. Mine mated without introspection then dropped me nameless in the nearest ditch to fend for myself. A sprat nibbled me, the ditch drained into a stream where a talba gulped the sprat and swam into a river to be eaten by a pike which the tides drove to the sea to be snatched in the jaws of a shark. And before the day was out, a fishing boat catches it and returns to shore, the shark slit to reveal the mess that was my original estate.

A black boy, fish-meal at best, one–two small English words in my mouth which Betty learn me, just enough to tell who I am – nig, pit, slug, dung – one–two small English words like coppers that weigh down the eyelids of the dead. How can Mr Pringle expect me to expatiate on Lady Montague's splendid presence and adornments of character, and the centuries' topiary which fashioned her nature, when my mind was as yet unsyllabled? No, all I am is a small boy sit near her, lock-jaw with fear in case she spike me and I lash and scream at the end of her point like fish we used to snare, Saba and me, who shave the tops of sticks to spear into the pond. And I watch all of her, all her neck, mouth, hands, arms, waist, feet, each breath and each time she shift, like how Saba and me wait dead still as we scan, and as soon as the fish move, swoosh! Spear throw, fish done! Scrape, cut, gut, fry, feast, and the day pass. Next day and next day and next day pass, the same. Start and end, start and end till what? Till I come here. What bring me here? O if I could think of my name I would know the sure of it.

V

I don't know nothing, so let Mr Pringle tell it as he want to, of Lord and Lady Montague, and I will shut my rambling mouth whilst he properize and give them pedigree, and make me present, and make of me a present to you, grateful reader:

There had been three children from their marriage, all female, now grown up and married themselves, their futures ordained from the time of their birth, as was Lady Montague's. A childhood of careless pleasures, a bevy of servants to supply their whims; a youth under watchful tutors who regulated their conduct, teaching the etiquette of dress and conversation, exposing them to a measure of learning sufficient for their determined roles; then marriage to this or that Earl or Lord depending on what advantages the family could gain by such an alliance. Lady Montague had successfully supervised the conduct of the children, preserved the honour of her husband's ancient title and lineage. Now that they had gone away to make their own families and consolidate England's pedigree, Lady Montague turned her devotion to her husband's career. She was the most esteemed hostess in London, their household famed for its brilliant soirees, attracting the best of European nobility and politicians from as far afield as Prussia. Lord Montague represented the King in foreign disputes. He was admired for his skills in diplomacy. He entertained lavishly, especially when England's traditional rivals were present. His house, adorned with the finest Old Masters from Europe and treasures from the East, was a display of England's universality. He could expatiate on the virtues of Chinese Opera with the same breadth of learning as he could discuss the brushstroke of an Italian artist. Civilized men from whatever part of the world could find an excellent example of their culture in his household, and therefore be reassured that he was a man of true catholic taste; one whom they could trust in any negotiation.

Lady Montague supported his ambassadorial duties, becoming an exemplar of patriotic duty, or so it appeared to him. She organized the household with an efficiency that would have been the envy of England's strategists. Each soiree was a campaign, Lady Montague in command of butlers, cooks and maids, ensuring that the table was set with a hundred dishes like so many pieces of artillery. She took utmost delight in such precision, a counterpart in the domestic sphere of her husband's diplomacy. And to humour her, Lord Montague would sometimes hold a classical banquet, with the table pieces specially made for the occasion. Like all women of breeding she had been schooled in the language and manners of the Ancients, and the classical evenings allowed her to display her erudition. Everything was cooked in clay pots and served on terracotta plates by servants attired in Roman costume. The drinking pots, beakers and wine-jugs bore familiar pictures of flute-girls and lyre-players. The sauces – crushed myrtle berries with cumin, pepper and honey for roasts; celery seeds, mint and vinegar for fowl; oregano, rue and dates for fish – were from the recipes of Apicius or Martialis. The table was set according to Petronius' description of Trimalchio's banquet, the centrepiece being an enormous pig crowned with a winecup and garnished with honey-cakes, boiled liver, beetroot and wholemeal bread. The men reclined on sofas, each allocated a personal attendant dressed in slave garb. They drank wines especially shipped over from the vineyards of Campania – celebrated in the writings of Cato – and debated in Latin the affairs of state.

In such ways Lady Montague complemented her husband's career, entertaining the palates of statesmen whilst he conducted subtle negotiations with them on behalf of the nation. And there was no gift precious enough that Lord Montague could present to her from his voyages overseas. He strove for more and more exotic things to amuse her. A gorgeous parrot, bought at a Spanish port, kept her company for many years, until it lost its tongue and succumbed to age; then, she had a monkey from North Africa, its teeth filed, its claws softened in honey and a silver collar embellishing its neck. It too died, and another amusement was needed to mark the beginning of their third decade of marriage. He had long resisted the idea of a pet Negro, such as kept by many of his friends, out of a vague moral qualm. He was contemptuous of the world of commerce, particularly the West Indian merchants whose manners were as unbecoming as their traffic in human bodies. Abroad they were a threat to peace, inciting war with rival countries, endeavouring to engross all the treasures of the Indies to themselves. They were secure in their counting houses, caring nothing for the English lives lost as a result of their competition. At home they paraded their wealth, tastelessly overdressed in their ornate coaches. They drove up the price of venison by their upstart appetite for noble game. At sea they brought into being the behaviour of pirates, too degraded to describe; on land they supported the whoring of country maids, nay, even ladies of quality, and a swarm of pimps. Altogether, in their lack of patriotism and the squalls bred by their newly acquired money, they were the greatest threat to the nation's ancient character, more so than the Jacobites. He could negotiate an honourable settlement with France, but merchants were immune to any form of reasoning that did not involve a hefty percentage in returns. Indeed they would set up in France or Spain, and turn hired guns against the British navy, if it brought in sufficient dividends. They would fund a mob to storm Court and Parliament and abolish England's ancient order, if it suited their purpose.

It was in such a frame of mind that Lord Montague travelled to Johnson's Coffee House to purchase Mungo. The notice of sale in the *Monthly Intelligencer* had caught his eye and moved him strangely. There were hundreds of such sales broadcast in the newspapers which never before affected him outside his normal repugnance at the ways of merchants. Was it that the advertisement for Mungo was juxtaposed with one for the sale of Mantegna's *Pietà*? Was it the description of Mungo as 'unblemished' and of 'uncommon dignity', in spite of 'scars' and the act of being 'blooded'? Like the exact image of Christ, His beauty barely surviving torture at the hands of men? Lord Montague had a fleeting sense of the Crucifixion as no more than a sale, the death of Christ not a deed of the most enormous and permanent consequence but a strategy for making quick money for a cabal of tradesmen, like the Bubble schemes hatched daily in the City. Could everything be so stripped of sacredness and made subject to barter and exchange? Were all the qualities invested in things, making them precious in virtue, heraldic or divine, so vulnerable to a trademan's calling? No, it was inconceivable that the Christian order which informed England's civilization – the result of centuries of Progress from the Dark Ages to the present time of Light and Reason – could collapse so catastrophically because of the doings of merchants; that the country could revert to the cannibalism of Sawney Beane, witchcraft, slavery to priests, civil war. And yet there was the spectre of the South Sea Bubble. Disaster visited the nation then, as the Plague of a previous time, reducing the noblest of families to lice, the most delicate of Ladies to sodomy. Once more the Crown threatened to topple, Britannia sprawled in the streets, her mouth gagged, her hands in a whore's restraints, and invaded by foreigners. Christ's torture; the depravities wrought by the South Sea Bubble; and the picture of his wife in the most indiscreet of positions, careless of the centuries of breeding that hallowed her, begging shamelessly the favours of tradesmen and their apprentices: consideration of Mungo's sale spawned such images in Lord Montague's mind which he slew as swiftly as they arose. He wished he had never set eyes upon the newspaper which disturbed him with a sense of his own involvement in the scheme of sin. Did he not, only last year, purchase a *Pietà* as expensive as that by Mantegna? Did he buy it out of reverence for art or the subject matter? Or was it a mere adornment on his wall to broadcast his taste to a respectful nation? Or worse, a sound investment? Did he not hesitate in temptation when Lord Beckford, visiting him for supper, sighted the painting and immediately sought to buy it for a full twenty per cent more than what he had paid for it? How could he scorn the merchant who dealt in the honest goods of sugar and tobacco, when it was he who, in dealing in *Adorations* and *Pietàs*, stripped the sacredness from the life of things as surely as the rough hands tearing at Britannia's undergarments?

Once more he read the advertisement, seeking confirmation of his guilt, or else escape from self-condemnation. He paused at Captain Thistlewood's name in acknowledgement of the real cause of his unease. Captain Thistlewood, a complete stranger, until two months ago when he became the subject of a dinner conversation, Magistrate Gonson asking his opinion of the Thistlewood case. Lord Montague was deep in his loin of mutton, which was unexpectedly tough, the seasoning somewhat indifferent. He felt a curious disappointment in his wife. He looked up from his plate, perplexed not by the question but by Lady Montague's lapse in providing such an uneven supper. Still, she had supplied them with a fine Burgundy. 'The Thistlewood case,' his guest repeated, and when Lord Montague didn't respond (for, against his will he remained distracted by questions about his wife's recent odd behaviour) the matter was politely dropped, and the male talk turned to Spanish manoeuvrings in the American colonies; the ladies preferring to converse among themselves, in French, on the latest follies. But Magistrate Gonson was slightly drunk and dribbled his wine. He hiccuped at the sight of his deeply stained napkin, the colour of blood bringing him back to his original theme.

'A veritable rogue and unchristian fellow, ought to hang! What's his name, Larwood, or was it Thistlefield?'

'Thistlewood,' Lady Montague corrected him, breaking off her conversation with the ladies, as if she was not paying attention to them at all but secretly following what the men were saying. 'Captain Thomas Thistlewood, once an officer of the Royal Navy, now in the African Trade.'

'Ought to hang,' Magistrate Gonson repeated, 'whatever his accursed name. A disgrace to the fair reputation of England!'

'You were abroad,' Lady Montague told her husband, noticing his perplexed frown.

'Imagine drowning all those poor fellows, and women and children too!' Magistrate Gonson continued, raising his glass as if in righteous anger. Lady Montague waved to a butler who replenished the glass.

'He shackled some forty slaves,' she told her husband, filling in the gaps between the drunkard's exclamations. 'He ordered them to be thrown overboard, all,' she continued in a matter-of-fact tone, barely pausing as she signalled the servants to furnish the table with new dishes. And then she ignored him, turning to the ladies, resuming from where she had left off, on the ridiculousness of the new pompons. The sudden casual introduction of mass-murder into the evening's conversation left Lord Montague speechless.

'They say he went mad, the horror of his business finally turning his brain,' the tipsy guest continued.

Once more Lady Montague intervened to offer a contradictory opinion. 'It was a calculated act. The slaves were sick. By throwing them overboard he could claim their insurance value as goods lost at sea. Surely you know that the law provides for such recompense.'

The ladies giggled, partly out of embarrassment at hearing of the killings, partly out of surprise at Lady Montague's boldness.

Lord Montague made an effort to maintain his composure. His wife had undermined his authority by speaking of a matter he was ignorant of, and pronouncing so decisively on it; in addition, a matter that was properly the business of men. He would raise it with her later, but for now he sipped from his glass and complimented her on her choice of wine. Lady Montague sensed his unease, but chose to ignore it, reverting to French and chevying the conversation on to the gaudiness of continental petticoats.

An unfamiliar silence presided as they took breakfast, Lady Montague stubbornly refusing to address him and Lord Montague unsure of how to initiate conversation. The servants moved around them quietly, laying down dishes or removing them from the table with the stealth of thieves. Today he was to set off for Dover and to France, to settle a fresh dispute in Calais. Perhaps she was displeased at the increasing frequency of his journeys. She knew though, without him having to explain in detail, that the times were peculiarly troubled, the unprecedented increase in trade resulting from the productivity of the West Indies creating new rivalries and tensions between England and its traditional enemies in Europe. Diplomacy was more needed now than in any other period of the nation's history. In any case he had never before felt the need to seek her consent in his various undertakings. But of late he had sensed an unhappiness in her, manifested not in any words she spoke to him, but rather in her silence when he returned from his duties. No longer was there excitement in home-coming, Lady Montague flustered at his return, unwrapping his presents with a child's untidiness; childishly impatient for the fullest account of his foreign adventures. Then she was in awe of his statesmanship, attentive to every detail of his negotiations, elated or depressed by his successes or disappointments as if they were her own. And during the few days he spent at home, she would organize the most convivial parties and entertainments so that he could be thoroughly relaxed in the company of friends. She dedicated herself to him with such completeness that when the time came to leave he felt traitorous, ensnared in guilt, as if the King's business was a harlot he was addicted to.

Was it that she was suspicious of his doings overseas, inventing mistresses who supplied him with pleasures she felt beyond her because of her age? Or was it a simple need for companionship, the children grown and departed and her life therefore useless? What was it that made her slacken in her service to him, providing bland food and independent opinion? He had no way of telling, for he knew not how to formulate the question, never before experiencing dissatisfaction from her.

'I have prepared some reading for you,' she said, suddenly making herself familiar to him. It was her custom, when he was away, to prepare a file of occurrences in the realm, cutting out items from various newspapers, always of a humorous nature, to distract him from the seriousness of his work. This he took with him during his new journeys.

When exhausted by examination of State documents, he would gratefully seek release in the accounts of human follies. They were typically exaggerated or improbable, satisfyingly different from the rigours and details of his Official reports: stories of the latest hauntings of the Cock Lane Ghost, fairground frolics, escapes from London Zoo, the ravings of lunatics, bankrupts and desperate gamblers, and brawls outside cockpits and beer-gardens. It was a world outside his experience, one he had only glimpsed through the blinds of his coach-window or in Hogarth's prints of crudeness and bawdy. But it was as English as his own estate, and though the trivia of people's lives was finally beyond his comprehension, he held no contempt for them. After all, it was from the ranks of the common people, misbegotten as they were, that England drew its superior strength over other nations; the hundreds of thousands of soldiers and sailors who defended its shores and safeguarded its colonies. Indeed, their fighting prowess – the careless spontaneity with which they plunged into battle, wagering their lives for a few shillings' pay – was his final appeal at the table of negotiations. Lady Montague's files entertained him but they were also useful memoranda of his obligations to the common people.

'It has made me quite unwell,' she continued as the steward presented her set of clippings to Lord Montague. 'Quite . . .' she struggled to find the exact word – 'fatigued.'

'But dearest—' he protested, but she dismissed him before he could formulate his concern.

'I didn't disclose it to you, for your duties must take precedence over domestic affairs,' she told him decisively, signalling that she would not engage in further discussion on the matter. Once more she appeared unrecognizable to him. Never before, throughout all their years of marriage, had she addressed him so immodestly. He opened the file in search of an explanation but she stopped him immediately. 'You can read it later, at leisure,' she said firmly, 'but now you must prepare to go.' She glanced at the mantelpiece's clock and then at him. 'The morning is nearly over, you must go soon,' she repeated, and he found himself rising solemnly from the table like a child being dismissed for his unmannerliness. She turned her cheek to him to accept a perfunctory farewell kiss, and when he left the room she sighed with relief, as if an iron weight had been lifted from her chest.

Lord Montague, fifty miles or so outside Dover, ordered his coach to stop and to turn back to London. The crisis at Calais, so threatening to England's peace, with the potential of engulfing the whole of Europe in war, would have to wait upon his own troubles. Lady Montague's file was humourless, consisting of a dozen clippings on the Thistle-wood affair, each contradicting the other. Why did she choose to confuse him (and on such a dismal subject!) when the prospect of war demanded (as she well knew) a clarity of mind on his part? Was it merely an error of female judgement or did it betoken a mischievous intent? Was the supper a (rare) lapse by their kitchen staff, or a conscious slight of a disappointed wife? And what was it about his behaviour that provoked her unseemly intervention in the evening's conversation? The twenty years of marriage were, as they ought to be, uneventful. Why now the prospects of accusation and malice? Why, after twenty years of marriage, should she select for his attention such an unconventional episode? Was it to make him doubt their marriage, sanctified by custom and tradition? Was she intimating to him acts of adultery, or the potential for such?

Lord Montague was as irritated by the secret purposes of his wife as he was by the contradictory accounts of the Thistlewood case in the newspapers. Some said the total cargo was drowned, others a handful of sick slaves only. The ship was going to the West Indies. It was going to Liverpool. Beside Blacks it carried ivory, gold nuggets, hides. It carried only hemp. Captain Thistlewood was veritably mad. The years of witnessing the horrors of the Trade had finally cracked his mind and he jettisoned the lot of them. No, it was a calculated decision to save the rest of the slaves, and his crew, for an African malady had broken out on board, and so the sick slaves were a necessary sacrifice. The situation was dire: even the young ship's surgeon (a Jew named Gideon, Gildeon, Gillian, Galton or Lillington) had fallen prey to the disease and was also tossed overboard. 'Captain Thistlewood ought to be tried for murder since his is a CRIME AGAINST HUMAN DECENCY, for though they were slaves they were also of the HUMAN SPECIES.' 'Captain Thistlewood is to be presented with a silver plate and a hundred guineas by Messrs Gillanders and Arbuthnot, the ship's owners, in appreciation of his EXEMPLARY ACTIONS in saving the vessel, even though it meant the OVERWHELMING LOSS of the Africans, through sickness or drowning. The experience was so dolorous and has left such a deep and grievous impression on Captain Thistlewood's mind that Messrs Gillanders and Arbuthnot recommend that he rests for two or three months on a full pension before resuming the trade. He is retiring to a small estate in Hampshire.' 'He was mad before the episode and killed out of such breakdown. The story of a mysterious illness on board is a smokescreen for his guilt, an attempt to ward off prosecution. He is a disgrace to the nation, AND THE PRICE OF SHARES WILL SHOW IT, for we are bound to lose our hard-won ascendancy in the African trade through such acts of monumental cruelty and wastage. Word will spread that our Merchant Navy is a refuge for lunatics who damage the goods in their care.' 'Last week, Messrs Gillanders and Arbuthnot, in an attempt to quell the controversy over the Thistlewood incident, re-affirmed their unqualified satisfaction in the Captain's management of ship and cargo, and their confidence that once he has recovered from the mental distress suffered, he would resume service with them.' 'Captain Thistlewood, Master of the ill-fated vessel, was FOUND HANGED IN THE STUDY OF HIS HOUSE AT HEMEL HEMPSTEAD. There was no suicide note.' *For Sale, a New Ballad and True and Authentic Account of the Notorious Life and Death of Captain Thomas Thistlewood, murderer of two-hundred innocent souls, to which is appended his suicide note confessing the wickedness of his deed and imploring of God's forgiveness.'* 'Yesterday, Messrs Gillanders and Arbuthnot issued a denial that Captain Thistlewood was dead, accusing STOCKJOBBERS OF SPREADING THE MALICIOUS RUMOUR FOR THEIR OWN PROFIT. They wish to reassure investors that Captain Thistlewood, who has given such sterling service to the African Trade, A PATRIOT OF THE HIGHEST ORDER IN THE REVENUES HE GENERATED FOR THE COMPANY AND THE COUNTRY, is enjoying temporary and greatly deserved rest in his country retreat, before taking command of the *Apparition*, the latest addition to the Company's fleet.'

A dozen newspapers, each with its own version of the Thistlewood case, convincing Lord Montague that the prodigious increase of journalists of late was prejudicial to mankind. No longer was there a simple and straightforward account of events. Now, each version was calculated to inflate or depress the value of shares. Truth itself was hostage to the designs of stockjobbers, another commodity changing hands at a price. He read again the brief notice of the auction at Johnson's Coffee House, the disposal of Mantegna's *Pietà* and of Noah, a Negro boy of Captain Thistlewood's ownership. An image formed in his mind of Christ's body being handed over to his disciples, like the return of damaged goods, or bonds found to be counterfeit, or a promissory note to be discharged. And then he pictured the living Negro child, still at the early stage of commerce, not yet bid for, betrayed and embarked on that brief journey to Golgotha. He resolved to interrupt his own journey to rescue the boy, a task that now appeared to be as significant as his international diplomacy. He would rescue him from the merchant whose true instinct was to return England to a state of savagery, a collapse which allowed for predation and profiteering. And he would present the boy to Lady Montague for instruction, for his mind was as yet unformed and she would imprint upon it, as much as his heathen constitution could bear, something of the learning and chaste qualities which defined England's historic character. What better way to mark the beginning of the third decade of their marriage than by such a gift, which would make her rediscover those very English qualities, bred and inbred by her ancestors, beautified by the passage of time, and bequeathed to them as the order and contentment of their lives.

Lord Montague scrutinized him as the coach took them home, doubting his judgement in making purchase of the boy. There was something odd about Noah, something foreboding, but of what?

Noah was unmoved as the coach steered a passage through scenes of degradation, the beggars with out-stretched hands, dingy women howling dingy wares, drunkards, pickpockets, vagabonds. A sudden downpour, or the horseman's whip, scattered them. The road was suddenly cleared, city gave way to green land and a carolling sky. A new life awaited him, but he remained unmoved by the prospect of it.

Lord Montague scrutinized him for any sign of familiar humanity, but he was as distant as an African mask or carving. In all his years of collecting, Lord Montague had never sought to possess African artefacts, preferring the lightness and delicacy of things Chinese. Perhaps he should not have acted on impulse, so uncharacteristic of his diplomatic temper. Perhaps he should have left the boy to the baseness of a merchant's house, a habitation more suited to his nature. Certainly the boy exhibited not the least sign of gratitude for being saved. He sat beside Lord Montague with the same unreadable look on his face, the same thick woodcut features he showed the auctioneer and the crowd of bidders. Still, Lady Montague would soften his stiffness and angularity, as she had softened the monkey's claw in honey.

Part VII

I

Lady Montague is aware that the boy is staring at her with curiosity and desire. Not since early motherhood has she experienced such feelings from like strangers – who were her own children. When she entered their chamber, they would stop playing, abandon the attention of their nurses and stare at her, caught between puzzlement and an urge to recognize her as their mother. Propriety forbade any intimacy with them. They were removed from birth and suckled on another's breasts. Maids were the companions whom they reached out to in hunger, sickness, wicked dreams or terror of ghosts. Hired tutors taught them to speak and read, instructing them in particular subjects, forbidding other thoughts. They were the products of several paid servants, and yet they sought to acknowledge her singly, wanting a love more reckless and innocent than the studied caresses of their nurses. And she too looked sadly upon them before quickly re-asserting her role (a paid role? Was she in fact not like the rest of them, in a paid role? The thought jolted her momentarily) by adopting a rigid demeanour, questioning the nurses on this or that trivial matter, making a cursory examination of the state of their cots, then abandoning them to the mist in their eyes, to their childish and inconsolable needs.

Lady Montague is aware of a mistiness in the boy's stare, and is discomfited by it; the same discomfiture that women of her rank avoided by handing over their babies to be suckled on hired breasts. She makes a wrong stitch, and in attempting to unpick it, pricks her finger. She takes up her lace handkerchief and dabs the blood. (*It was me who thief the kerchief. Yes me. But why? I just had urge to take it, from the time she blot her finger and it fell on the floor. The blood of her was bright with life, and I had urge to keep it, so as soon as she leave the room I hide it in my pocket. All the months or years I spend there I sleep secret with it. The red fade but I still keep it to dream the tear and wound she make for me, and even now as Mr Pringle is in my room writing, I have it in my pocket, but I will not tell the rip and wound she made in her heart for me so that I can see her with a child's clear eye.*) Then she replaces the handkerchief carefully in her sleeve (*No. In truth I swear she let it fall*), for it is a token of Lord Montague's love, especially made in Flanders for her, with her initials in raised gold thread. (*But it never. It was plain, no marks except of blood, unless my mind is as frail as I pretend to Mr Pringle. As soon as he is gone I will examine it again to be sure.*)

'He is to be called Perseus,' she tells the man in red, taking up her cloth again and resuming her sewing. 'When he has become familiar, and in ordinary company, he may be called Percy.' The man in red nods silently. 'Take him away and prepare him in suitable clothes. And give him Medusa's silver collar. My poor monkey . . .' She falters at the memory of her precious pet, suddenly resenting Mungo as if he is the cause of the monkey's death, and is (as yet) inadequate compensation for such death. Mungo looks at her arms, this time seeing not veins of gold but the scratching of an amorous animal he is destined to emulate.

(*So the Lady leak and the man bring me here as cork-piece or what? Everybody talking blood, from the time I land in England and the Captain's lap. The old blood of Dukes and Lords against the new blood of City men. Bad blood between England and France. Blood-feuds between this and that House. Blooding hounds, blooding whores. Bastards against blood-brothers. Mongrels against bloodstock. Blood-money. The bloody Irish. The Ladies wear jewellery of bloodstone. Bloodwort, Dane's Blood and so many other plants and flowers, like England is one slaughter-house. And all over the walls of mansions and palaces, pictures of Jesus with a bloody brow; Jesus dripping from a Cross; Jesus staining his winding cloth. Like England obsessed with blood or what? And yet little of it you actually see in the households of proper folk! It's all in the paintings and in the words. The most I ever see is the tiny drop on Lady Montague's thumb. All the real blood run overseas but I am cleaned up before I come into their presence, so they never know the gun-shot hole in Rima chest, the English bayonets boring lakes in faraway lands. Lakes, red seas, but how can they know, those who stroll on an English beach lapped by crystal water, for the seas rinse themselves before they come into England's view. Even the seas are in thrall of the decorum and manners that are to girdle me, by Lord Montague's command.)*

II

Perseus examines in the mirror Medusa's silver collar which has been secured around his neck. 'Poor Medusa, my poor monkey,' he says, mimicking Lady Montague's sadness. He hates the collar. He hates the dead monkey. He hates his name. Lizzie and Jane, mother and daughter, the two servants put in charge of him, enter the room and surprise him as he tries to remove the padlock holding the silver collar in place. Lizzie slaps his hand away, then pinches him viciously. He weeps. Jane too pinches him. 'Ma, look, water comes from the nigger's face,' she coos, as amazed as the Roman soldier must have been as he speared Christ's side. She approaches timidly, takes his hand in hers as if to comfort him, then digs her nails in his flesh, to see what would issue out of the wound. (*I will not excite you, dear reader, with an inventory of my tribulations at the hands of these mischievous creatures, for I do not seek to reveal myself as ungrateful of the charitable designs of Lord Montague in sheltering me in his house, nor will I besmirch the reputation of your race by charges of wanton cruelty. Suffice to say that these two were uncommonly sinful to me, as were the remainder of the servants, whose deeds will remain unspoken till that day come when God will blow their arses away and they will guggle for breath as gutters swallow them or beg of my spit and piss to fall upon their skin to put out the fires.*)

Lizzie shoves him away from the mirror to a shaving-bowl. Jane feels his hair, fascinated by the curly beastliness of it, then takes up a razor. After his head is shaven clean, Lizzie stanches the blood drawn by her daughter's clumsiness or malice, then bedecks him in a turban. She sings the latest tavern ballad as she dresses him, Jane aroused at the ribaldry of it. Its subject is a Turk making sin with a Christian Miss. 'Sick fucking Turk,' Jane says as a way of complimenting her mother's musical talent, but Lizzie glares at her. She is a child of fifteen, Lizzie being a concerned mother will not tolerate vulgarity in her young. 'Sick fucking Turk,' Jane mutters defiantly. Lizzie pauses from her work and slaps Jane with such force that her head goes limp. When she recovers her senses she raises her head and opens her mouth to bawl, then changes her mind. Instead, she reaches into her mouth and plucks out a tooth loosened by Lizzie's blow. She rinses it in the shaving bowl, examines it with intense curiosity, then puts it away in her apron pocket among the other playthings kept there – the broken-off handle of a soup tureen, a stub of candle-wax, a peacock feather, assorted buttons. (*Jane, truth be told, a wafer of flesh, thin as the soup of the poor, for she is full of worms, bribes me with the full contents of her pocket, which are of no fascination to me, but when I refuse her endearments she finds sudden strength, in spite of her wasted frame, pins me to the ground, snouts my neck, rips my shirt, bares her teeth at my chest, delves her hand into my breeches, milks me with her bony fingers. Her mother has brought her up on sausages, cow-heels, suet puddings, boiled pig-skin, porridges of pure grease, and yet she will not fatten. Born prematurely, she has remained skeletal all her fifteen years, but with what fury and invisible muscle she presses me to the ground, lifts a filthy skirt!*)

'Go brush his clothes again and fetch them,' Lizzie barks, and Jane withdraws to the wardrobe and brings back a linen shirt, a flowered necktie, a satin coat and breeches, and a pair of embroidered slippers. She stares with open mouth – a little blood trickling from it and running down her chin – as her mother removes Perseus' old sea-clothes. He is to be remodelled into a fantastic land creature, part Indian (his turban), part English coxcomb (his suit), part Chinese (his slippers), with a small Arabian scimitar strapped to his side. 'Careful, wretch, you'll stain it,' Lizzie shouts at her, snatching the shirt from her hand before her blood can drip upon them. 'Put them down, put them down, don't stand there like something from Bedlam.' She raises her hand threateningly. Slowly and reluctantly Jane turns her back to Perseus' nakedness to place the clothes on the dressing-table.

After much fussing, Jane suffering a flurry of abuses, Lizzie's preparation is complete, and he is taken to Lady Montague for inspection. He hesitates at the threshold of his chamber but Lizzie shoves him forward. He stumbles into a world of whimsy, leaving behind memories of wilderness, women nursing their hurts, women drying to heaps of salt, and the sea, the sea, where far from the sanctions of civilization a massacre takes place, no one to stop Captain Thistlewood's murdering with appeals to decency.

Lady Montague sits in her chamber, innocent of the sensations of hunger and neglect, or the imagining of sin. She sits before a looking-glass, examining the innocent fall of her tresses. The walls are hung with Indian paper, adorned with several little images of Pagods and Brahmins, and vessels of Chelsea china in which are set various coloured sprigs of artificial flowers. A mirror, enclosed in the fancy frame of Chinese paling, stands upon a Japan table, over which is spread a coverlid of the finest chintz. Several boxes of different sizes, all of which are Japan, lie regularly disposed on the table. They contain lip-salve, pills, sticking-plaster. In the middle stands a bottle of perfume and a roll of scented pomatum. Almond pastes, powder-puffs, hair-combs, brushes and nippers make up the rest of her fantastic equipage.

Lady Montague is displeased by his entrance. She glances at him, then looks away anxiously. His presence unsettles her but for no apparent reason. There is a sudden dryness in her throat.

Lizzie fetches a cordial of blackcurrant. She waits for a compliment from Lady Montague, some little acknowledgement of her taste in choosing the boy's outfit from the various patterns supplied by the tailor. She herself had taken up needle to make final alterations, for the tailor, proud of his reputation for dressing nobility and gentry, had thought it beneath his dignity to cater for a Negro, leaving the task to one of his apprentices. But Lady Montague is steeped in memory of her pet monkey, provoked by the sight of the collar around Perseus' neck. She dismisses Lizzie with a curt gesture, wanting to be left alone to mourn.

'You've come to plague me,' Lizzie growls, shoving him along the corridors back to his room. She is depressed by Lady Montague's snub. Her total happiness and the respect she obtained from fellow servants depended on being held favourably in Lady Montague's affections. For fifteen years, nearly the length of Lady Montague's marriage to the Master, she had given loyal service in spite of being burdened with a child – the doings of the gardener who had taken advantage of her naïvety, she a simple country Miss come to town and lucky enough to find immediate placement in the Montague household. Lord Montague had overseen the flogging of the gardener before dismissing him into the care of Magistrate Gonson. He had allowed Lizzie to remain, in spite of her shame, and the distraction from her duties necessitated by the infant's welfare. She now had the advantage of being able to breastfeed his own newly-born daughter, so she was retained. For fifteen years she had resented Jane's birth. It frustrated her youthful ambition to become Lady Montague's personal attendant, a kind of Lady-in-waiting, part servant, part confidante. She had intended to school herself in the arts of conversation and etiquette to qualify for such a position. Jane's birth put an end to her scheme. She would end her life as a kitchen-mistress, no more. Forty years in age she was now, and nothing to show for it but a sagging body and a daughter incapable of marriage because of her bastardy. She boxed the child from the time of its birth, relishing the sounds of its cries, for it must become habituated to cruelty. Throughout Jane's childhood she continued to beat her about the head, as if to induce idiocy, to make her future bearable.

It was a bearable future which, until Perseus' arrival, was unfolding according to plan. In five years' time, when she was too feeble for service, Lady Montague would place her with excellent references, and a small annuity, in an alms-house, where she would be cared for, until the time came to die. Jane, luckily, had grown up to be singularly ugly, as befitting the circumstances of her conception. She was as thin as a pin, no man would want to bed in nettles. And her toothless hiss would put off even the most craven of studs. Jane would remain with the Montague family, the object of universal pity, protected out of Christian charity by fellow maids, and after a lifetime of loyal service she would die peacefully in her sleep. Lizzie's behest to her daughter was the condition of ugliness. It was a precious gift, more than her own parents had given her. The crops had failed. The landlord was unrelenting. They died with straw frosted onto their skins, in an open field, like a pair of birds starved by winter, but they left her a virgin in full bloom, the scent of country upon her, inevitable victim to the cunning of men. The gardener was blamed, but there were others – a succession of gentlemen guests in the Montague household – who made her their target. Each and every one of them was Jane's true father.

The prospect of the future, meagre as it was, becalmed her, until the Negro came, like the bad odour and rancid breath of men. 'You'll be the ruination of me,' she scolds, shoving him into his room and banging the door with such force that the looking-glass slips from the edge of the table and breaks on the floor. 'God's mercy,' she whispers in fright, crossing and re-crossing herself.

'He's only a monkey-boy not the devil,' Jane says cheerfully as she picks up the glass, slipping a piece into her apron pocket whilst her mother is still distracted by the prospect of misfortune. 'Blub – blub – blub – blub – blub,' she says to Perseus, thrumming her lips to make infant noises, as she used to entertain the monkey. 'Blub – blub – blub – blub – blub.' The monkey-boy doesn't somersault and stretch out his paw for a treat, as she had trained the animal to do. 'Ma, look, he is crying again,' she says with the same astonishment as before. Her naïvety is as constant as a child's. Lizzie recovers her composure and grabs Jane by her hair, twisting her neck so violently that once again her head droops. 'Stop your stupidness now,' she growls at the girl, 'go fetch a brush and sweep up all of it.' Jane revives, her eyes widen, her neck straightens, like the stem of a flower that feeds and thrives on curses. (*In the heart of the wilderness was a stick of cactus that was like a stake in Rima's heart. She go to tear it up but the needles bore her hand, so she stand back and spit curses at it, but the more she do so the more*

constant it grow, and defy her, and it even flower, deep red
blossoms like the sores in her mouth.)

Whilst Jane is away, Lizzie undresses Perseus, all the time pulling his ear as if so habituated to violence that it has become her only mode of communication. She cannot resist pinching him, as she does everyone in her custody. The monkey had died prematurely because of her. At nights she had chained the animal to the foot of her bed, to kick him better, even in her sleep. She would leave no water out for him, his whining a sound that eased her into comfortable sleep. In the daytime, as soon as the monkey was released, he raced to Lady Montague's chamber, leaping into her lap, biting and scratching her arms. Lady Montague took it for love, but it was more desperate than that. He chewed the cloth she embroidered or licked the varnish off the table, and Lady Montague was much entertained and took it for impish behaviour, but it was more desperate than that. When Lizzie entered the room, the monkey hopped and hopped on the same spot, covering his eyes and screaming. Lady Montague laughed at his lively performance, clapping her hands like an excited child. He brought an unfamiliar child's glee to her heart. She could abandon the hoops and stays of decorum and laugh freely, nakedly. When she recovered she felt a twinge of shame. 'Dress the animal in a cape, and put a collar on him,' she told Lizzie. 'Summon the tailor to measure him properly.'

'He was a him yet she named him Medusa,' Lizzie muses aloud, undressing the boy with spiteful roughness. 'Medusa sounds like the name of a she, or am I wrong? But he was a he alright!' She pauses to remember the happiness it gave her to take up a stick and prod the monkey's testicles whilst he jumped so violently that his chains nearly broke. 'A he alright, even though he had a woman's name. Or was it?'

Perseus, up to now utterly still, twitches as if to speak but seems to remember some earlier mishap. He resumes his silent passive self, resisting the desire to tell the Greek mythology of Medusa's being.

'You've come to torment me, say it out loud,' Lizzie mutters, but Perseus adopts the blank face he had shown Lord Montague, a face without recognizable content. He stands naked before Lizzie, absorbing her cuffs and tweaks as if he is a piece of ebony carving, incapable of feeling, African in its alienness. Lizzie herself begins to doubt his relationship to the human race, and even his kinship with the lower species. At least the monkey moaned and even fainted when she taunted him. The nightly punishment enfeebled the animal. He moaned or fainted like a woman. Though there were no marks on him (Lizzie was too clever a torturer) he died within a year, and Lady Montague was utterly distraught. She was perplexed, but Lizzie put it down to some foreign ailment, or the strangeness of the English surroundings, which the monkey, raised in Africa, never grew accustomed to. But Lady Montague would not be consoled by reasonable explanation.

Lizzie laughs at the recollection of Lady Montague's exaggerated grief. Only her kind, with too much money and too much leisure, would behave so, when every winter hundreds tramped the countryside competing with pigs for tubers and roots, robbing the scarecrow, searching through its pockets in the hope of a copper or two; stealing its clothes to keep themselves from freezing. But no, Lady Montague grieved for a monkey which she dressed up in a woman's cape, and a silver collar like a woman's necklace, and gave it a woman's name, and played with it as if she were some – some—.

'Sapphic,' Perseus supplies her with the right word. It escapes against his will, and now he grits his teeth, widens his eye and pretends to be an alien mask.

'So it speaks?' Lizzie says, gazing at him with the idiot wonderment of her daughter. 'And what did it say?' But Perseus will not show weakness again. She pinches his nose but he keeps his mouth shut, even to the point of suffocation.

Jane enters with her brush as Perseus is at the point of collapse. She screams at the sight of Perseus' distress, the same piercing scream she makes whenever her mother discovers the playthings in her pocket and goes to dispose of them. She thwacks her mother with her broom handle to make her stop. Lizzie lets go of Perseus and turns on her daughter with the instinctive rage of a wounded animal, but instead of raining blows on her she reaches into her pocket and pulls out a soggy apricot. She squeezes Jane's cheeks to open her mouth, then stuffs the apricot in. Jane sucks with a simpleton's delight. Lizzie watches her approvingly. Her daughter's violence, even though directed at her, is a measure of the success of her strategy. It is all for the good that she has a brutish heartless constitution to match her ugliness, for then she is safe from conspiracies of lust. Lizzie strokes her cheeks, encouraging her to swallow the stone, which she does in an act of self-violence, reciprocating her mother's affection for her. 'Go fetch his other wardrobe,' she says, prodding her fingers at Jane's eyes to stop her staring at Perseus' nakedness. Jane cries, staggers backwards, then falls in the midst of the broken glass.

(*She is always bleeding and everywhere. Her mouth. Her nose. Her ears. Wherever Lizzie cut or cuff her. O many times I want to holler at Lizzie to stop. Stop, I want to holler, let her be, for I thank Jane for that time she saved me from suffocation, beating her own mother for me, but I stay quiet for it will only bring more torture on me. Jane don't seem to feel or mind the blows, as if she is become Negro slave so born or used to hurt that there is no more hurt. I read this once in a book, or else overhear a gentleman say it to Lord Montague, advising him not to bother to beat me thorough for my sin with Lady Montague, for in Africa we are no more than mules, we don't have proper human minds, the sun dry and thicken our skin to hides that in any case no pain can transmit through to our mule-minds, so quod erat demonstrandum, sell him, get rid of him, don't waste your strength with whip and thump, the gentleman say to Lord Montague. And Lord Montague look at me with that same longing the day he buy me and carry me home in his coach, longing for signs that I am of humankind, then doubting like Thomas, but yet he struggle to keep faith, for he give my hand a Christian squeeze. And though he did decide to sell me, believing I do sin with Lady Montague, he is a good man at heart, so I forgive him. When he pause from writing out instruction for my sale I hold my head high so that he can see the Crosses I bear on my forehead shining with forgiveness.*

Late at night when Lizzie sleep, Jane slip from her bed and come to me. Lizzie chain me to her bedpost like the monkey, I lie on a cloth so thin that the floorboards weal my back. I try to deny Jane but she block my mouth with her hand and sit on top of me to stop my wriggling. By the time of dawn when she leave I am a picture of Jesu self, weals on my back, bruises all over my body, and so weary that I cannot move. Lizzie shakes me, shakes me, O I have killed him she panics, as she try to wake me, bring water for my lips, bathe my face, and cry, O I'll hang I'll surely hang, and when at last I stir, her fright turns to hate, she says you wretch, you'll be the death of me, boxing my head, spitting at me.

So my nights spend. First Lizzie chain me, mock me, fall asleep. Then Jane start her devil's play, but how much more Christ can bear than me, for I yield to her temptation and I pleasure even as I retch inside, for Jane is bone like Rima. Like I am making the most sinful act with my mother, which makes me retch, but as I go to faint she revives me, like the shameless painted women of my village, how they cage and tease me till I stiffen like a cobra and strike, and they laugh at the venom drawn from me, running useless down the walls of the cage. So Jane draw the useless venom of me, night after night. She prove to me the curse of my barrenness, for she does not conceive. Her roundness is not child but all the cast-offs she stuff in her apron-pocket, and though she walk about the house with swagger, showing off her swelling, daring her mother to chastise her, Lizzie don't bother, knowing that button and loose tooth and soup-bowl handle don't make baby. She let the girl play at breeding, but if she only realize what Jane do to me night-time she wouldn't be so let-pass.

And not Jane only, but all the wenches brace me to kitchen wall, manhandle me to the floor, not just ones fresh with youth but even the old who spend thirty–forty years in crusty service, who know how to make exact stitch or wait proper at table. Like the Montague house where at first I find set place and gospel reputation gone rude, but I blame me, I bring curse on my own folk and wherever hence I go. So I let them pant and lust but I don't tell,

like in the coach I never did when Lord Montague look at me with
such Christian care, he try to lift the veil of me, spy the what and
why of my lost true self.)

III

Jane brings another suit of clothes and Lizzie dresses him
anew, hoping that this time her choice will please her
Mistress. It will be his first appearance in public, for Lady
Montague's card party will be meeting, as usual, in the
afternoon. But Lady Montague has no zest for the
gathering. When Perseus is ushered into her presence she
seems not to notice any improvement in his appearance.
Nor does she inspect the refreshments Lizzie has prepared
for the party. She has not bothered to change her morning
dress. She has not called upon the art of her hairdresser. As
usual, Lizzie serves her a simple lemonade so she can test its
strength, but Lady Montague sips it without opinion. When
she returns the glass, Lizzie notices a certain exaggerated
control in her movements, which makes the glass nearly slip
from her hand. She fumbles to place it on the tray.

The ladies arrive, her familiar companions, bearing
familiar gossip. Perseus, outrageously attired, and standing
decoratively behind Lady Montague's chair, goes wholly
unnoticed. The ladies, between their prattling, finger their
headdress or their patches. They are absorbed in their own
appearances, playing their cards indiscriminately, unlike
Lady Montague, who studies her hand with the detachment

of an astronomer, though in fact seeing nothing outside of herself. Her gaze is on the messy unfamiliar aspects of her recent thoughts; thoughts that existed within herself but not seeming to belong to her. She had no control over them, neither their origination nor their outcome. Hence she could witness their unfolding with the impassivity of an astronomer, as if they were exterior to her; and yet they caused her hurt, as a sudden flaring of light hurts the unprotected eye. Lady Montague is unseeing though she pretends to study her hand. She fumbles for the right card, chooses one at random, places it on the table and is promptly trumped.

Lady Cardew arrives late, on account of a broken axle. Lizzie announces her presence and the company pause to greet her. When the card-playing resumes, Lady Cardew realizes that she has left her spectacles in the coach. Lady Montague nods to Lizzie, sending her to the coach, but before she can obey Lady Cardew's servant enters with the spectacles. Perseus is stunned by his appearance. He is richly apparelled, with a laced cravat, its fringed ends appearing through a buttonhole; a snuff-coloured velvet coat with gold buttons and a red velvet waistcoat trimmed with gold. He is also black. Perseus recognizes him instantly in spite of his disguise. 'Saba, Saba, is it really you?' he asks in an African tongue suddenly restored to him. 'Saba, look, it's –, it's—' Perseus struggles to remember his name. The ladies continue their game seemingly not in the least disconcerted by his alien babble. The black page is also a picture of restraint, ignoring Perseus altogether as if the latter is without substance. He stands with quiet dignity behind his

Mistress' chair, awaiting her pleasure. Perseus is confused by his perfect stillness, and by the ladies' self-absorption as they lay cards silently on the table. It is as if he is at a dumb-show, or witnessing some pageant of ghosts. He begins to doubt their existence, then he begins to doubt his own. On an impulse, remembering a deed of the past, he goes up to the black page and strikes him in the face, to make him his slave again, but the black page refuses to cry out, preferring the bondage of foreigners. The violence has no effect on him, as if it had not occurred. The black page's attention remains fixed on his Mistress' every gesture. The ladies chatter and play on seemingly unconcerned by Perseus' rage, except Lady Montague, who with the slightest tightening of her hand alerts Lizzie to her unease. As Perseus is deciding whether or not to strike again, Lizzie slips her finger under his collar and leads him away from the black page with as much composure as she can muster. Perseus offers no resistance, stupefied by the behaviour of the gathering. Nor does he react when Lizzie punishes him once they are safely out of the room, for her blows are like a masquerade of violence.

The black page is horrified by Perseus' manner, though outwardly he remains composed as befits his years of training, and the particular status bestowed upon him by Sir Joshua Reynolds. For he figures in Reynolds' much admired portrait of the Cardew family, serving chocolate to the gathering. Lady Cardew had him attired in true finery for the occasion and made him put on his most dignified face as he served, to show the quality of his devotion to them. O how often he thrilled (but secretly, for it was unbecoming to expose emotion before his superiors) when noble guests to their house were effusive about Sir Joshua's genius, expressing certainty that the painting was the Master's finest specimen of portraiture. Although none of the gentlemen commented on his presence (*rightly so, for he was, admittedly, a detail, and after all, a servant, therefore – possibly – beyond the dignification of paint, for the true subjects were Lord and Lady Cardew, and the two children, blessings be showered upon them, for how adoring their appearance, sweet cherubs with not a trace of chocolate on their faces or clothes, though William had spilt his and out of mischief – that boy! Such a frolicsome temper he is sure to become a beau and famous Wit for already he has ready answers and rejoinders to his nurses' protests – knocked Henrietta's cup from her hand before she could enjoy hers*) he had acquired a degree of fame among the black servants who worked in lesser households and were therefore lucky even to get into the cheaper canvases of a Mortimer or Smith, or even into a Hogarth print. He was a Reynolds' black, and behaved accordingly, ignoring Perseus' uncouth-ness though inwardly revolted by it. (*Imagine being addressed in such a savage tongue, never mind the savagery of the blow! In spite of his rich suit, Perseus is obviously a maladjusted Negro, one perhaps best left in the bush, in the company of other bare savages. It is his kind that brings such shame on the race, making the English believe that no amount of exposure to virtue can cleanse us within. They live in secret fear of us, awaiting the inevitable outbreak of native manners; the household of a nobleman no less dangerous, for all its elegance, than a West Indian plantation. Still, I have to set a standard as a Reynolds black, and although the Ladies, quite properly, do not acknowledge it, I know that my equanimity in the face of Perseus' outburst proves me a hopeful specimen of Negro.*)

The ladies are pictures of calm, but Perseus' violence makes his Mistress tremble inwardly not with fear but with perverse pleasure. She feels her hand tightening to steady the cards. The enforced silence of her guests, or the inane chattering which disguises their fear, pleases her momentarily, before she recovers a sense of her virtuousness. It is the same peculiar emotion that had overcome her when she first read the account of Captain Thistlewood's killings, and just as swiftly she had suppressed it. Still, she had sought out more information, poring over the newspapers, impatient for the latest issues, in the six weeks or so during Lord Montague's sojourn overseas. That he was absent, unable to regulate her curiosity, was part of the pleasure she had derived from reading of Thistlewood's doings. And yet she had cut out each item and composed a scrupulous file for his attention. Was such scrupulousness a means of distancing herself from her emotion? Or was she wanting to inspire Lord Montague to similar emotion? The rage – however little it was, and so easily hooped by the manners they were bred to – had gone out of their lives. The three children retained no trace, no memory, of the passion which created them. And as the years passed, she herself forgot it, finding new satisfaction in organizing the household in accordance with her husband's career.

No, it was more troubling than that. She loved him, what did it matter that his nakedness no longer inspired her? She had no desire for such childish and messy self-indulgence. She was content with the small gestures of love, given to and received from him, albeit out of habit and duty. They were no less shy, the gentle embraces in bed or in public; the sudden careless touching of hands as they walked the gardens absorbed in serious conversation or in their own thoughts, yet keenly aware of each other; the perfunctory kissing at his departure, yet both of them agitated by feelings of loss. The rage belonged properly to a previous age, and reading about Thistlewood was not a means of resurrecting it. That would be too simple an explanation, and she had sufficient regard for her intelligence not to settle for such simplicities. And when she thought of it, the killings provoked no surge of excitement. No, it *was* fear after all, and an overwhelming disgust at the whole business which took place far away but which engulfed her in her own drawing-room. It was as if the massacre had taken place among the china pieces, the wardrobe of silks, the shelves of poetry.

But when she thought again, she doubted. There was no denying the pleasure – an inexact word, but she could think of no better – in following the news of the massacre, like the sharks (so it was sensationally reported) scenting blood and swarming to the tragic spot. Her imagination, so bounded by her surroundings, found sudden release in the descriptions of sharks feasting on men's flesh; men bound and chained, unable to resist or to retaliate with the violence glimpsed in Perseus, violent utterance, violent act.

Her hand tightens, but within the terror is a nerve of pleasure, and when Lizzie leads Perseus away the terror subsides; but the nerve of pleasure so long quiescent in her remains exposed.

IV

Lord Montague brought the terror home in his coach, in the person of the Negro youth, survivor of massacre yet bearing its scars on his forehead. She will spend the coming time trying to control it, control herself, by schooling him in the ways of the civilized. In the daytime she will introduce him to Greek myths, Roman fables. She will immerse his tongue in Latin. She will take him on a tour of their possessions, explaining the origin of books. She will teach him the notation of their music, the historical and religious subjects of their paintings. But at nights, he will visit her in dreams of such adventure that she will not recognize herself in them, her trespassing beyond the bounds of permitted aspirations.

Each morning she is awakened by convulsions in her body. The chambermaids rush to bring bowls of water, clean towels, spoonfuls of sugar to calm her sickness. The doctor is fetched. He bleeds her. She rests. The bruises in her stomach subside, but she knows they will return the next morning, and the next. She comes to dread the approach of night, taking pills to stave off sleep, but finally surrendering to the assault of dreams.

She rises from her bed at noon, dresses, and immediately summons Perseus to her. All day she makes him recite a Latin ode repeatedly until he does it to perfection. She tells the meaning of a painting, dwelling on the minutest of details to prolong the lesson. She teaches him a single note of music, and makes him perform it again and again on the flute. There are a thousand odes, a thousand frames and melodies to occupy the time to come.

Perseus too is afraid of the night, for he too awakens

from it with bruises, the effect of Lizzie's and Jane's doings. Gladly he remains by her side, as in the shadow of a rock, for then he is secure from cruelty. Gladly he learns from her the arts of her civilization, finding refuge in them. No clause, no conjugation, no skill in recital, no instrument, is too difficult for him to attempt. And she is amazed at the rapidity of his learning, not knowing of his Greek ancestry; what has lain dormant in him for centuries now flowers, a Negro renaissance he dares not try to explain to her, passing off his scars instead as Thistlewood's brutal doing so as not to frighten her away from him.

Lady Montague abandons afternoon card parties for evening entertainments. She summons her friends to dine each night, plying them with endless courses to prolong their presence. But the quality of the food suffers, for the cooks cannot make adequate preparation for such regular feasting. And the servants are exhausted or bored by the repetition of nightly duties. They grow inefficient in their waiting, supplying the wrong wines for game and fish. Lady Montague herself is too frantic in her conversation, too frantic in her desire to keep them entertained, to be a proper host. Her eyes betray signs of sleeplessness, and although she is bedecked in the most costly silks, her appearance still lacks the elegance of former times. Perseus waits behind her chair, but she keeps glancing back to make sure he is there, behaviour most unbecoming of a lady of quality. The company suspect some physical malady, or else anxiety over her husband's welfare (they forgive her such openness of feeling, for Lord Montague's latest task was particularly fraught with dangers, since he planned to meet directly with the ringleaders of the English Jacobites in Paris, rather than negotiate with their protectors in the

French Court). The company is loyal to her, staying until midnight, to begin with. But over time their own household affairs take precedence. They seek their leave at an earlier hour or else make excuses not to attend. After two weeks of constant banqueting, their numbers dwindle, a widow or two, beyond household cares, remaining; and even these eventually disappear.

In her panic, she orders Lizzie to issue dinner invitations to the lesser rank, the draper and his wife who supply her with such fine Venetian cloths, Lord Montague's lawyers, the manager of the Opera House, some local politicians. Lizzie is speechless. Lord Montague offered hospitality to such people on the King's birthday, or at Christmas, and then in the parlour. It was inconceivable that they would sup at his table!

That night, after the humiliation of having to wait upon people a mere two notches above her rank, Lizzie chastises Perseus with uncommon vigour. The guests, unaccustomed to such splendour, had taken full advantage of the victuals on offer, taxing the energies of the servants, and staying until the early hours of the morning to clear the table of the last wine. They had left a memorable mess behind them, the dining-room more like a stable than a stately quarter. 'From – the – time – you – come – here – I knew you – were – trouble' (punctuating each word with a slap on his head) 'but – you'll not – drag – me – down – like – you've – done – Lady – Montague – andmadeherthelaughingstockofproperfolk' (a flurry of blows ending her tirade). Afterwards, Jane makes him even more giddy as she spreads her legs and rides him with idiot fury.

(*Of none of this I can talk to Mr Pringle. He don't want no dirt of woman but Moll's kind so I cannot tell more of Lady Montague's madness. Mr Pringle is a true gentleman, not the nigger that I am who make baseness wheresoever I go, turning gold to dirt by heathen alchemy. To him, a Lady is not ever improper, and if she is, it can never be in print. Life and print: two different things. Moll yes, the Jew yes, but Lady Montague will not be his topic, however much she bear down on me with the same sickness as Jane. He rest his pen and frown at me like he is chiding me for making up false things about Lady Montague, like if I don't know love, that's why I be nasty about women, give them sickness out of my own corrupt geometry. When Mr Pringle depart I pick up from the floor and unscrew the piece of paper he was doodling on whilst waiting for me to speak. He draw circles and squares and triangles all muddle and mess up, the points of the triangles poking and stretching and deforming the circles which trap them, like bumps on the shaved heads of Bedlam folk; and the squares lying on top of other squares in all directions like the cards of a drunk gambler. Why they all deem me bringer of disorder, why they watch me and only see an egg hatching in themselves, the shell break, a red beak show and then the body too blasphemous for print?)*

V

Three months have passed since the first signs of illness, and the doctor's ministrations have proved to be useless. Some mornings the pain is so cruel that Lady Montague abandons all dignity, lying messily in her bed and moaning. She wears her clothes as if they were thrown upon her with a pitchfork. Urgent messages have been despatched to Lord

Montague in France and he is expected home at any moment. Lady Montague, though, cannot bear the morning pain any longer. In preparing details of the Thistlewood affair for Lord Montague's file she had noticed a newspaper advertisement for Sampson Gideon's Amazing Eastern Cordial, with bold claims made for its various properties. She had cut out the advertisement and kept it for no particular reason. Now, as if she is the victim of some unfolding plot, the pattern of which is beyond her control, she finds herself summoning help from a stranger from the East.

Perseus opens the door expecting to find a crooked-back and bearded Jew, hook-nosed, darkly complexioned, his hands worn by a lifetime of counting money, like one of the Magi in Galdi's *Adoration* which came in the coach with Perseus (or was it a *Pietà* that the postillion had brought into the house that fateful day when they arrived from the auction at Johnson's?). Instead, he is confronted by a fresh-faced man, dark-haired, handsome, in his mid-twenties. He beholds Perseus with momentary alarm, as if the door had opened to an inevitable fate. Recovering his composure, he attempts a benign smile and announces himself modestly as Mr Sampson Gideon. He waits politely for Perseus to stop gaping, then follows him to Lady Montague's chamber, bemused by the boy's soft growling in a Negro language which sounds bizarrely like dog-Latin.

Lady Montague dismisses all servants from her chamber, except Perseus. Lizzie presses her ears to the door but can hear nothing. She peeps through the keyhole, but it is blocked by Perseus, as if out of malice. She hates the boy for supplanting her in Lady Montague's affections. Before he

227

came she was constantly at Lady Montague's side, but now it is Perseus who is favoured. Like one love-struck, Lady Montague cannot bear to be parted from Perseus, but she, Lizzie is not afraid of whatever Negro charm he works.

'What did the two of you do to Mistress?' she asks, tugging Perseus' ear as soon as the Jew has departed.

'Go see for yourself,' Perseus taunts her, knowing that she is forbidden to do so until called for. He suddenly feels protective of Mr Gideon in the face of Lizzie's accusations about conspiracy. Mr Gideon had shown utmost concern in treating Lady Montague, his voice gentle and reassuring as he felt her forehead, peered into her eyes, measured her pulse. Never once did he touch her indelicately, or seek to examine her more closely.

'He's poisoned her and you let him,' Lizzie groans, listening intently at the door but hearing nothing.

'Move aside,' Perseus orders her, pushing her away and re-entering the chamber. In the daytime he was Master of the house. There was no ill that Lizzie could do to him, not when Lady Montague was still awake. He locks the door in her spiteful face, gloating at her impotence.

Mr Gideon has left letters of recommendation from other patients for Lady Montague's scrutiny. 'Read them to me,' Lady Montague says, sitting up in her bed. 'Come, sit beside me,' she says gaily, smoothing the coverlet to make a place for him. Perseus approaches the bed with lowered gaze. He rests shyly on the edge, his back to her, for it would be improper to face her. Her hair has loosened immodestly, falling like vines upon her shoulder, and her gown is slackly pinned, threatening to slip and expose her breasts. But she is unaware of any impropriety, turning him around to face her and ordering him to begin his reading lesson. Perseus takes up the letters, shuffles them nervously, clears his throat. 'Read,' she says, laughing at his hesitancy. She pulls him to the centre of the bed, so close to her that he can smell Mr Gideon's cordial on her breath, a smell of a young, freshly-cut melon which brings him curious relief. '*Sir, for the sake of doing justice to your extraordinary abilities, as well as to inform the enemies of public practitioners in that science, that they should not be too precipitate to censor ingenious and honest men, I do hereby inform the afflicted, and the public in general, of the most surprising cure in the known world, perfected by your Restorative Eastern Cordial. I was afflicted by a nervous complaint, palpitation of the heart, which so distracted my head, so that I could scarcely sleep night or day; took sometimes my sight away, that I could hardly see half a yard before me. I applied to many eminent physicians, but all to no purpose; in which situation I was for fifteen years; but by applying to you, Sir, I was cured in a short time.*'

Lady Montague sighs deeply at the happy outcome. 'Read more to me,' she says, and as Perseus does so she attends closely, her breathing stopped at the details of pain, loudly released at the proclamation of cure.

'*Sir, by the advice of an eminent physician in London, I went to the Hot-Wells, Charing Cross, where I attended to every means possible for eight weeks; but, to my great disappointment, could obtain no relief for a most violent nervous complaint, which I had for a long time laboured under, which was attended with violent tremblings, depression of spirits, etc. So that at the least sudden surprise, I was thrown into strong fits, sometimes crying for hours, which I could not avoid; in short, my whole frame was so impaired, that I was obliged to be carried to my bed. My father, appalled at my distress, obtained a two-guinea bottle of your Eastern Cordial which before I had taken half of it, I was able to walk without assistance, and strictly adhering to the doctor's advice to bathe at Brighton, am now happily restored from the very verge of the grave to a better state of health than I ever enjoyed. Signed by me, Jane Baker, and witnessed by my father, Jonathan Baker Esquire, at Mr Gideon's Office, 40, Allbright Avenue, Richmond.'*

'I, Clarissa Richardson, in consideration of the great benefit I have received from Mr Gideon's Eastern Cordial, voluntarily depose, that I was violently afflicted with an inward complaint, that settled on my brain, and terminated in deep decline. During the extremities of my distress I could not obtain any relief, until my husband fortunately heard of the great benefit that was dispensed to such miserable objects as myself, by the administration of the above truly excellent medicine, which was a sufficient inducement for him to make a trial of its efficacy: the result of this experiment has been to me a blessing of the first importance, since, after being given the medicine for a short time, I am now completely restored to my health; which induces me, for the good of my fellow creatures, to make oath before Our Lord; and that I shall ever consider Mr Gideon as the Agent of the Almighty in putting a period to my calamities, and fervently pray, that he may continue to dispense the blessing of health to objects like me, who have long been a stranger to so inestimable a blessing. Signed by me and witnessed by my husband at Mr Gideon's Surgery, 40, Allbright Avenue, Richmond.'

'More. More,' Lady Montague urges, addicted to the rhythms of sickness and salvation.

'But today we are to do Petrarch,' Perseus complains, but Lady Montague insists, preferring the odours of tonics, syrups, medicinal barks and powders to the sweet airs of Italian poetry.

Perseus reads to her, of palsy, inflammation, dropsy, colic, obstructions of the biliary duct, night sweats, spasms, spitting of blood, excessive discharges, swellings, despondency and a host of other maladies unpicking female intelligence, infecting blight into the most certain beauty, cancer into the certain frame of happiness. She is fascinated by the ease with which the world she inherited can convulse and become disfigured, but with traces of its original state persisting – a wedding ring caught in the splinters of a finger-bone, unable, even in death, to free itself; buried in mud, pieces of stained-glass still bright with tragedy; a gilded tooth from which laughter roars, or the jaw to which it belonged redolent of rich wine, pleasurable meats.

The morning pains return but Lady Montague bears them with fortitude, knowing that she will never be obliterated by them. Something of her will remain, some token of nobility, the dignity of her class surviving the fractures of centuries and bequeathed to her intact. The Jew and the Negro who attend to her are two who have emerged from the fractures; strange dirty creatures spawned by the passage of time; creatures that thrive in the creases between floorboards, in nooks and chinks, in the cracks that cheapen the richest porcelain. They witness her decay, they feed on her decay, but she will finally withstand their designs, out of inherited strength.

Mr Gideon makes her drink an emetic, rubs ointment in

her skin, and bathes her face in a decoction of rue and bay-leaves. He mixes maiden-hair into a syrup of mugwort and orders her to sip it throughout the day. The immediate pains lightened, he departs from her presence to care for his other patients. Lady Montague resents his going as much as she is relieved by it. Placing herself at the disposal of a Jew marks the extent of her degeneration, and yet his medicines becalm her, however temporarily.

Each morning however brings new distress, Mr Gideon's ingenuity is fully taxed. He experiments with camomile pills, tinctures, aloes, infusions of Jesuit-bark, to no avail. Lady Montague's condition is such that Mr Gideon no longer observes the rules of gentility. He unbuttons her smock to inspect the coloration of her skin. He makes a plaster of Genoa soap, olive oil and ceruse, and applies it to her navel. He parts her thighs and inserts a finger, feeling for any growths. More scandalously he turns her on her belly and studies her insides through a looking-glass. He takes a specimen of her bowels with a long-handed silver spoon normally used to serve truffles. Lady Montague offers no resistance as the Jew manhandles her. Her pride disinte-grates with each wave of pain. Gladly she slackens her muscles to accommodate his enema, and evacuates without shame. Afterwards she collapses into a deep exhaustion, utterly apathetic to the Jew's further probing. But she wills herself to remain conscious, dreading worse humiliations that would visit her in the shape of the Negro, should she fall asleep.

It is in such a dire condition that Lizzie discovers her, barging into the chamber, although expressly forbidden to do so. She is too overcome by suspicion to pay heed to her

Mistress's command. She shrieks at the sight of Lady Montague as if the latter's pain is transferred to her. Mr Gideon stops his scraping and delving, dropping the silver spoon like a startled burglar. Its contents spill onto the floor, making an ignoble stain on the Arabian carpet. Perseus goes to intercede as she lays hand on Mr Gideon but Lizzie shoves him away with such force that the turban topples from his head. His ugliness is revealed, making Lizzie shriek even louder. Lady Montague raises her head weakly from her pillow and waves Lizzie away, but the servant remains insubordinate. She takes hold of Mr Gideon by the neck and leads him unceremoniously to the door. She opens it and pushes him out of her Lady's chamber.

Perseus gathers up the instruments and vials, stuffs them into Mr Gideon's bag and rushes after him. He is offended by Lizzie's behaviour and offers an apology in his best English. Mr Gideon is not in the least perturbed, accustomed all his life to such rejection. He thanks the boy graciously. 'I know you love your Mistress, but there is no need to mourn, there is nothing physically wrong with her,' he assures Perseus. 'It is a passing hysteria, particular to women of her age and condition. Her pain is ghostly, that is all.' He mounts his horse, but then halts, turning back to Perseus. 'You can come with me if you want,' he offers. 'I have noticed how quickly you learn. I am in need of your help.' But Perseus is too puzzled by the sudden invitation to respond appropriately.

'You will be wanting your fee,' he says instead, searching his pocket for the money entrusted to him by Lady Montague. Mr Gideon's face quickens with hurt. He refuses the money and rides away. Perseus, ashamed of his baseness, replaces the coins in his pocket. He is overcome by an urge to follow the Jew.

Part VIII

I

Mr Gideon purges and vomit-pills so strong that Lady Montague smell up the whole house, all the servants run about opening windows to let out fumes like offal boiled in horse-manure. And so many clothes to wash, carpets to scrub clean, bedsheets, handkerchiefs, for Lady Montague don't care what and where she soil when the medicines seize her. 'Please God bring back Lord Montague soon,' Lizzie moan, and she look at me with the same vileness that crawl out or seep from Lady Montague's mouth and behind. 'The Master will hang you when he come home,' she threaten me, and she start prepare me for that happy time by special hurts and scourges every night, like I am a Lenten creature waiting for Lord Montague to come to judge and sentence me. But I have other plans, the more she torture me the more I will not be a Christian saint nor Son of God, for the pain become so beyond bearing that I must purge myself of her and of her hawk-child too. So this is what I do: I steal a fresh silk handkerchief from Lady Montague wardrobe and lay it out on the mirror-table like altar-cloth. Then I clench my jaws, whisper to myself a grace-before-meals prayer, take up the razor Lizzie use to shave my head and in one quick slice sacrifice my right ear. Then before the pain can hit me I wrap the ear in the handkerchief, run up the stairs, along the corridor, into Lady Montague chamber. She look up from her bed to see the bleeding cheek of a mutilated Negro, like a figure from her nightmare, but before she can beg and sob to be left alone I let go one almighty bawl that break the water-glass in her hand and cut her. Then I fling myself upon her bed and mercy, our blood mingle, all the time I am crying out Lizzie's name while she is fighting me off and also crying out Lizzie's name, till our mingled voices summon Lizzie to the room, pale as ghost. And when she come I unwrap the ear and hold it up in the air like a bloody wafer and I point at Lizzie, blaming her, baying at her like a crowd of Pharisees, but Lady Montague too staring at my ear to pass judgement but will pass water and wind and what-not instead, for the disgusting spectacle of my ear loosen all her muscles, she vent and puke and squirt from every available hole like the legion of demons cast out by Our Lord. Hear O Israel, for this is the Lord of the Word (so the pain make me rave) given to you for the salivation of sins: a madman, coming out of the tombs meet Him so fierce that He cannot pass, and the nearby uncooked swine scent trouble and start fidget for when Jesus cure the madman the demons seek salt-pork and drown the swine in a pickling sea whilst the cow jump to safety over the moon and the cat run away with the spoon and Jesus move to the next town for His next miracling.

Truth is, the pain make me sudden hunger and thirst so that I eat the daffodils in the vase and drink the water, but want more, eat my own ear, swipe the pisspot from under the bed, downed it in one go, dab my mouth politely with the handkerchief like a tea-table conversationalist. Lady Montague faint quite away.

When she awake she is wholly cured, God's truth, and

treat me like boy miracle and offer me three wishes: so I make a swine of Lizzie, I make a swine of Jane her daughter, and I reserve the third wish for a fateful day when I face trouble and will need saving.

'Do you want me to summon Magistrate Gonson?' Lady Montague asks, believing that Lizzie has mutilated me, but Christ's pity take hold of me as I behold Lizzie. Magistrate Gonson will transport them sure, I know his lust from the way he cast a cruel eye at the serving-maids, stab and carve his meat at the table like a wedding-guest hateful of women. Nothing will please him more than to have Lizzie and child stripped, flogged, salt rubbed in their wounds, sent to sea. 'Save them both,' I say, changing my mind and using up my final wish. Lizzie is so moved by my self-sacrifice that she fall at my feet and wash them with tears more precious than pure nard. I raise her up and say unto her, 'Hop it, verily, back to your village in Yorkshire, and sin no more, or else . . .'

Or else what? What if Lizzie had stayed? I look in the mirror at the bloody landscape of my head and wonder whether my freedom is worth a fig, much less an ear. Slaves revolt, burn house and crop, hide in the bush, but how can they enjoy freedom in the company of snakes and wolves? I revolt, I destroy my face, I am free of Lizzie, but where to? What I know of London is a jungle of poor white beasts with savage looks who will eat me. And nothing remains of my village to go back to. I bandage my head and regret that Lizzie and Jane are gone away. At least I had a certain place – taking learning in the daytime, taking Jane at night. And the blows from Lizzie were no more than what I got from Captain Thistlewood, after a while they never ache, till I look forward to his novel ways of arousing me.

Now that she no longer fear the night, and her bellyache vanish, Lady Montague no more learn me things. Instead she dote on me. All she want to do is feed me walnuts as if I am a new pet monkey. She put a chain on my silver collar and take me for afternoon walks in the grounds of the house. Her talk to me, once of the High Latin of the Ancients, is now gurgle. She gurgle at me and make silly faces. 'Who's my goody-good good little boy, my little Percy-worsy-green fields of Jersey-boy,' she exclaims, echoing Jane's night-time ecstasy. And the gardeners, though stiffly upright in her presence, laugh when her back turn. And the other servants, now that Lizzie dismiss and is not here to bully them, slacken in their tasks and laze and disrespect, for Mistress don't care for nothing more worthy than a nigger-boy and she let a Jew unsex her, she truly gone mad.

II

Lord Montague returns at last, but to a curse rather than a miracle.

He sniffs the air, puzzled by a certain fetidness, for although Lady Montague has decorated the entrance hall with gay sprigs in preparation for the Easter festivities, traces of her malady remain. There is a curious untidiness about the house, and the servants are not as prompt in their attending to him. The ritual glass of mulberry wine brought to him, welcoming him back to the household, is stale to taste.

He enters his Lady's chamber, expecting to find her in her sick-bed, expecting a fervid greeting, a wife's relief at the safe return of her husband, a wife's relief that now that he has come, all her worries will be allayed. He has brought her a fashionable French parasol and the latest book of French recipes. He would have acquired more precious gifts but news of her illness interrupted his business. He had broken off his negotiations and left hurriedly. She was certain to understand and receive them with customary grace, if not excitement.

He is met by a stench which unsettles his stomach. The room is as prim as ever, but the odours of soiled coverlets, night-gowns and towels remain. His wife is sitting by the window, her brows furrowed in concentration as she sews. She looks up as he enters and greets him with a wan smile. He kisses her and hands over his gifts which she takes hesitantly. She can think of nothing to say, mumbling perfunctory thanks. He in turn mumbles apologies for his delay in returning to her, but she seems not to understand. She examines his face as if seeking to recognize him.

'Where is the physician?' he asks, looking around the room for signs of mental decay but noticing nothing out of order.

'The Jew came and went away with his quite useless cordial.'

'Jew?' he asks, slowly becoming convinced of some disastrous occurrence in his absence. She goes to explain, then her voice trails off.

'Jew?' he repeats, but she will not answer. She makes idle stitches in her cloth, loosens them, and lets the cloth fall from her lap. She feels suddenly exposed and folds her hands in her lap protectively.

'Where is the Negro?' he asks in sudden inexplicable realization of the boy's role in her distraction.

'Leave him alone,' Lady Montague barks, hunching her shoulders aggressively, as if the slightest movement from him would cause her to pounce.

As soon as he see my missing ear my fate seal. His jaw drop. His hand twitch. The blood drain from his face. Like he watch a ghost. He sit down to catch his breath.

The very day Lord Montague returned to England, new conflict broke out in Europe, precipitated by the loss of an Englishman's ear. I can quote for you reports – as you would expect, as confusing as ever – from the journals of the day which I have saved over all these years to give some semblance of meaning to my life; to try to understand why it is that a simple nigger like me was deemed to be the undoing of England, darkening its bright historic fabric; black moth, black adder, black beetle, blackfly, black bryony, infecting and strangling and poisoning and blighting England's heritage. In moments of self-doubt (or sheer malice, my enemies will say) I would take out these clippings and study them, seeking confirmation or denial of my characteristics, for what my Negro brethren do (though thousands of miles away in Africa, or on the High Seas, or in the New World) is charged on my own head. From the *Craftsman*, the *Monthly Intelligencer*, the *Spectator* and *The Daily Journal*, as well as from Grub Street broadsheets and penny-ballads, I have, over the years, created an archive of

my own morals and manners. I believe no such compre-
hensive compilation on the Negro exists in one place
(though hidden under my bed in no more than two or
three fish-boxes, such is the scantness of our history), and I
plan to donate it one day to the Abolition Committee ('the
Perseus Collection': I can see the silver plaque gleaming at
the head of the bookcase in some fine London library,
though sometimes I try out other titles in my mind like 'the
Mungo Collection', which I instantly dismiss as too
common for the ambience of learning; 'the Noah Collection', also not quite right since it confuses a sea-bleached
story-book Jew with the actual black me, the blacker-than-
midnight me, blacker-than-crow/molasses/spade card/sin/
shoe-polish/peppercorn/pimplehead/eyepatch/billiard-ball/
coalpot me; 'the Barambangdodo Collection', a trifle too
comic; 'The Augustus' or 'The Gustavus Collection',
splendid names indeed, except that no owner blessed me
with such title. And vanity of vanities! I blush to recount
the number of times I have dignified the plaque with
appendages like 'Negro Gent' or 'Esquire': 'Donated to the
London Library by Mr Perseus Esquire/Negro Gent/Man
of Taste/Famed Antiquarian/Servant of Scholarship'). Or
else I plan to sell the archive to supply my small needs, for
why should I not generate money from the sale of myself
when the sale of the Negro has generated fortunes for
foreigners? As a collection of newspaper items, I am a false
parcel and counterfeit story but I will pass hands as easily as
a forged banknote in the City's markets.

But I have hesitated out of honour, or perhaps shame, to
capitalize my self, for only the lewd or the morbid will
invest in me. Or is it out of concern for public morals that I

refuse to be circulated in the hands of pornographers? To be sure I have sought out alternative and more hopeful headings for the files, but my English falters, or else English itself falters. The headings made years ago remain like stubborn stains: 'Slave Revolts', 'Mutinies', 'Runaways', 'Suicides', 'Infanticides', 'Executions by Hanging', 'Executions by Gunshot', 'Executions by Burning', 'Executions by Hand'. In the faraway plantations of the West Indies, in the barracoons of the African coast, I have rebelled, stabbed, poisoned, raped, absconded, and sought escape by killing myself and my offsprings. In return I have been strangled, flogged to death, roasted alive, blown away and lynched. Truly I have made havoc in the hearts and minds of whitepeople, compromising their civility, sharpening their Christian principles to breaking-point.

A war come when a Spaniard ruffian cut off the ear of one Mr Jenkins, sailorman and true servant of the King going about his proper business in the Caribbean Sea. And Lord Montague who did go abroad to make peace and spend so much effort to heal whatever sickness grip the foreigner, whatever make him want to rave and froth and bite up like a rabid dog, now face fresh trouble which undo all his great work. Like the foreigner is chronic, you can't balm him, that thought must have passed through Lord Montague's mind when he look upon me and see the missing ear. He look on me as if my black arts caused the war, that the very hour I raise the razor to my ear is the very hour the dago put a dagger on Mr Jenkins. O how his heart grieve to think of me as evil sprite or at best omen of disaster, for he did buy me out of true pity, reading the crosses on my forehead (which now appear like upside-down crosses, for my growing skin stretch with time, sure marks of devilry). And he did bring me to his Lady's house, and lock her up and me in it, so that she can breed the badness out of me with nothing to distract her from such a duty; but he fail, for I infect all of them, the Lady, the servants, even the animals (things make worse in his mind when the very day he find me no-ear, his best horse that always bring him safely home burst his chest and die). And then the gossip that a Jew come, unpick the padlock of the Lady's treasure-box and shower fool's gold in it. And the gossip too that the Lady overfond of me, as if not just my ear I slash but her very and most precious flower (though the truth is that all I rob from her to eat was a bunch of common daffodils).

No, he must rid me for he think I bring chaos to his house, corrupt his wife, and one day I may even rise up to slay him for I have the instincts of a savage, no feathered turban, silk and silver ornaments can enslave them for too long. Yet he take up only a pencil, for in writing out the English bill to sell me, he can change his mind and rub out this or that lettering. O how I grieve for him when I watch him labour and sweat like a Negro, and he of noble birth. He is in so much sadness that he press down on the pencil and when the point break, so my very heart. He take out his snuffbox to revive his spirits, but seeing the tears rolling down my cheeks, all of a sudden he hand it to me. 'Take,' he says, for although I am to go he will not be unkind.

'But – but – but – but,' I stammer as if to say, 'How can I take your love-present from your wife?' but it is adding up I'm really doing in my mind, counting my blessings between one 'but' and the next, for instantly I figure that the snuffbox worth ten–twelve pounds, and the Lady's handkerchief I done steal is two–three pounds, so I let the gift drop in my hand, and with as much grace as my Saviour teach me I slip it into my pocket.

III

Perseus flees the Montague household before he can be sold to a West Indian merchant. It pains him to abandon Lady Montague to the wreckage he has made of her life. He takes with him a sackful of various items belonging to her – two bottles of French perfume, a silk handkerchief, a leather-bound volume of Petrarch's poetry, a bust of Cato carved in sandstone and a Japan fan ribbed in ivory. It strikes him, as he gathers her belongings, that he will or should also miss Lord Montague, so he stuffs in his sack a pigtail wig, a gold-nibbed pen, a snuffbox, silver toothpicks, a Bible with gilt-edged pages, and his Master's favourite tankard of Spanish silver. As he is about to depart he realizes he has no mementoes of the house itself, which has given him such splendid refuge from the poverty of the world he is about to enter (had he been sold to a merchant or tradesman he would have languished in cellar or basement, ignorant of finery and the artefacts of taste). So he takes a candlestick, wrought in the new rococo style, and a small painting of Ganymede riding an eagle (not so much for its subject but the convenience of its size). Laden with these valuables he sets off for London. He does not depart at midnight like a common thief, but in bright daylight. It is Easter week, the servants have been released for their holiday and Lord and Lady Montague departed for church and thence a period of recreation in Surrey, guests of one of their daughters. Perseus has the house to himself, hence he can pick and choose at leisure, selecting this or that object judiciously. Of course when the household returned there would be a hue and cry, servants running here and there, calling out their discovery of missing treasures, their own disorder suggesting that Perseus had exercised no profound decision in compiling his haul, experienced no love and pathos as he furnished his sack. He would be deemed a common thief, Magistrate Gonson would be despatched after him.

It grieves him, as he saddles Lord Montague's swiftest horse, to think that he would be so profanely misunderstood, but the prospect of slavery in the West Indies – his certain fate when the Easter was out and Lord Montague returned – overcomes his pride, overcomes the fleeting desire to replace the items (worth at least one hundred and fifty guineas, by his instant computation, the very sum Lord Montague had paid for him) and leave as empty-handed as he had come.

He get me cheap anyway, a Christian already and with a hidden store of the classics. You have to pay fifty guineas for your normal nigger, and he comes with nothing but sadness in his eyes. You have to beat out of him all his pining, till he break and be new, and even then you have to pay for him to learn English, learn manners, learn to call you Ma and Pa and no more dream of another place. But with me, I already done forget. 'Forget the land! Forget the land!' Thistlewood done teach me.

On a fine steed – fleeter than Christ's or Euclid's ass – I set off for the city and the Jew's address (40, Allbright Avenue, written on the hymn-sheets to his Cordial I sang for Lady Montague), the only sure and proven place I know of in the realm, but when I get there what mishap and what revelation! But halt! Mr Pringle commands, as trenchantly as a highwayman. He pulls me up, telling me that I must think of my readers. They must know the intimacies of my voyage, not merely my arrival. He chides me for the vagueness of my descriptions, advising me that I will never sell a book of generalities such as I offer the reading public. But what do I care? I have a hundred and fifty guineas' worth of goods in my sack (the steed itself is worth an additional fifty), altogether more than the subscriptions I can expect from any publication, howsoever novel, bizarre or exotic in the telling. I care not for this business of writing, the necessity of plot and verisimilitude. In any case I am an African, and old beyond the recall of exactitudes. But Mr Pringle, stalwart of reason, stalwart of Abolition principle, insists, for upon my honest Gospel word depends the salvation of my enslaved brethren. Suffice to say that as I cantered towards London, the only details I recalled were hosts of daffodils crowding the path that took me there, bowing reverentially as I passed, for it was springtime and the Lenten hour. If you wish, dear reader, I can invent familiar perils and comforting ideologies. I can make of myself an exemplary and heroic Negro thus: there were twelve hours, twelve stations, of my journeying to the Jew's domain. In the first hour, and the second, and the third, there were taverns and brothels, between my departure from Hertfordshire (the Montague seat) and a place called

Hemel Hempstead, a few miles outside the city. Gamblers and gorgeous whores all besieged me at various points but I would not surrender my booty to them, in spite of their promises. The gamblers showed me dice, a lucky throw would double or treble my future they said, but I spurned their offer, content with the venerable tokens I possessed of England's past. The women wiped my brow with their kerchiefs, and would relieve me of my burden, but I dismissed them, content with the sack of sorrows slung over my shoulders. Then they bared all, but yet I would not stray from the thorn-strewn path. In the fourth and the fifth and the sixth hour, between Hemel Hempstead and Putney, thieves set upon me, replacing earlier beguilements with brute force, but though weakened by the heaviness of my load I still managed, by inward prayer and rapprochement with my human fate, to rebuff them. To put it more plainly, I bashed one thief with the candlestick, I scooped out the eye of another with a long-handled spoon, I cracked the skull of a third with Cato's bust, I tickled the fourth to exhaustion with the wig's pigtail, and the fifth I stilled by opening the Bible to Matthew chapter 27 and reading aloud the story of Barabbas. As the last thief listened his hand slowly relaxed, dropping his weapon, and then he too dropped on his knees, begging my forgiveness, God's forgiveness, and offering to follow me to the ends of the earth as my bodyguard and disciple. But in truth I was glad to save myself, never mind him, and beside my least wish was to have some wretched whiteman hanging around me, needing to be fed daily, depleting my meagre store; but I put on a benign face and gave him benediction: 'Go forth and multiply,' I told him, and after grovelling at my feet for a while in absolute gratitude, he scampered away into the nearest bush to form a new religious movement. My latest convert. What can I say of the final six hours? Word of my coming must have preceded me, for between Putney and Richmond, beggars appeared in Biblical numbers, thousands of them, and all Gospel-garbed, leaning on crutches, carrying pallets, and the rest. I knew them to be a masquerade of rogues, seeming to be destitute, seeking alms instead of work, and felt no pity for them. They stretched out their hands but I was no easy touch, I tightened the neck of my sack, hugged it to me, giddiupped my horse and cantered through them. I had nearly escaped from their carnival of entreaties when an aged woman threw herself on the ground, and though I instantly reined in my horse, it was too late. She was trampled under its hoofs. I leapt from my horse to tend to her. Her last tooth was dislodged. Her nose was split. She opened her mouth to breathe. I noticed her naked bleeding gums. I searched through my sack to make appropriate amends. I alighted on a silver toothpick and gave it to her. It will remind her always of a time when her mouth was fresh and full, even though mockingly, for there was never enough to eat but every Matin a piece of bread and sip of wine, and now and again when the Thames became choked and poisoned by human ordure, a miracle of dead fish washed up on its banks, fought over by five thousand other beggars.

Why I seek out the Jew? I can't tell. Is it that he once say to me, 'Come follow me'? Is it that from the time I land in England all I hear is curse, but after a while I too believe: vile Jew, rich Jew, rob − and − cheat Jew, Jew carpenter who shave and plane the wood into Christ's Cross, then charge extra for the nails? Everybody scorn him, is that why I go to meet him, to find a soulmate, two tribes in the same craft and storm that bring us to the same soil, soiling? All I think I am sure of is that the very time I set eyes on him the scales drop, I seem to know right away that I will become his slave.

'Leave the Jew alone,' Ellar buzzes angrily in Perseus' ear. 'Lead him not to the time of his suffering,' and a chorus of female voices arise to support her.

'Your name is Legion, you are many deaths in one living body. Please, I beg of you, don't go to Mr Gideon, or you'll kill him.'

'Like you kill the lot of us.'

'Like you killed your own father by putting breta-bark into his drink.'

'And your mother by selling her as meal to Captain Thistlewood.'

'And Saba with one blow to his head.'

'Like you killed Lizzie and Jane by getting them banished to a country hovel there to starve.'

'And soon you'll widow Lady Montague,' Ellar says, drawing a cry of protest from Perseus. 'In a few weeks' time Lord Montague will go to Spain to negotiate an end to the war you caused by slashing your ear. Jacobites will lure him unwittingly to a tavern and there cut his throat.'

'Lady Montague will howl with mirth at the news, jump up and down like her pet monkey.'

'She'll run amok in the house, wreck the dining-room, overturn the dining-table, dismiss all the kitchen servants.'

'No more grand parties, no more the throng of nobles and Latin conversations.'

'She will sell her estate and give all to missionaries working in Africa. She will seek refuge in a nunnery, protected from temptation by prayer, scratching Crosses in her skin, sleeping with a Bible under her pillow.'

'All because a nigger like you landed in her house and terrified her beyond words.'

'What was it about you that so moved her to self-disgust?'

'Leave the Jew alone,' Ellar repeats, 'or else you'll send him to his suffering.'

'He'll come among us in the ship.'

'He'll relieve our fevers with his medicines.'

'He'll massage our feet with gentle movements.'

'He'll make us speak our names calmly even when the pain makes us want to speak nasty words instead.'

'Then he'll die, by choice, of our common diseases.'

'Then they'll toss him overboard like a common slave.'

'When he does not rise up from the sea (look how anxiously they scour the surface, fearing for their lives) they will mock him.'

'Deny that there was anything special about him.'

'Preach that his healing gifts were mere quackery.'

'They will come to us again to make fresh tortures and bolder sin.'

'For he is no more there to show mercy by his example.'

'But I will not curse him for abandoning me.'

'Nor I.'

'Nor I.'

'None of us will, but instead endure in body the sickness they visit on us.'

'And though they gag me I will call out the torch of his name.'

'And though they thrust themselves on me I will call out the sword of his name.'

'My last word as I die will be the vengeance of his name.'

'I will rise up from the dead to plan their extinction.'

'I will pack them live in cages, ship them to some wasteland, but many will thirst to death and suffocate before they arrive.'

'And those that survive will be shot in the head and shovelled into pits.'

'But, for sport, some will be reserved as logs for the huge furnaces we will build.'

'And others we will release into the poisonous vapours of marsh and swamp.'

'The rest will be worked to death, or starved to death, no matter.'

'Leave the Jew alone,' Ellar says, 'or else you'll bring suffering beyond meaning to the world.'

I think him arrogant and worldly-wise, from the tone of his newspaper advertisement and the letters announcing his genius at curing the sick. And yet he treated Lady Montague with utmost compassion. I am uncertain of his character, but there is no alternative to slavery in the West Indies, my certain fate by Lord Montague's determination. My plan is to make some compact and alliance with him, the only alien I am familiar with in the realm, the only address known to me. Reckoning on his greed (in spite of his previous refusal of a physician's fee), I bring with me tribute from the Montague household: ornaments and specimens of England's noble civilization. If as a philistine he cannot appreciate such articles of faith, he can at least sell them for pieces of silver.

Imagine my confusion when I eventually come upon his dwelling and find a structure that is more a stable, more humble than the humblest hut I remember of my village. And a dozen women crowded therein, whom at first I take to be the women of my tribe, until they turn to me and lift their veils to show blanched faces. They look at me with awe and foreboding and turn to Mr Gideon for protection. Mr Gideon, though he sees me as a comet blooding the sky, foretelling his death, still greets me warmly. He kisses me on both cheeks, identifying me to the company not as a traitor but a fellow woman and sinner. I hand over my sack to him, and he receives it graciously, not chiding me for my robbery. 'You are safe with us,' he says, gesturing to the gathering who listen to his every word with the intentness of disciples. I behold them with pity and desire, knowing them to be sluts, fens, malkins, diseased posture-molls, all of them my mothers. Pity for their venereal condition, the abuses which cripple them beyond their years. Desire to heal myself of my murderous past by being of some posthumous service to them. Mr Gideon understands my purpose in coming to him, without any explanation on my part. From the moment he set eyes on me, at the Montague doorway, he seemed to have known that the true patient was not my Lady but myself. Hence his call to me to follow him; hence my arrival at the barn bearing gifts. But Mr Gideon puts away the sack of treasures. I had doubted him, thinking he would be tempted by it, but he put the sack away as the possessions of the living, useless to him, useless to the company of ghosts who are his disciples. For though they show the most eerie signs of life – they cough, they vomit, they shiver, they cry out in desperate pain – they are already dead. He moves wordlessly among them, for there is nothing he can say to give meaning to their death. And yet the women carry the shrouds of their skin with longing, tormenting him with a sense of his quackery. They wear their sickness like desired ornaments. They dare him to transform their suffering into raiments denied to them in life: the whiteness of pus becoming rolls of silk; sores, sequins; abscesses, beads of pearl. They want to be gorgeously arrayed, and challenge him to resurrection in colours and textures denied to them in life, but his medicines are ineffectual. And I pity him, for I remembered Ellar (the chastest of our tribe, in life, her crippled body securing her virginity) transformed into gaudy beauty, because of slavery. I remembered Ellar sporting the swelling on her lips like haughty ornaments. I remembered her skin brushed with colourful bruises, her cheeks streaked like a mask of desire. She was radiant in the midst of death, but Mr Gideon's women remain veiled by sexual diseases, unable to glimpse any sign of beauty about their bodies. Mr Gideon administers cordials and applies plasters, but none of these can restore vision to them. One by one they die, believing with blind faith in the promise of his medicines.

'What nonsense you talk about me,' Ellar abuses him. 'Why do you write that I flit and glitter like if I am some winged frivolity? No one will take me seriously now.'

'I want to present you in the best light, as you said I must,' Perseus protests.

Ellar sulks, still not satisfied that Perseus is offering proper compensation to the tribe for causing their death. His duty is to write them into life, but she questions his competence. 'But how can you say that my lips and face and body are gorgeous from all the blows I took? Are you wanting to excuse what they did to us, and excuse yourself too?'

'I was praising you, I was saying that in spite of all you remained beautiful within.'

'But I didn't,' Ellar persists. 'Outside I was covered in my own shit, and inside too. I couldn't take the lash any more, I just gave up and died. And still the sailor continued to do it to me, can you believe? What are these people made of, that they sleep with the dead?'

Perseus is stilled by her outrage but he knows he cannot write it, for fear of alienating his readers.

'Perhaps you should curse them outright as white devils, tell the story as it is and not bother with the consequences,' Ellar says, sensing his anxiety. 'What more can they do to you worse than slavery?'

'They can refuse to buy my book, and I'll starve,' Perseus says quietly to himself.

The last thing on Perseus' mind is the emancipation of his brethren. Unlike Mr Pringle he is not foolish enough to believe that a single book will alter the course of history. Not even a whole library testifying to the plight of the Negro would deflect the English from their common pursuit. Money, not ideas, is what holds the nation together, and as long as it is profitable to trade Negroes, slavery will thrive, and the state of England remain intact.

Imagine what catastrophe will befall the English should his book miraculously succeed in abolishing slavery! No longer united by the endeavour, things would simply fall apart. Imagine the hundreds of thousands of sailors, carpenters, shop-keepers, rope-makers, coopers, gunsmiths, iron-workers, sugar-refiners, ship-builders, bankers, insurers, lawyers, who will become workless and worthless, without the likes of him. As his slavery gives them labour, so his emancipation will give them a terrifying freedom. No, he Perseus has caused enough destruction for one lifetime. He will be content with a hundred pounds or so in royalties, which will keep him comfortably in his old age. And to ensure that his book sells, he will not repel his readers by calling them necrophiles.

Ellar, possessing the clairvoyance of the dead, knows his secret ambition but still will not condemn him outright, sympathizing with his need to live. Her own ambition is to live otherwise on the page, differently from the way she died on the soiled plank of a whiteman's lap.

Is Mr Gideon no more than me? I watch him crush and boil herbs to make his cures, though they don't work, and I ask whether he is no more than me, proud and false and of bad faith. He makes his cures like I make my book but of what use? My book lies. The whores die.

'One by one they die, and yet you do nothing,' Ellar accuses him. 'Even now, after all you have done to us you care nothing for women?'

'But what must I do?' Perseus asks, angry that Ellar deems him Mr Gideon's accomplice in murder.

'Can't you see, what they want is proper doctoring. Insist that he sells these things you stole from Montague and buy proper remedies. He is no god, even though he acts like one, and gathers the women around him. Faith won't heal them, only real medicines.'

'Leave him alone,' Perseus cries, coming to Mr Gideon's defence. 'He has given up the whole of his life to serve the destitute. A man like him can make great money for himself, but he has surrendered all such ambition.' (*The Jew used to put his name in the newspapers, self-praise his special cure, with epistles from many women to prove the truth. Rich people like my Lady call him, give big fee, and his young career thrive, but the bubble burst when he look upon the Crosses on my forehead, his conscience prick. Me it is who call him unto me and from that time all he want to do is serve the cast-offs. Me it is who change his life and without a word from my mouth speak to him of Godliness. Me it is who convert the Jew.*)

'Writing don't make you a god either,' Ellar says scornfully, mocking Perseus' achievement. 'Just because you are making a book of fancy words and the whiteman mark your forehead don't make you better than us.'

In a fit of anger Perseus resolves to scratch her name out and all her history from his autobiography, but Ellar anticipates the plot.

'You and Gideon are one,' she says dismissively, 'I want no part in your doings. He'll come to me soon to massage my feet and rub oil on the iron lock to soften the chafing. He'll tell me his name in an oily voice and ask me my own. But what is all that but false ministry? Damn his name, his massage and his penny cures, what I want is the key or skill to pick the lock, and a gun to blow a hole in the whiteman's crotch, bayonet to stick in his guns, a match to make of him a wick of death. I used to dream of the wax of the whiteman's flesh, how I torch it, look how it melts, how it runs and runs, filling the hold, filling the mid-deck, top-deck, spilling over the sides into the sea. Afterwards, what a holy candle-smell conquers the ship! And in the depth of candle-smoke I start a canticle and all the women join their voices in thanksgiving.' She pauses and sniffs the air, savouring the prospect of slave revolt, the blasphemy of it.

Forgive her song and heathen rage, dear reader, for when her pain becomes unbearable, her mouth opens involuntarily, centipedes spill out, but she knows not the creatures she utters. Nor is her venom against Mr Gideon meant. I can vouchsafe that he was no charlatan as Ellar claims, that the wretches in his care were not apostles. The truth is that he gave up all his worldly ambition so as to wait upon the most despised of women. They were beyond salvation, being practically dead by the time they reached him. Their lives were a journey through kennels and stinking alleyways, and it was Mr Gideon's mission to make their final passage hopeful. They expired with blessings on their lips, blessing for a love they never thought a man was capable of. And the last meal he fed them was not his famed cordial – for he had repented of such trickery which once promised him a fortune from the gullible rich – but a preparation of England's ancient verdure; ancient beyond the slum, marketplace, pawnshop, brothel and Bridewell that their lives had become in the city. I helped him crush willow bark and saffron, I helped him make poisonous draughts of poppy and belladonna. I thought of Captain Thistlewood who fed me stories of England's ancient properties. We could not save the women but we restored to them a taste of the innocence of their childhoods. They gasped and died. They swallowed up the air, returning to their villages as Manu had swallowed up the sea to reach our own childhoods.

'You poisoned them!' Ellar whispers in astonishment. The rest of the women are stunned by my revelation.

'What more could I do?' I ask, appealing to the memory of their pain, when all they begged for was a sip of poison to end their lives. Onya, suddenly remembering her dead children, bursts into tears. Her sorrow revives them. They look to Ellar to speak their condemnation of me, but Ellar is silent. She is too astonished by my deed to put it in appropriate words. I have reduced them to silence, even I am shocked by what I had done to them. I will give my own life to hear them speak, even if to condemn me.

'What more could I do?' I ask again, but they are incapable of speech. 'They were already dead, I only helped them to free them of their flesh.' And as soon as I utter such I realize with dreadful clarity the nature of my final sin. Men had driven them from their villages, lured them to the city, whored, diseased and abandoned them. And when I brought them to their death, I had at last arrived at the state of manhood. It was not my mothers dancing nakedly and all night in the chatree hut which initiated me into manhood but this deed in England, this feeding of poison to women.

Men had started them on the path to their death, I had brought such Progress to completion.

'I cannot do more for them,' Mr Gideon says, confessing his failure to me. 'They are beyond the genius of England's best physicians. The most I can do is to make their exit swift and painless.' He hangs his head in guilt.

'Go far from here, where your gifts can restore health to the sick,' I tell him, sending him to my folk in slavery. I release him to work among my folk who are still hopeful of freedom. I will stay with the dying English women. I will be their executioner. I will take upon myself the sins of men. Mr Gideon is overwhelmed by my kindness. He looks upon me not as a foreigner but as a fellow man. He looks upon the marks of my forehead and wants to say something but cannot find the words.

'Go to my mothers,' I say to him in benediction. 'Remember to call them by their names, Ellar, and Baju and Onya and Sanu. The men are Manu and Kaka and Tanda and Nara.' I am glad for him. He is a Jew, therefore without family, except a community of curses; Christ-killer, child-killer, stock-jobber, and countless other maledictions keep his company. He will find the blessings of family among my tribe. He will free the ache from their feet as from his own mother's. He will purge their speech of execrations. He will abduct the darkness of the hold. The love that radiates from him will be the light they surge towards, breaking their chains to catch the raining of it for their parched mouths. He will part the sea to show an ancient trail leading back to Africa; a trail gleaming with human bones, pearls, bullion, goblets of silver, ivory horns. Guided by the light of previous wrecks, they will reach home.

Part IX

I

One by one the women died until only Moll was left.

She was always different from the others. Their bodies were abscessed, but her outward appearance was marbled beauty, not the least chip, not the least cavity to show the philistine abduction and shipping of her. The signs of men's handling of her were all within. To look at her was to look upon perfect form, Greek in the grace and symmetry of its conception. I recognized and loved her instantly, not out of physical want, but a different necessity.

The other women treated her with suspicion, drawing away from her, leaving her to occupy a lonely corner of the stable. They were jealous of the smoothness of her face. They were jealous of her youthful scented face, that of a girl on the brink of womanhood. Even Mr Gideon, wise as he was, could not reckon her condition. When she first came, he had examined her and found no trace of disease. She was in no obvious physical pain. Outwardly there was nothing doleful about her. She was not a picture of Bedlam distraction. He could not appreciate her inner sickness, but as soon as I saw her I recognized the imprisonment of her spirit. Like the other women she spoke nothing. They spent their final days sobbing because of the pain, or in a silent daze. Looking back I remember no complete and lucid sentence uttered by any of them, the pain always halting their speech, converting it into a desolate cry. Moll too was beyond utterance. That was her only kinship with the other women.

She differed from them in covering herself from head to toe with a blanket. Roasting with fevers they cast off their clothing, they rolled around the bare earth, seeking its cold damp vapours. One day, all of a sudden, as if wanting to separate herself from the company, Moll cocooned herself, refusing to emerge from under the blanket. When she wanted anything – a drink of water, a piece of bread – she would gesture and I would supply her. It was only when she slept, and the blankets slipped from her, or on awakening, that I glimpsed the proportions of her beauty. And later, when she became too frail, and I uncovered her against her will.

Mr Gideon, believing the darkness detrimental to her health, sought to coax her from under the blanket, but she would not. Thinking her healthy, except for such oddity of mind, he was glad to leave her in my care, so as to attend to more urgent cases. Only I knew the extent of her plight. She was my fair Alexandrian who had wandered into a jungle of hurts. She moved through the sky's discharge, the earth's slush of human ordure, until the inhabitants of this cannibal region called London trapped her in a cage. Nightly they bled her of virtue. Their chief was one called Magistrate Gonson. He had the choicest meat of her. When she was plundered and vandalized beyond remembrance of her origin, they let her go. Having converted her into a beast they released her to move among them, as one of their own tribe.

None of this I could tell Mr Gideon, for to explain

Moll's plight in terms of the decline and fall of the Ancients would have been to expose myself to ridicule. One by one the women died, then Mr Gideon departed, and whilst I wept at their passing, I was glad to be left in the company of Moll. I renamed her Ceres, goddess of harvests, even though she hid under her blanket like a heap of barren soil. She hid under her blanket so that I would not be distracted by her outward beauty, but would see her true degenerate self. And yet I was determined to restore her, to re-awaken her mind to the genius of our ancestors, the traces of which we bore within ourselves. I looted the sack of treasures taken from Lord Montague's house. I placed the bust of Cato in her hands, and held my breath as she felt it, tracing the contours of his eyes, forehead, lips, as if on the brink of recognition. But she suddenly flung him to the ground with such force that his nose broke off. Ganymede's fate was no better. She ran her fingers promisingly over the surface of the painting, then ripped it from its frame. She scraped away at the colouring, disfiguring the boy's face beyond the desire of the gods. I withheld Petrarch from her, for given her mood, she would simply have broken his spine and made him fall limply from her hands.

I scolded her, but she seemed not to comprehend, stretching out her hands for me to place in them some other item to be vandalized.

My attempt at renaissance failed, I decided to leave her to her barrenness and should have kept silence except that anger moved me to lewd expressions. 'Pedicabo te et irrumabo,' I cursed her in language that even Catullus would have envied. I was addressing her from some store of knowledge buried deep within me, which alarmed me by its sudden revelation. Even more alarming was her response, for she withdrew her hands to the cover of the blanket as if she understood the violence of my speech. Could it be that modern life had so debased us that the only trail back to our past was through lewd intercourse? 'Puella defututa,' I said to her, encouraging her to react, but she would not utter. I rose to greater heights of pornography, but she remained silent. Once more I began to doubt my talent, my descent from a lost tribe of Ancients, when she revived my spirit with a sudden commotion of hands. I listened intently, but could not make sense of the beat of her gestures, the broken signatures she made in the air. She willed me to understand, but I could not. She strained so much that I expected her to burst into speech, but after a while she grew exhausted by the effort. My fair Alexandrine! The rhythm of her hands waned, her wrists slackened, she withdrew once more into the cocoon of her blanket.

She grew more and more sick, her decline unseen since she would not throw off her blanket to let me examine her. I could tell her condition only by the green blotches which suddenly appeared on my skin. They grew in size according to the rate of her decay. They were the outward signs of her decay, which I bore on my own flesh. They itched and tormented, but I endured them for her sake. My sole concern was to cool the abscesses multiplying within her. I made her classical fare as best as I could from Mr Gideon's meagre store. I made sauces as close as possible to the recipes of Columella learnt at Lady Montague's table. But she would not eat, however erudite my presentations. Reduced to despair, I offered common broth such as Betty and her kind consumed, but this she also declined. She fasted throughout the time I spent with her, hastening her passage to death. I summoned up ancestral resources from deep within me, so desperate was I to save her life. From Mr Gideon's cabinet of herbs, oils and powders, I made cathartics according to Paracelsus, and even more ancient fermentations according to Galen. Although she was persuaded to imbibe these (she believed them to be poisons) the medicines failed. In the end I reverted to Hippocratic oaths, invoking the name of Zeus. I beseeched him as Lord of Creation to rescue her, to transform her into flower, nightingale or creature of divinity, like the thousands of other women He desired or took pity on. But at the very moment of invocation I realized the nature of my blasphemy, and knew that the true Christian God would remove her from me as punishment. He who smote the Amorites, the Sodomites, the Moabites, the Canaanites, the Hivites, the Jebusites, the Perizites, and other countless tribes; He who reduced cities and kingdoms to rubble for their worship of false gods; He who sent plagues to sterilize vast regions of the earth; would revenge on me, an ordinary misconceived Negro, in less merciful ways. He would take Ceres away from me, and put in her place Mr Pringle and then Mr Hogarth.

In her final days I took advantage of her weakness by throwing off her blanket and lifting her bodily to the tub to be bathed. She gasped when she set eyes on me, for I was a patchwork of green like areas of the desert Rima and I would scour for food, after the rains conjured forth miraculous blooms. She gazed at the strange green landscape of me with such intensity that I was moved to look upon myself. For the first time I marvelled at strange growths my skin nurtured. Skin that was the curse of my race, bringing slavery upon us, was now a harvest so plentiful that even my planter-father would have been astonished at me. And when I looked upon her I too was dumbfounded by her appearance. I had expected to lift the blanket to a sight piteous beyond words, but was faced instead by unblemished form. Her disease, though it raged violently within her, could not break through to the surface of her. She was the very image of the Virgin depicted in many of Lord Montague's paintings. I lifted her to the tub, and although there was not the least sign of impurity about her, I still bathed her as a means of cleansing myself of the desire I felt for her. My hands explored all the nakedness of her. The trials of slavery were insubstantial compared to the temptations suffocating me with their weight. Each time I touched her I cried for the King's Pardon, for Christ the Executioner to stay His pressing of me, but He let me bleed from the shameful parts of me so that I could better understand my sinfulness. It was not the village Elder marking my forehead nor the women of my tribe dancing nakedly for me, nor Captain Thistlewood's missionary acts, which brought me to an understanding of sin. It was the helpless beautiful body of a harlot which, after I had done with it, I lifted out of the tub with remorse as final as that of the apostle as he lifted Christ's corpse from Calvary.

II

There is nothing more I will speak of Ceres. You will forgive my closure for I fear that whatever I utter will be misconceived. You have, as evidence of this, Mr Hogarth's prints. Go to Mr Hogarth's prints on Moll to sate your curiosity, for he has fixed her for all time on the point of his burin. How can my halting feeble art release her from such agony? Countless years ago, when Mr Gideon was still in life, attending to his stable of diseased women, Mr Hogarth visited. I had newly arrived at the stable, seeking refuge from Lord Montague's execution of my sale. From a distance he resembled Magistrate Gonson, a short fat swaggering man, a man whose brooding forehead suggested that he was constantly rehearsing in his mind the punishment to be meted out to others. He pushed through the stable door and approached confidently. The women looked at him and screamed, thinking that it was Magistrate Gonson come to visit them with posthumous sentences. I too flinched from him, thinking him Lord Montague's emissary come to claim me, until I smelt paint about him, not death. I calmed the women as best as I could, and greeted the stranger in case he was a benefactor, fetched him a stool and a cup of water. He did not acknowledge me, thinking my action no more than a slave's duty. Nor did he have money to give. When his visit was over, he gave me a Bible, that was all, as if a pagan needed neither bread nor soup nor silver like other humans, but only nourishment for his soul.

And what was the purpose of his coming? He wanted us to reveal our lives. He promised to represent us in the best light, to immortalize us by his art. The women opened up to him, vying with each other to be heard. Such was their agitation, such the flood of stories, that for a moment I believed I was witnessing a miracle; that Mr Hogarth had restored them to life, when before they were husks, shadows, faded stains. But in the very moment I believed, I also doubted him, for I remembered Ellar, Kaka, and all the others of my tribe looking to me to resurrect them in happy stories. 'Say that I am graceful,' Ellar had demanded. 'That I am visionary, bountiful, compassionate, vivid, endless,' others had demanded, and they trusted me with their expectations of alternative lives; lives which they did not live, but which were possible, for they could imagine the possibilities of them. So the women trusted Mr Hogarth, but I doubted him as I had doubted myself.

Did he betray their faith out of malice? Or for money, an account of sensationalism being more marketable than the sacred in our age of Commerce? Or was he not gifted enough to portray the sacred, as words were beyond my own grasp? Whatever the reason or reasons, he broadcast their lives as everyday and bleak, evoking nothing more worthy than pity in the viewer. He portrayed them as lice-ridden carnal hags. Moll to his mind (for she would not be uncovered for a sitting, refusing his farthing's bribe) was also a foul spectacle and willing victim to her fallen state, an object of pity and desire.

Yet for all the seeming realism of his art, he lied. He lied about Mr Gideon, making him whore Moll, the Virgin Mother, so that you, dear reader, will be roused once more to ancient hatred of the Jew. But it was the Jew who sought out the tragedy of my people, who sacrificed his life to free

272

us from hatred of the whiteman and the Christian. Mr Gideon acted thus not because he wanted personal glory, nor to redeem his race for nearly two millennia of condemnation. He acted out of ordinary human feeling. History will forget him. History will continue to be a chronicle of massacred Jews. But in attempting to succour a single life aboard the slaveship, by applying a single salve to a single wound, he begat the moment of a new history. And however unseen his deed, because of the blanket darkness of the hold, or witnessed only by Negro eyes (and therefore unworthy or untrustworthy of record), the deed will be the potential brightest star of a new firmament.

And as to me, Mr Hogarth lied too. I wanted him to make me ordinary, for that is what a Negro is, ordinary man and woman, deserving of the ordinary human feeling that yet creates and recreates glimpses of new worlds; a New World Negro was what I craved to be, but the glimpse he offered of me was as servant to Moll and to the oldest profession. And servant too to the Jew who was the oldest Jew in the book, in terms of his cunning, his hoarding of coin, his purchase of Christian women. I fear that I will forever be associated with the indecencies of merchants and whores, for Mr Hogarth's prints will last forever. Centuries from now, when your descendants think of a Negro, they will think of a pimp, pickpocket, purveyor of filth. Mr Hogarth's pictures sold uncommonly well, spreading the message of me throughout the realm, that for years afterwards I could not venture out of doors without being accosted by strangers. He had made me so familiar to the public that they greeted me with good-humoured saluta- tion, or outright curses, depending on their character. If I walked among the sinful, they would run up to touch me. A crowd of molls, punks, cripples and tax-collectors would follow me everywhere, cheering and applauding and begging me to bless them by swearing most outrageously in their presence. Others – stern widows in Sunday black – crossed the street and crossed themselves at my approach. Young women of all classes reacted to me, the kitchen-wenches jigging their waists in invitation, the proper misses glancing away and quickening their steps to their quickening hearts.

For though Mr Hogarth's art was not affordable to many, a dozen ballads and a dozen pirated versions of his pictures appeared, cheap enough for mass purchase. Once I was affordable only to the very rich, a slave worth countless guineas, but because of Mr Hogarth I was possessed, in penny image, by several thousands. To be sure I thus became an historic and memorable figure in the birth of democracy in the British realm. Thankful as I was for such status, I still resented the ways my Ceres was portrayed, for the hacks and picture-makers embroidered our doings, sensationalizing them, spawning fresh scandal. They showed us in a tavern stinking of sweat and tallow, a picture of moral ruin. Its windows were patched with brown paper, its ceiling beautified with smutty names and shadows sketched with candle-flame and charcoal. Men stuck pipes of sotweeds in their mouths, sucked, watched the whores getting drunk on cock-ale, spat. Ceres was seated at the table, arranging her feathers and powdering her face for the night's engagements. I was in attendance, making her first appointment, by signalling her readiness to a man seated at the far end of the room. He was an old gent, in the winter of his lechery warming his grey hairs with a dram of brandy. His hand was deep in his trouser pocket, in self-arousal for the arduous act ahead, at the same time counting out the fee. 'Subscription fee' the print's caption called it in an attempt at wit. Ceres was described as 'a bawdy tail', the old gent 'an incurable bookworm', and me, 'Moll's pageboy'. Other prints didn't bother to give their contents a playful turn. They appealed directly to the pornographic eye. Ceres stripped or was stripped in ways so ingenious that no caption could distract the curious eye. And in all these novel spectacles I was present as her familiar, my black presence an ancient and reassuring sign. The buyers of such prints used me to steady their eye. They reeled at the sight of Ceres' posturings, but the sight of me (rifling through the client's pocket whilst he was preoccupied with Ceres; entering the bedroom afterwards with refreshments; count-ing the money while she cleaned her thighs for another venture) restored to them a sense of the orderly. A Negro, a devil. A Negro, a creature of mischief. A Negro, a thing of lawlessness. Devil, mischief, lawlessness: such familiar notions helped them to resist total surrender to Ceres' nudity even as it highlighted their enjoyment of it.

Mr Pringle too will replicate Moll and me in lies, for he believes Mr Hogarth's prints and the dozen pirated versions of them. 'A beginning, a middle, an end,' is what he demands, promising a novel story. I know though that he will chain me to the old firmament of stars, making me familiar in my Christian hatred of the Jew, my Christian distress at the sexual sin he financed and made me slave to.

Mr Pringle's story will see Moll and me at fairgrounds, cavorting with Tom-fools and merry Andrews; at churches, seeking out new gentleman clients; at galleries and concert halls, Moll acting like a Lady of worth. He will have Moll and me riding a handsome coach through London for all the world to see her quality, or else to Hampstead to take the country air (it will be on one such peregrination that we will encounter Captain Thistlewood's ruined estate). High Life and Low we will indulge in, visiting disease and heartbreak upon whomsoever we touch. The ruin of our Christian lives will be his theme, for Mr Pringle is obsessed with such. I piece together the odd remark here, the outburst there, and come to believe that Mr Pringle sees danger to England's Christian fabric everywhere, in the shape of Jew and Papist, Jacobite and callous merchant. I sense it in the doodles he makes on his paper as he waits for my confession. He draws and re-draws the moon, shading in its crown so that it resembles a skull-capped Jew or Papist. He draws ruptured circles and broken triangles. Collapsed shapes, twisted and ruptured shapes. Sometimes I want to appreciate more of him, but it is not my place to ask questions of his intimate life. Young in face, his eyes steady, his hands steady, a mask of composure, his heart and mind confirmed in Christ, and yet what is it that has so afflicted him that he comes to me for relief? Why his obsession with ruin? What dreadful thing has happened to *his* mother that makes him seek of me the story of my mother? What conflagration has engulfed *his* family that he insists on knowing my Ellar, my Kaka and others of my tribe? I sense he carries an epic pain with him, but I am a black man, it is not my place to enquire, much less be ambitious of writing an Englishman's history.

So I keep quiet. As we should have kept quiet when Mr Hogarth enquired of us. He made a hue and cry of our lives but heard not their unfolding into mystery, as I did in my final hour with Moll. She shuddered. She twisted. She buckled. She grew taut. She convulsed in agony. I lay my body upon hers, weighing her down to stop the pitching and the yawing which would break her spine. Her throat was a slurry of senseless noises. All the senseless existence emptied from her. She struggled again, but I clung to her like bird-lime, refusing to let her go, wanting a melody from her, but she would not fake a miracle for me, satisfy me with a trick of harlotry. Once more she heaved, with such force that I was thrown bodily from her. She sucked in air for the last time, a huge and lonely breath; her own breath, not that forced into her mouth by men's purchase of her. Then, having recovered herself, she breathed it out freely. Forever and forever, the giving up of her life.

A full seven days I bear her on my back, from bed to tub, cleanse her, powder, put fresh clothes on her, beg her to sup and take cure of pill, but she will not. She just stare at me like a child at a raree-show. Like she put her eye to me, peep through the hole and see . . . what? A star that loosen from its roots and fall from the sky, like God's aged tooth. A star that of a sudden flare and whirl like a wheel of fire, scorch heaven's door, the angels huff and puff but can't blow it out, only by God's Flood the flames expire. Another star slip straight down the side of the night and dangle from a ribbon and noose of colours. Another star shoot across the sky like a sick man's cough. She peep in at me and see the middle of the beginning of the end of the way things are; the end of the middle of the beginning of what things will become. Or so I console myself, that I give her hope of another life, that only by her sickness and death can she bring the new creature of her into being. A black snake disappears down a black hole, there to die unseen, and emerge again into the light of our astonishment with its new green and glittering skin. Look at me! Look at the greenness of me! I say, displaying the miracle of my blotches to console her and me.

I bury her with hopeless hands at the doorway of the stable. The tears run down into my mouth so that my breath forms bubbles, the taste of salt in my mouth, as if I am a drowning slave. I dig and dig, trying to free Saba from his burial place, Rima from where the sands closed over her, my mother, my father, all the shot, the massacred and drowned ones, and when I have made a hole deep enough in the earth and in the sea, I lower Ceres into it. 'Go and sin no more,' I tell her for the last tired time, being old, useless words but the only learning I have. I keep the pigtail wig but empty my sack of chandeliers and crockery and silver toothpicks and Petrarch and torn picture and broken-nosed Cato into her grave, so that she will arrive in the New World laden with treasures, not bare-headed like we. I put in some bread for succour, and a bottle of Mr Gideon's Amazing Eastern Cordial in case she get sick on her journey (*God be my witness, it was the only time I cursed Mr Gideon as a nasty quack Jew and murderer of Christian women. Forgive me, for it was the grief of her death; grief at the uselessness of Mr Gideon's cordial; grief at the only thing that worked, the solution of poison*

he taught me to make which I forced down her throat at the last).
When the hole is filled with her and her rich possessions I
cover her over with ordinary dirt, flatten it so that no trace
is visible, in case grave-robbers come. I sprinkle a brew of
boiled nettles and stinking herbs over her resting place, to
repel rats from digging her up.

Everything gone, but me, years and years in this dark cell
and garret which I come to, after I bury her, to hide from
memory of the killings. I live by Mr Gideon's eleven
guineas, his total worth, which before he leave to join the
slave trade, he give me, to buy my freedom from Lord
Montague. But I keep the money, for whilst man does not
live by bread alone it still come in useful. In an age of
Commerce the greatest sin is to be without. That much I
learnt from Betty. Plus I sell Lord Montague's possessions,
those I didn't bury with Moll. I sleep. I wake up. I cut out
and save scraps from the newspapers. I go back to sleep.
That is all to tell of my later life, or all that I will tell. After a
while my skin clear up of green, though Mr Pringle's visit
bring back some blotches. And with Ceres' death the voices
in my head gone, as if her death give final rest to my tribe,
though Mr Pringle's visit bring back one or two or three of
them. But I don't listen! I press my hand to my one ear and
sing a Christian hymn to myself so that I can't listen. For all
the voices will be Ellar's, I know it, jungle howl, loud
cackle or big-bosomed laugh, that make birds shoot from
the trees in fright. I press my hands to my ear and sing and
sing, but she still insurrect into my head, for there are some
women – Ellar in particular – who no matter how strong
the poison, secure the grave, will break out, torch the

katran bush, blow with disobedient angel breath, fan the flames, that not even God's Flood can drown them out, for when the waters ebb, there is smoke still, the first smouldering thing that arise is the spirit of Ellar.

Acknowledgements

I am grateful to Martin Carter for permission to quote from his poem; to Marjorie Davies for typing and retyping manuscripts; to colleagues at the University of Warwick (especially Susan Bassnett and Piotr Kuhiwczak) for their ready support; to Wilson Harris, George Simon and Pauline Melville for reminding me of Amerindian myth; to Andrew Latiff for his shining intelligence; to Michelle Remblance for her severe criticism and shaping spirit; finally, to Cheddi for the canine imagery.